An Invitation to Hitler

An Invitation to Hitler

Bernard Neeson

Bigpa Publications

Published by Bigpa Publications

ISBN: 978-1483974064

Typesetting services by BOOKOW.COM

For Dee

CHAPTER ONE

He left his driver and bodyguard by the cottage. They knew he wanted to be alone and let him walk away unaccompanied. Here, of all places, he should be safe – deep in the garden of England, where an assassin or a landing party would stand out against the tableau of the age-old landscape. Still wearing drab army battledress from his earlier engagements of the day, the solitary figure walked slowly past the redbrick country house, barely glancing up at its fine gabled walls. Until recently so welcoming, it now stood closed and shuttered – an appropriate symbol, he mused, for the country at this perilous time.

He walked on past the terrace, the gravel crunching beneath his feet, until he reached the edge of the garden. For a few moments he hesitated, looking around and quietly absorbing the sadness of its current neglect... the flower beds unkempt and weed-strewn; the once-manicured lawns almost meadow-like. He counted out the months... eight, nearly nine, since he had left this place and moved back to London. Nature had moved quickly to reclaim ground no longer tended.

A hundred yards further on, Churchill came to a stop on a sunlit, grassy bank by the lakeside. So often over the years he had come to this special place to enjoy the tranquil scene, the calls of the wild birds and the rustling of water through the sedges. On this glorious

June afternoon, however, there was no such pleasure. Instead, he could only stand and watch sadly as the lake's last waters drained away. So painstakingly constructed just fifteen years ago, it had been deemed too recognisable a landmark from the air and had to be expunged.

Earlier that morning a squad of Canadian engineers had arrived to prepare the execution. Cordoning off the area, they surveyed the earth and stone construction to select a suitable spot from where an out-flowing torrent would do least damage, directed well away from house and garden. They drilled a hole deep into the retaining wall and inserted a few ounces of plastic explosive, just sufficient to make an effective breach while minimising the damage to the surrounding structure. Retiring a safe distance, they detonated the charge and watched with quiet satisfaction as the lake began to empty itself along the intended channel. Tomorrow they would return to finish the task, to plant on the drying bed the shrubs and trees that were already stacked nearby in hessian sacks. Within a few weeks the recently visible contours of the lake would blend back into the green countryside, the work of camouflage complete.

The engineers had completed their task professionally, without emotion, a small diversion from their routine of technical classes and weapons drill. For Churchill, arriving on the scene a few hours later, it was different. This was *his* lake. He had created it, had planned it here in the secluded eastern acres of the estate. He had measured out its perimeter and checked the levels with the greatest of care, then supervised the men over the months as they excavated the ground and raised the banks, helping out from time to time with the brick and stone laying. With the long work of construction finally complete, he had watched with a deep glow of satisfaction on the day the waters from the Chart Well began to fill it, giving it life. When it settled he had planted freshwater weeds and rushes, then stocked the new-born lake with trout and carp. He had maintained it over the years with diligence, perhaps even love, enjoying it immensely as it came to life with fish and waterfowl, and gradually merged into the landscape until it looked as if it had been there for centuries. He had painted by its banks, catching all its seasons and moods, and paced by it for hours at a time, deep in thought.

Now it was gone, an unsung casualty of the conflagration. Only a few muddy puddles remained, and in them a few carp, flapping about in their death throes. For all the carnage, the deaths of hundreds of thousands of people, the mass destruction of cities and towns throughout Europe – for all of that, the demise of this small lake and the plight of its few poor fish brought a tear to his eye.

He stood quietly for a moment, his mind churning, feeling the pressure from the dozens of issues confronting him until, just as the blackness threatened to enfold him, he sensed the evening sun begin to warm his face. He steadied himself. His words to the House a few days earlier echoed in his mind and gave him sustenance. He spoke them aloud, across the ravaged site.

We shall never surrender!

He turned his back on the emptied lake and walked towards the garden, still moving slowly but now taking time to look around. For all the obvious lack of care the wonderful charm of the place still endured... the familiar shapes and shades, the aromas, and in the background the comforting sounds of country life. Slowly he felt his spirits start to lift. Along the lower path the azaleas and the roses were in bloom, the scent from the flowers almost overwhelming in the early summer warmth. He lifted his eyes from the untidy palette of colours in the beds and looked over to the long curtain wall built a decade ago, much of it with his own hands. For a few, almost sensual moments he enjoyed the splendour of the scene, as the late afternoon sun brought out the lustre in the brick, bathing the garden in a warm, russet light.

He relished this small island of peace in an unpeaceful world. Those glorious views across the Weald of Kent, the very finest of English countryside, meant so much to him, reminding him of what the struggle was ultimately about – freedom, peace, prosperity. Almost a thousand years had passed since an invader had last come this way, and the passing time had left the land matured, gracefully aged. For countless generations it had been nurtured by yeomen of England, who had toiled and cared for their holdings without fearing the ravages of the next passing horde.

It was here in this lush corner of the country that he had chosen to make a home for his family, a haven from politics and the bustle of daily life in London. For almost twenty years it had served that purpose admirably, as Clementine and he slowly adapted to the country life and their children grew to adulthood. Closing his eyes for just a few seconds brought back pleasant memories: bright spring days gardening or painting; crisp autumn days engaged in building work around the grounds and, most of all, long summer evenings relaxing with friends, enjoying both their company and the good-humoured debates that often developed.

But there had been serious purpose here as well. Far away from the treadmill of London, he was able to marshal his thoughts on the national issues of the day as he went about the work of the estate. In the midst of all the physical activity he found an oasis for concentration, where he could assimilate the latest news from the Continent, mull over the opinions of others he respected, and contemplate parallels from history. Then, most evenings, after dinner with Clemmy or friends he would retire upstairs to his study, there to pen the articles and speeches that had tried to alert his countrymen to the threat posed by Hitler.

His 'wilderness' years, some called them, and he often smiled at the irony.

Wilderness! Here... in this verdant place? This nursery of fauna and flora... this seedbed of political manifesto!

He knew that history would be the judge. But whichever perspective was accurate, his idyll was not to last. Peace, hard-won through the 'war to end wars', had been fervent desire of many. But, sadly, not of all. Across Europe the sound of jackboots began to echo, first in alleyways, then in wide streets, and finally across great squares... Rome... Berlin... Vienna... The thunder was increasing, and it became clear that events on the Continent were drifting ominously back towards war. To his great dismay, he had watched his own government vacillate in the face of Nazism, temporising and seeking compromise. With his incisive mind and great power of oratory, Churchill became the leader and the voice of those opposed to the appeasement. The discussions in his country house had moved on from Socratic debate about the threats to democracy posed by Bolshevism and Fascism to the hard practicality of fighting Hitler and his apologists. Far from being a refuge, Chartwell became instead the centre of political opposition.

It was now nine long months into the war and, to his great regret, his visits here were rare. Today's had been finessed into the schedule on the way back to London from a tour of beach defences, some less than thirty miles from where he stood. He was glad of the short break in his gruelling programme and the few minutes of sanctuary afforded in the garden. Realistically he knew that he would not be able to spend much time here in his beloved Chartwell in the months and probably years to come. The demands on his time, since the outbreak of war as a member of Chamberlain's Cabinet, and now as Prime Minister, were just too heavy. Even as a place of occasional retreat the house did not serve well. Its very position, elevated above the surrounding countryside, which made for those heart-warming views, also made it far too visible to the Luftwaffe's pilots. They would be sure to see it, and him, as prime targets in the brutal conflict.

He started to head back towards the cottage, passing again by the great house. In the courtyard stood a makeshift bomb shelter: squat, almost obscene. He glared at it as he walked past, knowing that, for all its ugliness, it offered little protection against the munitions now in use. Dealing with it would be the first item on his list when this damned war was over. A few yards further on he came to the foot of the steps down from the French windows. He paused and looked round to the side of the flight. The scowl left his face and a wistful smile appeared. His eyes were focused on a small stack of bricks, still resting where he had left them almost a year ago. He sighed, pondering on how much had happened since he had last put down his trowel and finished, as he had thought, for the day. Bending down he lifted a paver from the top of the pile and turned it over in his hands, caressing its rough clay surface.

He was desperately worried. His calls over the years for the country to ready itself had been clear and cogent, but he knew that he had been only marginally successful. Few of his countrymen and, amongst politicians, neither friends nor opponents had wanted to listen. Less than twenty years after the First World War, and all its horrors, there were few indeed who would allow themselves to countenance a renewal of that conflict. Surely no-one who had lived though that maelstrom of blood and steel, trenches and mud, bayoneting and gas could allow it to happen again. Reason, they assumed, would prevail in Germany, as in England.

Eventually, but much too late, people had realised that reason did not prevail when it came to Nazi Germany. That nation's hatred of war had been replaced by a hatred of defeat. The humiliation of Versailles and the debilitating depression that followed had outweighed the painful memories. New leaders had arisen who carried deep within them a lust for revenge against the countries, and the race, seen as responsible. Chamberlain and Halifax had tried valiantly, but naively and ultimately in vain to negotiate and compromise with Hitler. It had all been to no avail. Perhaps the year's breathing space between the doomed Munich Agreement and the outbreak of war had allowed for some improvement in Britain's defences; but not nearly enough. No one would ever know whether a stronger stance at an earlier time would have caused the man to stop before he had acquired the taste of victory; before his generals had demonstrated the superiority of their soldiers and weaponry to those of the democratic countries.

It was too late now. He placed the brick back on top of the stack and walked on along the terrace, his thoughts moving to the present dire situation. The 'Phoney War,' they were calling it just a month ago. Not phoney for the hundreds of civilians drowned on the SS *Athenia,* or the thousand sailors lost on HMS *Royal Oak,* although compared to the hell of the last few weeks... Denmark and Norway, Holland and Belgium, and now France!

That the neutrals had been overwhelmed by the German juggernaut did not surprise him – but that the combined armies of Britain and France, nearly a hundred and forty divisions, could be smashed in a matter of weeks by Hitler's panzers... He shuddered. *Thank God for the deliverance at Dunkirk.*

A deliverance certainly, but also, by any measure, a disaster. The weapons and equipment of the British Expeditionary Force, the prime of the Army, lay strewn across the fields and dunes of northern France. The RAF had lost hundreds of aircraft, shot down or abandoned at dusty airfields; dozens of destroyers and small craft had been sunk during the evacuation. Now, just two weeks later, the Battle of France was almost over. The remnants of the French army were still hanging on in the south of their country against fierce German pressure, but he knew from his last meeting with their leaders that it would be only a matter of days, a week at most, before they capitulated. Their famous élan was all but extinguished. *Then Britain alone would fly the flag of freedom in Europe.*

He took a deep breath as he contemplated the enormity of the challenge. Then he paused, steadied himself, and tried to focus on his lush surroundings. The sun was setting lower now, and for a brief moment he was able to indulge himself, enjoying the rich colours and sounds of the countryside. In the middle distance he could hear cattle low as their milking time drew near, while in the high branches of a nearby elm tree a blackbird was loudly proclaiming its tenancy. Around his head dozens of bees pirouetted noisily. He smiled at their furious activity, untroubled by the world, as they ferried nectar from the shrubs on the terrace down to the hives in the lower garden.

Then, indistinct to begin with but gradually becoming audible above their drone, he heard a different sound – the distinctive tone of a Merlin engine bringing a sharp injection of reality to his cloistered setting. He looked up and, far above, could just make out a solitary aircraft straining for height as it headed east towards the Channel. A Spitfire, no doubt, on a reconnaissance mission. A lone, brave pilot setting out for the final check of the day on the French ports. It was a poignant reminder of where the photographs came from that appeared on his desk each morning. For just a moment the sun glinted on its wings. Silently he wished the pilot Godspeed, and watched and listened until the aircraft disappeared from view, its engine note faded away and, gently but persistently, the sound of the bees regained the ascendancy.

He looked at his pocket watch. It was nearly six o'clock, the time when in those not so distant days he would have been finishing up work for the evening, before heading to the house to wash and dress for dinner. He found himself half-listening for the church bell in Westerham village to ring out the hour. On this day no sound came from the tower. Instead, its deafening silence rang out a different message: *England was waiting.*

It was time to go; there was much work still to be done in Whitehall. He headed back towards the garden cottage where his companions had waited, stretching out the small talk over a pot of tea. Coming in from the light he saw a young woman watering the geraniums in the porch. He hesitated. The woman had her back turned to him, but he knew it was Jessie, his housekeeper. He had spoken to her just a few days ago on hearing the sad news that her brother, Ted, had been killed at Dunkirk; one of the brave rearguard who had held off the German advance so that the mass of the defeated army could make its escape to England. A fine young man. He remembered him well.

"Good evening, Mr Churchill." She turned and greeted him, in a warm but subdued voice.

"Evening, Jessie. I thought those were looking a bit dried up." It was easier to talk about the withered plants than the sadness that enveloped her.

"They are." She continued watering. "I'm afraid they weren't seen to last week... while I was off helping my mother."

"That's understandable." He paused for a moment, then lowered his voice. "How is she?"

"Bearing up, sir. She's been through it before." The words cut through him. He recalled that Jessie's father had been killed in the First World War, at the Somme, leaving behind a widow and the two infants. He struggled for the right expression, but could only grunt sympathetically before gently making his way past her into the kitchen.

"Time to be on our way, gentlemen," he said quietly, not really wanting to leave but conscious of the tasks that remained to be done that evening. As they rose to go, he turned again to the young woman and took her hand.

"Goodbye, Jessie. Please give my deep condolences to your mother. It's hard to offer any consolation at a time like this, but you should both know that Ted's sacrifice, and his comrades', may have saved the country."

He looked at her. He saw the tears welling in her eyes, and heard her voice falter as she struggled to reply.

"I will, Mr. Churchill. Thank you. And may God's blessing be with you too, sir. We're all depending on you now."

CHAPTER TWO

He didn't say much on the drive up to London. Jessie's grief had brought into sharp focus the immediacy of the threat they faced, and her parting words lay heavily upon him. She had meant them as encouragement, but instead they made him feel the weight of his burden. As the car sped through the Kent countryside he slouched low in the back seat, barely sensing the blurred shapes of trees and hedgerows as they flashed past the window. When he did look out at the world, it was only to be reminded of England's green and pleasant land, its splendour – and of what might befall it if he failed... concentration camps... deportations... executions...

The car slowed as they came into the village of Warlingham, as the driver carefully steered his way through the narrow streets. Here there would often be a friendly wave for Churchill as he passed through, but this evening the footpaths were empty; the tidy homes, shops and taverns all beginning to darken under the evening black-out. Past the village green they went, then braked to a stop as they reached the main road to allow a long convoy of trucks to pass. They waited, unrecognised, as it trundled by. From a pub on the corner he could hear the faint sound of singing and a piano playing. He rolled the window down an inch and listened, picturing the scene inside; the happy, probably slightly intoxicated youths. Servicemen, he guessed, many of them, on a few hours' leave. 'Run, Adolf, run,' they sang. It was a cheery chorus, and spoke to him of the country's spirit. They would fight and he would lead them. But, surrounded as he was by so many conflicting images, he couldn't bring himself to smile. The carefree young men in the pub, relaxing from their duties; the others, much grimmer he suspected, in the convoy on the way to their battle stations. And over there, standing proud in the centre of the green, was the village war memorial, a brooding obelisk, inscribed with the fallen from the First World War. Was it hungry for more names? The granite would not refuse the chisel. How many of these young men? He thought, in sadness, about the price that would be paid to see this through.

The car drove on, and Churchill closed his eyes for a few minutes of fitful sleep.

An hour later he was back in Downing Street, being met by his private secretary, Jock Colville. Any lingering thoughts or doubts were quickly dispelled as he went with him into his comfortable office and began to immerse himself in the pressing tasks of leadership. There were several urgent messages to deal with, and then, as ever, the ministerial boxes. He could see that the young Cambridge graduate had done his usual professional job getting them into shape. Just as he opened the first buff-coloured folder a senior officer appeared at his door. He beckoned him in. It was General Ismay, 'Pug' to his friends, his representative on the Chiefs of Staff committee; a tall, imposing figure with the bluff military looks to match his nickname.

"Good evening, Prime Minister, how did the tour go?" Even his opening question was reassuring. If there was anything of note on the military side he would know about it, and would have been quick to raise it.

"Fine, Pug. The defence works are coming on well, and the men seem very determined... I'm glad to say. Chartwell, though, is looking a bit run down. I supposed that's to be expected... How are things here?"

"Not much changed from this morning, sir. The withdrawal from

Norway is going to plan, and you're well aware of the situation in France." A steadfast and trusted advisor, Ismay had the good sense not to burden the Prime Minister unnecessarily. This evening there was little to discuss that couldn't wait until the Cabinet meeting next day.

"Fine, Pug, you'd better leave me to this lot." He nodded at the boxes. "I'll see you in the morning."

With General Ismay gone it was time for his correspondence. He took a cigar from the humidor on his desk, lit it, and settled down to the files, with Colville hovering close by, in case he was needed.

"These look fine, Jock. I'll give them a couple of hours and then take supper in the dining room." He looked at the carriage clock on the mantelpiece. "Let's say, about half past ten. Give Beaverbrook and Bracken a call and ask them to come over."

He knew that he needed occasional escape from the pressure cooker. These two Tory MPs were his great friends, friends he could talk to and share his deepest thoughts with. Though much disliked by many within the party, they had been close to him for years. The pair had much in common; both were pressmen, both colonials, both lightning sharp. Max Beaverbrook was Canadian, a pushy and hard-hitting businessman who had arrived a few years before the First World War, leaving behind a slightly cloudy background in his home country. Settling quickly in London, he had thrown himself into the world of the popular press, taking over the *Daily Express* and driving it to great success. Within a year of his arrival in his adopted country, friends in high places helped ease a path for him into politics, and he had entered Parliament.

Brendan Bracken, a younger man, had come a decade later with his fortune still to make. He was an even more complex individual than Beaverbrook: a tall, wiry-haired extrovert with a reputation as a schemer, a manipulator, and regarded as frequently economical with the truth. The troublesome, truant son of an Irish Republican activist, he had been exiled from his native Tipperary to Australia as a teenager, there to live with relatives for several years. At the tender age of 19 he had returned to Europe, to England, now reinventing himself as an orphan who had lost his parents in a bush fire. He had bluffed his way into a minor public school where he stayed for a single term, just long enough to wear the old school tie, before setting out on life as a journalist and re-directing all his unusual talents in pursuit of that career.

In time he, too, had become a successful entrepreneur, chairman of the *Financial News* and *The Banker,* before turning his attention to politics. Along the way he had become totally committed to Churchill, the politician and the man. He had managed to befriend the iconic figure in the mid-1920s, when the statesman's political fortunes were at a low ebb, and had now been at his right hand for fifteen years, helping guide him through the twists and turns of his turbulent private and public life. In 1929 he had been elected as a Tory MP, and had earned Churchill's eternal gratitude for his unwavering support during the long, lonely fight against appeasement.

Over the years these two rumbustious pressmen had become influential and well-respected, both in Fleet Street and in the political establishment – if not much liked. They were, after all, outsiders... radicals... perhaps not quite gentlemen. But they both were experienced and pragmatic politicians, equipped with acute antennae and, very usefully, with influential public voices through their newspapers. Most of all, they were totally loyal to Churchill.

A month earlier, in mid-May, Bracken had been at Churchill's side as the political crisis unfolded. With Prime Minister Chamberlain's government tottering towards collapse, the Tory party began the process of choosing a successor. The Foreign Secretary, Lord Halifax, had been first to show his hand. A tall, patrician figure, he was the epitome of an English gentleman, a devout member of the Church of England and a friend of King George VI. It looked as if he would be the natural choice. As the party grandees set about taking soundings in their traditional, club-like manner to confirm the selection, Bracken had coached Churchill. "When they ask if you support their recommendation, just sit there, for as long as it takes. Say not a word."

The long silence had been enough. It dawned on the elders, and on Halifax himself, that he did not have the breadth of support needed to unite the party, never mind the country. He had been too closely associated with the policy of appeasement to take over the torch of leadership once that policy had failed. In a momentous decision they nominated Churchill, and advised the King to appoint him head of a National Government.

Even as Britain's politicians deliberated on the succession, Hitler's divisions smashed across their western frontier. The Phoney War was over. It was no time to be faint-hearted, or think about longer-term political consequences. Without hesitation Churchill invited Clement Attlee, leader of the opposition Labour Party, to join the new Cabinet, and appointed him Deputy Prime Minister. Wryly he thought to himself that working with Labour ministers in government should not be too challenging a task – he often felt that he had more friends on their side of the House than among his fellow Tories. But he then had to decide on the remaining Cabinet positions. With German panzers sweeping into France, Holland and Belgium there was little time to ponder. Beaverbrook had been quick to offer his advice, not mincing his words.

"You're going to have to be careful, Winston. You'll be working away with your new Labour buddies, making them part of the team – and at the same time you'll need to…" He hesitated for a moment. "To be brutally frank, you're going to have to watch your back… from your own right wingers. You can't be fighting a war with them as well as the Nazis. It's not going to be easy."

"Hmm. I'm conscious of that, Max," he grunted. "And I agree… the Labour side should be fine… Attlee's dependable and so are their other ministers. On our own side, if I can still call it that, Eden is solid – and I'll rid myself of any of the juniors I'm not sure about. The real question lies over one or two of the others…"

Bracken knew there were some tough calls to make and voiced his opinion bluntly.

"The big threat's still the old appeasement mob, Winston... trying to undermine you... maybe even making secret contact with the Nazis. I still hear mutterings in the House. Some of them were a bit too impressed by that Austrian corporal before the war. Too bloody dangerous to leave the ringleaders of that lot sitting on the back benches, like vultures, waiting for things to get worse," he hesitated for a moment, looking straight into Churchill's eyes, "which they undoubtedly will."

Churchill pursed his lips. "Chamberlain and Halifax? I've been thinking about that. Keeping them in the Cabinet certainly reduces the chance of a rebellion, although, to be honest, I don't see Neville as a problem."

It was clear that Chamberlain was seriously ill and deeply disillusioned by the collapse of the agreement he thought he had reached with Hitler. He had, nonetheless, earned the respect of the nation for his honest endeavour in trying to stop the Nazis by diplomatic means. Even after his failure in that quest, and despite failing health, Churchill knew he would offer his final reserves of strength to serve his country. He then sat silent for a few moments, pensive, before adding quietly, "Halifax is more of a question mark..."

He knew that, while in every sense a patriot, the Foreign Secretary believed that it was still possible, indeed necessary, to seek a settlement with Hitler that did not compromise Britain's vital interests – particularly in the Empire. His position was the one that Churchill needed to make a decision on.

"Yes," he murmured, "there are risks whichever way I go." He looked up. "However I'm coming to the same conclusion as you, Brendan. It does make sense to keep him in the Cabinet. And if I am to pursue the logic in my line of thought quite relentlessly, that means the inner sanctum, the War Cabinet."

Beaverbrook had been quietly signalling agreement, and added his support.

"Damn right, Winston, keep him as close to you as possible... up to his neck in it... totally involved with every decision. That'll reduce the chances of him ratting on you at the worst possible time, based on some 'noble' principle or whatever."

There was consensus. With some reservation, and with his friends' words of counsel still ringing in his ears, Churchill decided to retain Halifax as his Foreign Secretary.

A month had passed since the new government was formed; a nightmare month, with the crisis deepening from day to day. Defeat after defeat, withdrawal after withdrawal, the Allied forces had been driven back inexorably by the Nazis. The Battle of France was reaching its disastrous, almost unimaginable conclusion, with the surrender of that proud country imminent. However for Britain, mercifully, the immediate danger in the train of Dunkirk seemed to have passed; the German armies had turned towards Paris instead of pursuing the defeated troops across the Channel. After the previous few weeks of panic there was now a breathing space, a brief interlude, allowing some semblance of defence to be created from out of the chaos. Nazi paratroopers had not come swarming from the English sky; the panzers had not come rolling up the beaches to continue their assault upon the broken army.

Even as the French army still lay writhing in agony, the defeated British troops were being transported to camps around the country, there to recover, regroup and, as soon as possible, re-arm. In the naval dockyards the Navy's battered destroyers were being patched up; riveters, welders and fitters working round the clock to prepare the ships for sea. At airfields throughout the land, the RAF stood bruised but ready. There was no time to relax. As the new Prime Minister had counselled the House a few days previously, *"Wars are not won by evacuations"*. But he knew that there was, at least, some time to ready the country for resistance. *And, by God, resistance there would be!*

Refreshed by his few hours at Chartwell, Churchill worked on into the evening, preparing for the Cabinet meeting in the morning. Even though the final fate of France was still to be determined, he had to start preparing the nation for the next battle – for Britain itself. He was satisfied that the new Cabinet was functioning well, but knew it was now time to direct his attention to the leadership in the Services. The performance of the British forces since war began had been most dispiriting – Norway lost, the British Expeditionary Force in France defeated. He had to take action, had to stop the rot. He had already shared his deep disquiet with Ismay. Though conscious that Pug might naturally feel some loyalty towards his military colleagues, Churchill knew that he also recognised the leadership problem. His military service in the Indian Army, on the North West frontiers rather than in the trenches of the First World War, gave him a certain independence of mind, and he knew he could be trusted to give a balanced, professional view. However, for the second time in a month, he had decided to call on his old friends for advice. They were not military men, but they would know the mood of parliament and the nation. He would seek their input over supper.

As he sat contemplating the problem, there was a knock on the door and Colville entered.

"I'm sorry, sir. There's an urgent call from the Admiralty. I'm afraid it's bad news."

He lifted the phone and listened with dismay. It was yet another devastating blow; the aircraft carrier HMS *Glorious* and its two small escorts had been sunk in the North Sea. He listened, appalled. "*Contact lost twelve hours ago... German battleships spotted nearby... unlikely to be many survivors...*"

He smashed his fist on his desk in frustration, railing at the loss. The stupidity of allowing one of the navy's few carriers to sail almost alone in an area where German warships were known to be active; the disgrace that it had failed to spot the enemy in time; the shame that it hadn't been able to fly off a single aircraft in its own defence!

With his experience as First Lord of the Admiralty during the First World War, he was well aware of the danger from the German navy. He knew how close to starvation Britain had been brought by the U-boats, and was very conscious that it could happen again. But that threat came from under the sea, not from the tiny number of surface ships that the German Navy possessed! At the Battle of Jutland, in 1916, the German fleet had learned that they could not challenge the Royal Navy on the open seas, and had retreated to port for the duration of the war. Yet now, with this new war only nine months old, they had inflicted a humiliating loss – a capital ship lost without reply in a surface action. First the Army had failed the country... *and now the Navy?*

He tried to calm himself for a few minutes, then called Admiral Pound, the First Sea Lord, to check that a full search was underway. "And not just for survivors, Admiral," he bellowed. "For the assailants!"

It was close to midnight, and with no more to be done he rose slowly from his desk to go to the dining room. He stopped in mid-corridor, deeply dejected, his hand gripped tightly on his cane. *The great ship itself... more than a thousand men... dozens of Fleet Air Arm and RAF pilots, so desperately needed for the battle ahead.* He took a deep breath to compose himself, then, still tormented by his thoughts, went in. The room was empty apart from his two friends, and he could tell by the anguished looks on their faces that they had heard the news. The mood was sombre as he sat down.

"Another appalling disaster! When will it end? The Army routed in France and now the Navy losing major warships in the North Sea. I don't believe the country will stand for it much longer."

He put his hands on the table and looked down, slowly, disconsolately, shaking his head. "How do I keep the men fighting if they see, yet again, the incompetence shown in the last war? How do I stop them rebelling or simply throwing down their arms in disgust?" He paused again, a catch in his throat, then looked up at his friends. "I feel it necessary to sweep right through the Services and replace the failed leaders, before the men simply give up... or worse."

Bracken was alarmed by the anger and despondency in his tone and, glancing at Beaverbrook, saw the concern reflected. They both knew the signs. Over the years they had often seen Churchill experience extreme mood swings, sometimes to elation, but occasionally into deep depression, his 'black dogs' as he termed them. With all the problems the country faced, this was no time for the Prime Minister to slip into the darkness. Nor would it help to lash out indiscriminately at the Services, hurting as they already were from the exertions of the last month. As often before, it was Bracken who pulled him away from the edge.

"You're quite right, Winston. We've got to stop this run of defeats. There have to be changes. So let's fire the generals, certainly, and the admirals, and the colonels as well... maybe the sergeants too, while you're at it?"

Churchill glowered at him, but Bracken held his ground. "You know exactly what the problem is. *Where do you stop?* I'm no expert on military affairs – but I know you can't sweep away the command structure in any organisation and hope it will survive."

Churchill scowled. "Someone's got to take these hard decisions – while we still have the ability to do so."

Bracken wasn't for turning. "It's not a question of ducking tough decisions; it's simple practicality. You've got to balance the change you want against the disruption it'll cause – not to mention the damage to morale."

Beaverbrook added his voice in support of Bracken, but in a more conciliatory way. "Winston, look, we know there's sense in what you're saying... but only up to a point. Of course the Army has done badly, but in my opinion – and it's what I hear on the street – the RAF and the Navy are doing OK. Sure, the RAF caught some criticism from the troops for its lack of visibility over Dunkirk, but most people I talk to, at least most intelligent people, say that's nonsense. It was our pilots who kept on fighting even after the French Air Force had given up. The very fact that our troops got away shows they kept the Luftwaffe at bay."

He paused for a moment, then added ominously.

"Our planes will be a lot more visible over the fields of Kent."

Churchill made a rumbling noise, somewhere between a snort and a sigh, before relenting slightly, to the great relief of his friends. He looked at them balefully. "That much, I grant you, is true. The RAF did fight, and bravely so. Perhaps also I should exclude their leadership from the sweeping charge of incompetence. I did give Dowding a lot of grief last month about not deploying more fighters across the Channel, but, though I don't often do so, I'll admit that I was wrong. Thank God he held back the squadrons I wanted to send over, or we'd be in an unbearable situation now."

Bracken continued while the two held the initiative. "As for the Navy... they're the heroes of the hour after Dunkirk. Apart from this disaster with *Glorious,* which sounds as if it was due to the stupidity of a few men – probably now dead – it's doing pretty well. Does it make any sense to insist on sweeping changes there?"

Churchill looked at them and grimaced as he seemed to accept their counsel, but only partially and grudgingly. He drummed his fingers on the table and raised his voice. "Must I remind you that we lost in Norway? We lost in France! Now we're losing major warships in the North Sea. You think I'm being too hasty in my drive to stop the rot? I have to act, and act quickly. But enough, enough! I've listened to your arguments and, to be fair, Ismay is saying much the same thing. I will be more focused. The Army is the problem: out-witted and out-fought by the enemy. It must bounce back immediately from the defeat in France, or we're all dead men; and it must bounce back in a way that's visible, clearly, to the man in the street. As our warriors are fighting the good fight on the battlefield we must ensure that the home front doesn't crumble behind them."

He thought he saw a slight sign of disbelief in their faces. "You think that's unlikely? Look at Germany in 1918!"

Bracken knew that they had made important ground, and now began to align himself with the Prime Minister's thinking. "So, Winston, it's desirable, even necessary, to make changes in the Army. But back to my original question, is there enough time, with the invasion perhaps just weeks away? Who would you fire?"

Churchill addressed the second part of the question first. "General Gort is an obvious candidate, as he commanded the Army in France – perhaps not too well, brave soldier though he is. I've decided to appoint General Dill as the new Chief of Staff. He's got the grey matter needed to handle this new type of warfare. And I'm not convinced about General Ironside as commander of the Home Forces. Is he up to leading the grim battle against invasion? He will also have to go. It must be clear to everyone that we've drawn a line under the defeat in France. I need someone with energy and new thinking to get the Army ready for the coming battle. I have someone in mind... Alan Brooke. The skill he showed in France was one of the few redeeming features of the campaign there. I've already bounced it off Pug, and he supports the choice."

He then came back to the earlier point, and looked directly at Bracken. "You asked if there's time, Brendan, and my answer is yes, I do believe there is – but I have to move fast. I will get Pug to start the process immediately. It may make sense to leave an overlap of a week or two to avoid a sense of panic, but no more than that. And, of course, we'll treat the departing leaders with respect. No night of the long knives here. But believe me, change is essential, and change there will be... before the storm hits."

They ate in silence for a while before Churchill continued on a different theme. "When I asked you over, I wasn't planning to spend so much time discussing these military affairs. I wanted to ask for more help from both of you. This is a completely new type of war, different from any seen before. There are new weapons we must learn to wield, over and above those carried by the fighting men. Industrial production, on an immense scale, is one. This war will be about steel – and aluminium – as much as men. Max, I've already asked you to bring your huge talents to the task of aircraft production. Drive harder, harder, and harder still. I don't believe that our war economy is out of first gear yet. If we're going to survive over the next few months we've got to build more aircraft than the Germans: in particular, more fighters. It's as simple as that. Do whatever it takes, with my full authority."

Beaverbrook looked directly at him and answered formally. "I understand, Prime Minister. It won't be pretty."

Churchill turned to Bracken.

"Propaganda is another crucial weapon. It's already plain how radio broadcasts are spreading news, or what purports to be news, almost instantaneously across the world – with scant regard for truth, only for effect. You, Brendan, have been my most insightful advisor in my political battles over the years. Now I face the biggest battle of my life. I want you to turn your attention to the outside world; to take responsibility for the propaganda war, using all your skills and influence. Start thinking how we can best employ the great range of channels that are available to us – the BBC, the national, and indeed, the international press. Consider how we can use to the full perhaps the finest asset that we have as a nation – our native tongue.

"Our communications, our propaganda as I said, though I still don't like the connotations of that word, must become clinically effective. It is imperative that we maintain the nation's morale in the tough months ahead. We must also influence, in so far as we can, opinion overseas – in the Empire and the United States. We cannot win this war without their support. Sadly, the Germans are ahead of us in this battle and are already trying to sow the seeds of defeatism here and in America. However I like to think that anything the appalling Mr Goebbels can do, you, Brendan, can do at least twice as well."

Bracken wasn't quite sure, but assumed it was meant as a compliment.

"And hurry, both of you. We don't have much time."

Chapter Three

As Churchill entered the Cabinet Room he could taste the bitter irony. Since he had first entering politics, forty years earlier, he had aspired to reach this pinnacle; to sit in the centre of this room, surrounded by his colleagues, and direct the affairs of the great nation. The room at 10 Downing Street had been the epicentre of British power for more than two hundred years. It was steeped in history. He thought about the immense issues that had been debated here over the centuries: the American War of Independence, the ending of the Slave Trade, the Napoleonic Wars, the First World War, the Emancipation of Women – and now a Second World War. On this bright morning the room was looking at its finest, the light streaming in through the tall garden windows only slightly tempered by the criss-crossed security tape on the glass. But he knew that the splendour was out of keeping with the grim reality of the hour. The war was getting too close. It was the last occasion that they would meet here, for many years in all probability. Having climbed to the top of the greasy pole, he had to say farewell to the physical trappings of that achievement. From tomorrow the fight would be directed from the new Cabinet War Rooms which had been hastily constructed under Whitehall, a few hundred yards away – much less pleasant, but safer.

Despite the dreadful news from the North Sea, the Prime Minister was in renewed vigour. He had shaken off his brush with depression and was ready for battle again. The rest of the Cabinet were already in the room and he greeted each of them individually, being particularly conscious to spend a few moments in political small talk with Chamberlain and Lord Halifax. He then took his seat at the centre of the long rectangular table with his back to the great marble fireplace, and began the meeting.

There was no good news to cheer them. They reviewed the details of the final evacuation from Norway, and then read Admiral Pound's short note on the loss of *Glorious*. His report made stark reading, but there was little sense of recrimination. The time for enquiry would come later.

They moved on to France. The situation there was deteriorating fast and they explored a range of measures which might be taken to shore up the French defences. It was rapidly becoming clear, however, that things were almost beyond salvation. Churchill said, somewhat despairingly, that he would make one final visit to try to salvage things, but it seemed to all that the end was approaching. There was little choice but for the remaining British troops in France to fall back towards Cherbourg, and hope for evacuation before they were cut off and annihilated by General Guderian's rampaging panzers.

With the military discussions concluded, the Prime Minister switched to the diplomatic situation; the recurring topic of possible negotiation with the enemy, and the growing threat of Italy entering the war.

"We need to consider our response to the latest communication from Mussolini. His language is bellicose. He shows no interest whatsoever in our efforts to get him to stay neutral. Clearly our defeat in France has emboldened him in his support for Hitler. It does seem likely that soon, perhaps within a matter of days, we will find ourselves engaged with the Italians. That is indeed sad, considering the long and warm friendship between our peoples. However we must now prepare ourselves and be ready for an outbreak of hostilities."

Antony Eden, the Secretary of State for War, was quietly support-ive. "Prime Minister, I agree that this, most regrettably, appears to be the case. Is there no further word from Foreign Minister Ciano? No follow-up to his ambiguous message last week?"

Churchill shook his head sadly as Eden continued.

"Are we even certain that there really is a peace faction in Italy, or could it all just be part of an elaborate ritual – hard man, soft man?"

Churchill responded. "Unfortunately we have not been able to de-termine which precisely is the case. In reality, however, there's not a great deal of difference between the two interpretations. On the one hand, from Ciano, and indeed via the King of Sweden, we hear sug-gestions that it might still be possible to make a deal with Hitler, un-doubtedly on most unfavourable, even squalid terms. On the other hand, all we hear from Mussolini is more drum-beating to show that things are going to get worse if we don't. But, in any event, we can-not delay our military preparations. We must proceed to increase the establishment level of our forces in the Mediterranean and, of course, their readiness. I recognise this will have implications for the battle on the home front, particularly with regard to our naval resources. I know the balance won't be easy."

Halifax remained keen to look for any chance of a negotiated agreement to the conflict. "These developments in the Mediter-ranean are indeed disappointing, but should we not, at least, main-tain the communications channel via Sweden? In our current, weak-ened state this may be the last opportunity to reach a reasonable settlement with Germany."

Instead of looking for common ground, Churchill exploded – not so much at Halifax's words as at the thought of a supplicant Britain looking for a sordid deal with the aggressor. "Reasonable, Foreign Secretary? With that man? When has he ever shown reasonable-ness? In his dealings with Czechoslovakia? Poland? Norway or Denmark? Holland or Belgium? Why would he be reasonable now, when he has just one more nation to conquer before he controls all of western Europe?"

"That is an understandable sentiment, Prime Minister," replied Halifax coolly, even coldly. "However it is possible that even in the flush of victory in France he may harbour reservations about the final battle. He still has the Royal Navy to contend with. It may be that we could negotiate from a position of some strength, before we've suffered further losses at sea or in the air."

Churchill took several deep breaths, quite deliberately, wanting to calm himself. He knew that Halifax, like Chamberlain, was a decent man, trying desperately to do the best thing for the country. He addressed his words not just to him, but to the group as a whole, his voice growing stronger and steelier as he spoke.

"The Foreign Secretary states that the Royal Navy is our strongest card and that, certainly, is true. But we have other great strengths as well: the Channel in front of us, the Empire behind, and the RAF above. Undoubtedly he fears a great naval battle – and rightly so – but we are also far stronger in the air than he thinks. Remember we chose not to send any of our Spitfire squadrons to France, keeping them back instead for the titanic battle in our own skies. The Luftwaffe is going to find Britain a much tougher nut to crack than Poland or France. And our soldiers may have come off worse in France, but they'll fight like Trojans in defence of our country."

Halifax persisted with his argument. "Prime Minister, those strengths are visible to the enemy as well. They all point to the conclusion that we're in a much better negotiating position now than we may be in a few months time, with our forces severely weakened by the ongoing battle."

Churchill wasn't interested, waving his hands in dismissal and raising his voice "We will not negotiate with that monster. Even if we all lie bloodied and dead, other men will rise to take our places and carry on the fight... here on this island, on the seas surrounding, and in the far corners of the Empire."

Halifax made no reply. There was an uncomfortable silence around the table. For a few moments it looked as if he might walk out, which was not what Churchill needed at this hour of crisis. The Prime Minister sat back in his seat, not looking anyone in the eye for a few moments, or inviting any more discussion as he waited for the tension to ease. He then straightened himself up and began to speak in a more collegiate tone, addressing himself directly to Halifax.

"On the other hand, Foreign Secretary, I suppose it can do no harm to keep open the communications channel via Sweden. It may come in useful if Germany wants to surrender!"

He pushed aside his chair and rose to leave.

Halifax looked distinctly unimpressed, but one or two of the others at least managed a wry grin. In the midst of Britain's darkest hour, they knew that the incorrigible Winston was the one thing that would keep the country fighting.

Chapter Four

The Cabinet's deliberations were quickly overtaken by events in the Mediterranean. Anxious to gain a share of the spoils before Hitler completed his victory over France, Mussolini declared war on England the next day, and the faint possibility of using Italy as an intermediary vanished. Britain's battle front now extended from the Arctic Ocean to the Eastern Mediterranean, and the country steeled itself for an onslaught from across the Channel.

In mid-morning, Churchill met with Foreign Office staff to prepare a response to the Italian declaration of war, before heading over to Admiralty House to confer with Admiral Pound on the changes to naval deployments. He decided to stay for lunch in his old haunt, and invited Beaverbrook and Bracken to come over from the War Rooms to join him. Beaverbrook was first to arrive and, after listening to Churchill summarise the previous day's Cabinet discussion, he voiced his annoyance.

"Huh. Halifax as dogged as ever? Sounds as if he hasn't really accepted the decision from two weeks ago." The issue of negotiation with the enemy had been hotly and closely debated in Cabinet in the last few days of May. "Are you worried he still poses a threat?"

"Bah, to some small extent, Max, but nothing that troubles me greatly. I can assure you that if positions were reversed and he were sitting in my seat, as Prime Minister, talking about negotiation with the enemy, the challenge would be much greater! Not just from me, but from the rest of the Cabinet, the General Staff and, I'm quite confident, the country at large. In any event, Attlee is supportive, as well as Eden, and we are the new men come to tackle the dreadful task ahead. Even if things were to get tight within the War Cabinet, I know that emotions run much differently in the full Cabinet, and I'll go there again for support, if necessary."

"Perhaps even before it becomes necessary?" suggested Beaverbrook.

"Hmm, perhaps. In any event, as far as the Swedish link is concerned it doesn't do any harm to keep playing tag – as long as the contact is kept absolutely confidential. Of course, should this discretion be abused howsoever, or should there be leaks from anywhere, it must be utterly deniable. To have it any other way would risk great damage to morale. So, in the event of any leak occurring it must point straight back to Halifax – a member of the War Cabinet certainly, but acting beyond his authority. He doesn't command the degree of personal loyalty in Parliament, or in the country, that would make such a denial problematic. And the House of Lords would be an unlikely place to start a coup!"

Bracken had joined them at the table, and had caught the end of the conversation. "Nothing new on the diplomatic front, by the sounds of things, gentlemen?"

"No," said Churchill. "Halifax still grasping at straws, but he has no support. The news from Italy is obviously regrettable from a military point of view. Perhaps even more of a risk, in the wider scheme of things, is the possible effect on our relationship with the United States. The Italian lobby there will probably line up with the isolationists, making Roosevelt's position in Congress even more difficult. Fortunately Mussolini is so pig-headed that he seems to be missing the opportunity to gain a subtle advantage. Now that you're here, Brendan, tell Max about the last telegram that Signor Mussolini sent to the President."

Roosevelt had stayed in contact with the Italians, trying to keep the country from becoming a belligerent, despite the pact they had signed with Hitler in May. A friendly, and bemused, source in the State Department had leaked Mussolini's latest telegram to Bracken, who now began to recite the bombastic missive almost verbatim, sticking his chin out in mimicry of Il Duce as he recited... *the country's honour... the noble rights of Italy... the unfairness of the treatment they had received over Abyssinia...* Finally he finished, shaking his head in disbelief. "In terms of helping our cause, I couldn't have written it better myself!"

Churchill had already read the telegram, but still sat spellbound, listening to the animated performance. He raised an eyebrow in jest. "Are you quite sure you didn't, dear Brendan?"

"Certainly not, Prime Minister!" Bracken recoiled in mock horror, but his eyes twinkled at the suggestion.

"Not on this occasion."

Chapter Five

The hiatus came as a surprise. It was as if none of the players quite knew what was in the next act. In Britain, the people awaited their trial of fire under the mocking blue skies of the finest summer in decades. Cities and towns basked in glorious sunshine, lifting the spirits of the beleaguered people and making the privations of the wartime austerity measures slightly easier to tolerate. In the countryside the effects of the good weather were even more spectacular. The rural landscape looked glorious, lush despite the early hot spell. The fields of barley and wheat were ripening quickly; the meadows and uplands filled with healthy animals; the hedgerows alive with birds.

For all the benevolence of the weather, however, there was little opportunity for leisure. By July the nation was moving rapidly to a war footing. Mobilisation was in full swing, and the race to recruit and train servicemen rapidly gathering momentum. The sound of marching could be heard in city streets and country lanes alike, as the military presence became more and more pervasive. The sadness of parting was felt across the land, as young men and women turned their backs on families and sweethearts, and left to do their duty. From all walks of life came volunteers, determined to defend their country and to fight Fascism. For many it was personal; young men wanting to carry on the fight their fathers thought they had finished twenty years earlier. For others there was no option, as the long finger of conscription plucked them unceremoniously from civilian life. At hundreds of centres, volunteers and conscripts alike began their basic training and the hard physical education to toughen them up for war. They had all that soldiers needed – except weapons and ammunition. Broom handles and pikes were poor substitutes. But gradually rifles, at least, started to appear and the new battalions began to form up, ready to take their place in the front line.

In the tillage fields the continuing good weather promised a bountiful harvest. Away from the immediately threatened corner of the realm, where military activity predominated, the English countryside seemed to have been transported back to an earlier age. With almost no private cars and few buses running, the country lanes were filled with bicycles and even older conveyances: carts, side cars and pony traps unearthed from dusty barns and sheds. There were even horse-drawn ploughs reappearing, helping to supplement the tractors as the nation adjusted to life under strict petrol rationing.

The faces in the fields had also changed. Farming was a reserved occupation, with the workers exempt from call-up, but many farmhands had signed up in response to the threat to their country. With so many of the young men gone to war, their places were now taken by their sisters, wives and mothers. Young and not-so-young, these land girls made the hard adjustment to the tough, physical work in the fields. In the propaganda newsreels, shown in cinemas across the land, they may have looked cheerfully innocent, but they knew the deadly seriousness of their work; knew the part they were playing in the nation's fight for survival. Every ton of grain gathered from the fields meant one less to import. Every thousand tons meant a ship freed up to carry munitions instead of food.

In the ports and railway stations there were many other signs of change. Strange accents began to be heard as soldiers from abroad started to make a welcome appearance. Driven by the strong bonds of kinship, the dominion countries, Canada, Australia and New Zealand, had sent seasoned troops and airmen to support the mother country in its hour of need. Strange languages could be heard, too. From the defeated countries on the continent had come, by a myriad of routes, thousands of escapees. For these young soldiers, sailors and airmen, the call was different. For them it was a common cause, the defeat of Nazism. Deeply embittered by the fate of their homelands, they bravely donned new uniforms, khaki or blue, determined to continue the fight.

The stress of mobilisation brought other severe challenges to the war economy. With hundreds of thousands of young Britons enlisting in the Armed Forces, it was vital that the wheels of industry kept turning. Twelve-hour days became the norm in the munitions plants, as production ramped up to meet the desperate needs of the troops: the guns and shells, small arms and ammunition. Most critical of all, output soared in the aircraft factories, as Beaverbrook slashed his buccaneering way though red tape, ignoring objections and blind to compromise as he carried out Churchill's clear instructions.

The nation's physical defences were also steadily improving. Across the south-east corner of England, squads of navvies and army work details laboured round the clock to build fortifications. The warm, dry spell gave a fillip to the work. Even under the threat of imminent invasion, concrete could not have been poured into water-filled trenches or cement blocks laid in lashing rain. But under the high summer sun the construction teams made rapid progress, fortifying towns, villages, hamlets and farmhouses. With close supervision from Army engineers, they created choke points at river crossings and in tight country lanes to impede the enemy's advance. On the vitally-important airfields the defences were greatly strengthened, turning each of them into a tough bastion. Earth and stone revetments were constructed, scattered around the dispersal areas at obtuse angles, to protect the aircraft against bomb blasts or strafing attacks. Buildings and runways were camouflaged. Trenches were dug beside the busy hangars and workshops to provide shelters for the vulnerable ground crews. Ominously, it was not just for air attack that the airfields were being prepared. The blitzkrieg on the Continent had shown the real threat of direct assault on airfields by German parachute and glider troops. The bitter experience had been heeded. Large numbers of concrete pillboxes and other ingenious defensive positions were hastily constructed on and around the air bases. The RAF was determined that its fate would be decided by the battle in the skies, not by a grubby defeat on the ground.

Every day that passed gave more precious time to prepare, and for several weeks the work was untroubled by a strangely quiet enemy. With victory achieved over France, the Fuehrer seemed to have paused, perhaps sated for the moment, or perhaps the Nazis, too, needed time to recuperate from the battle and consider their next move. But gradually, as the month wore on, German attacks began to increase. The naval skirmishes in the Channel became more frequent and intense, with E-boats and the Luftwaffe's bombers making life increasingly difficult for the little tramp steamers ploughing their way along the coast in makeshift convoys. Losses of ships began to mount, and the RAF was gradually drawn into an unwelcome battle over the Channel, trying to protect them.

On the other side of the narrow seaway, the first signs could be seen of serious preparation for invasion. Reconnaissance photographs showed immense troop encampments being set up across northern France and the Low Countries, and airfields filled to capacity with fighters, bombers – and transport aircraft. There were equally ominous signs on the maritime side. Hundreds of steamers and barges had been appropriated from their civilian owners, and were now being plotted heading south from the North Sea and Baltic ports. Although German shipping had no easier freedom of the Channel than British, groups of vessels began to sneak their way down the coast under cover of darkness, trying to reach the relative safety of the heavily-defended French and Dutch ports. But even when they made it, they were not to have too comfortable a stay there. The RAF responded to the unwelcome arrivals with a fierce campaign of bombing during the short summer nights, inflicting considerable damage as they tried to disrupt the build-up of the invasion fleet.

Away to the west, in the Atlantic, the submarine war was growing more vicious by the day. Their commander, Admiral Doenitz, had transferred his U-boats to the new bases on the coast of Brittany, from where they could strike more readily at the convoys, little more than a day's sail away. The southwest approaches to Britain gradually became unsafe for passage, forcing merchant shipping from the Commonwealth or the Americas into long detours to the north. The Atlantic battle could now be recognised for what it was: the other flank of a great German assault whose pincers were slowly, painfully beginning to close.

In the skies above Britain, the RAF appeared to be holding its own, to the enormous relief of the War Cabinet. The Luftwaffe had stepped up its pressure, and switched its focus from the coastal convoys to Britain's defence infrastructure, the airfields, radar sites and control centres. Losses on both sides were growing, although at least Fighter Command was now getting the planes it needed. Driven hard by Beaverbrook, the factories were producing twice as many fighters as just a few months ago, more indeed than the RAF was losing. But aircraft numbers were not the only issue. As the battle continued, the focus came more and more on the shortage of pilots to fly them and fight in them. There were not enough new men coming out of the training units to replace the losses: the dead, the missing, the burned.

Even the Army had put the defeat in France behind it, and was being brought to a battleworthy state. With General Brooke now in firm command, the demand for reform and improvement was relentless. His approach to defending Britain was based cogently on his experience from the cauldron of France, and was closely aligned to Churchill's own conviction – that speed and mobility were key. The best infantry divisions and tank regiments were redeployed to new locations, selected with great attention to their road links. The message to their commanders was clear; the defending forces were to be at the ready to strike in whatever direction was needed to smash any enemy breakout.

The static defences were no longer seen as the main plank of defence, but they too were greatly strengthened. Along threatened coasts, fortified emplacements were constructed. Razor wire was strung across dunes and cliffs, and minefields laid. Behind this coastal crust, serried defence lines were established using the natural features of rivers and canals, forests and embankments. Where these didn't exist, steep anti-tank ditches were dug to stop, or at least slow, the Nazi panzers. Deep in the countryside, work continued at the same frenetic pace. Pillboxes and concrete anti-tank pimples began to appear by roadsides and in laneways. Bridges and dykes were wired with demolition charges. Anti-glider posts were embedded in potential landing fields. Even signposts were removed from roads.

There were other, less visible, preparations. In secluded woods and barns, hides were constructed where small groups of stay-behinds would secrete themselves, ready to strike in the rear of the advancing German formations if the worst were to happen. They prepared for their covert missions in the full, grim knowledge of how the Nazis would treat any *franc-tireurs* they captured.

From Land's End to John O'Groats, Britain was readying itself.

CHAPTER SIX

On the first day of August, the Cabinet and the Chiefs of Staff gathered in the War Cabinet Room. Churchill had demanded a full review of the nation's defences against invasion. He remained particularly concerned about the readiness of the Army, and had asked his two most senior generals to attend: Sir John Dill, Chief of the Imperial General Staff, and Alan Brooke, just two weeks in his new post as C-in-C, Home Forces – the army responsible for defending Britain. The two generals entered the room together, deep in conversation. Every moment was precious as they continued their critical evaluation of the senior officers in each division, deciding who was up to the job of command in the coming battle, and who was not. A few minutes later the First Sea Lord, Admiral Pound, arrived. He would report on the Navy's anti-invasion plans. Just behind him came Air Chief Marshal Dowding.

The senior officers took their places in the cramped room, followed a few minutes later by the members of the Cabinet and then the Prime Minister, swathed in cigar smoke, to the distaste of the non-smokers in the group. At least the ventilation system seemed to be effective, though noisy. Last to arrive was Pug Ismay, who had to duck under the reinforced concrete ceiling beams and squeeze his large frame round the table to reach his seat.

Churchill asked Dill to begin. There was no need for a preamble;

they all knew why they were there. The General started with a candid review of the Army's lacklustre performance since war began, the clipped Northern Irish tone underlying his public school accent being well-suited to the abrupt message he brought,

"Prime Minister, the Army suffered a calamitous defeat in France. We must accept that, and come to terms with it. Just a few words can be said in mitigation. The tactical situation was extremely unfavourable. We were left badly exposed by the collapse of Belgium and the poor disposition of the French army. The troops suffered from a lack of air support, and they had difficult logistics to contend with. It's also true that in some battles, particularly at Arras and Calais, the men did fight extremely well."

He looked up, ahead of his damning conclusion.

"But, that having been said, we must be frank: the Germans fought better. Our forces were overwhelmed by their tactics, especially the fast moving *blitzkrieg* and their use of air power to support their troops. We are extremely fortunate to have saved the lives of so many of our men, and, from the country's point of view, their fighting skills. But we have much to learn, and learn fast."

He paused for a moment while his blunt words were absorbed, in silence, by his audience. As instructed beforehand by the Prime Minister, Dill then handed over to General Brooke to continue the briefing. Brooke was the man now carrying the responsibility

He took the floor, and didn't waste time on preliminaries. Despite the short time since his appointment, it was clear that he had mastered his brief quickly.

"Prime Minister, in the aftermath of Dunkirk, the German army was at least twice as strong as us in men, and possibly four to five times stronger in tanks and artillery. If they had been able to cross the Channel in May or June we would have been put to the pins of our collars to stop them. Fortunately they didn't, and we've been making good use of the breathing space."

Brooke paused and looked down at his notes.

"The re-organisation of the regiments is well underway, and their refurbishment. The regular and reserve infantry divisions are almost up to strength in terms of men and basic equipment – rifles, machine guns and mortars. Re-equipment is also proceeding well in the artillery regiments. We have received the consignment of 75mm field guns from America – almost a thousand weapons. They're old, but adequate for a defensive battle, and are being distributed to the regiments as I speak. We're also building up production of our own guns, particularly the anti-tank weapons which are urgently needed. Looking at the armoured regiments, the situation is also improving, with the factories delivering almost four hundred new tanks since May."

Churchill interrupted his flow, with an almost casual aside. "That is progress, although I suspect that the Germans may have built even more."

It was Brooke's first challenge, and he looked directly at the Prime Minister. "With respect, sir, that doesn't actually matter. It's not how many tanks they have; it's how many they can get across the Channel. The real problem would be if they were building many more tank landing craft, more perhaps than we could sink."

The Prime Minister accepted the mild rebuff. "That is fair comment, General. Pray continue."

Brooke returned to his theme. "It is our great good fortune that almost all our gunners and tank crews got back, even if they had to abandon their weapons. At least we are not faced with a huge training task. Our re-equipment also benefits from the short time it now takes to get tanks and guns from the factories to the front line – contrast that with the long supply lines that the enemy has to contend with. For all that, the Germans would still have a considerable advantage in numbers if they were able to deploy their full strength against us, in pitched battle. But, as I said, we won't be facing the entire German army, only those forces that they can convey across the Channel. We know that the RAF and the Navy will see to it that that will be a not-insignificant challenge for them."

He paused, and Churchill interrupted again, though this time with a supportive comment. "That is moderately reassuring news, General, both in regard to the troop levels and the progress on armaments. Now will you please share with us the situation regarding the tactical deployment of our forces."

This was an easier ball for Brooke. The main reason that General Ironside had been replaced was his penchant for static defence, which experience in France had shown to be an outdated concept. Brooke had already demonstrated to Churchill a much greater awareness of the need for rapid mobility.

"Sir, as soon as I assumed command I reviewed the disposition of the troops, and have made changes. In France we saw the speed with which the German panzers can cover ground once they achieve a breakthrough. In Holland and Belgium we saw the threat from their parachute and glider forces, which were able to overwhelm static defensive positions with startling speed. We also discovered, to our cost, how quickly they can move their air squadrons, to stay abreast of the armoured units – often within a day or two of capturing an airfield. I've now assigned a much larger part of our forces as mobile reserves rather than to the fixed defence lines, so that we'll be able to bottle them up if we see any risk of a breakout occurring."

Clement Attlee was most concerned about the civilians living in towns near the battle zone.

"I assume you will not be abandoning the defence lines completely, General?"

"No, Deputy Prime Minister. They still have an important role, namely to blunt the initial assault and slow them down. However the General Staff now recognise that behind strong coastal and inland defences, we must be able to bring forces to bear rapidly, and I mean within a few hours, on any location where the enemy threatens a breakout, in particular where there's risk of loss of a vital asset such as a port or airfield."

Churchill knew the direction in which Brooke was driving, and indicated his approval. "I am very pleased to hear that these steps are underway. Unquestionably the Nazis were faster to adapt to the modern technology of warfare, and it is essential that we respond quickly. Please advise me of progress or of any obstacles you encounter. On a different topic, how are we doing with the big guns for the coastal artillery? I had asked General Ironside to keep me informed." He had long had a fascination with these, which he maintained even though they appeared be at variance with his proclaimed belief in mobile defence.

"We're making good progress, sir. There are six batteries already in place along the coast between Dover and Portsmouth, each with a pair of 6" guns. So just about all the potential landing beaches now have some heavy artillery cover to supplement the Army's field guns. Dover itself is being built into an exceptionally strong fortress, with a number of large weapons, including a powerful gun from an old battleship."

"What about the big railway gun?"

"It's almost ready, sir. It's been re-commissioned on a railcar, and will shortly be moved to a tunnel in Kent, which is being kitted out for it. Unfortunately it doesn't have the range to bombard the French ports, or the accuracy to engage the enemy invasion fleet at sea – but if any German forces get ashore it will rain havoc on the landing beaches."

"That's good. I suspected it might come in handy at some stage" said Churchill, almost chuckling. He had been personally involved in saving the huge siege weapon from being scrapped at the end of the First World War.

Brooke looked down at his notes and took a sip of water, before continuing. "Clearly it's vital that we guard against these emplacements being taken by direct assault by airborne forces, or from the rear by air- or sea-landed parties. I have issued orders for their land-side defences to be strengthened... machine guns... barbed wire... mines... anti-tank weapons. I've also ordered a large increase in basic provisioning – ammunition, food and water, medical supplies – so that they can continue fighting for many days, perhaps weeks, even if surrounded."

It was hard, practical soldiering, and Churchill was quietly pleased. The discussion continued for another half hour, largely as a dialogue between the two men, with the Prime Minister's tone gradually becoming more positive. As the debate began to wind down, Attlee, who had been listening quite passively, involved himself again in his usual civil manner.

"General Brooke, the information on the regular forces is encouraging, but, if you could enlighten me, what are these reports I'm hearing about weapons being withdrawn from the Home Guard and other reserve forces?"

"Ah... yes, Deputy Prime Minister, you may well have heard some complaints. I should explain what's happened. After Dunkirk we were so short of equipment that we had to withdraw rifles from the reserve units to bring the regular divisions up to strength. Unfortunately that included the Home Guard's Lee Enfields. They've had to survive for a few months with shotguns and .22s, admittedly not much good for facing up to a professional army. But I'm afraid that with the challenge we faced re-equipping the regulars, we had to be quite single-minded in our approach. We've encouraged the Home Guard to use makeshift weapons... road mines... Molotov cocktails... various other incendiary bombs... That has been quite effective. However the good news is that the first of the half million rifles ordered from America have just arrived in Liverpool. They are old but serviceable, and will be distributed over the next few weeks."

Attlee persisted in his polite questioning. "There would also appear to be some confusion about what their precise role is in the event of invasion." Brooke hesitated for a moment. He had been dismayed at the lack of planning he had found when he took over, but did not want to be too critical of his predecessor.

"That's a fair observation, Deputy Prime Minister." He hesitated, searching for the right words. "I think that we, perhaps, let our enthusiasm to recruit volunteers run somewhat ahead of our thinking on how best to use them."

Having dealt diplomatically with the issue he had inherited, he proceeded in a more positive vein. "We now believe that their most important role is the defence of static installations against fifth column or parachutist attack, so as to free up the regulars for the front line. We are issuing them with their new orders, and they'll soon have the appropriate weapons to carry out those responsibilities. But, again, I must be honest. With so many other priorities at home, and now the Middle East as well, we have to be selective. We can't afford to dissipate the finite amount of modern weaponry we've got into areas where it's unlikely to be needed, or into the hands of semi-trained soldiers."

Brooke had been precise, but perhaps, in his Northern Irish way, too blunt. The Prime Minister intervened with a note of caution. "That's all very laudable, General, but do keep a weather eye on morale. We must be careful that what may be sensible decisions from a quartermaster's point of view do not get misinterpreted by the civilian population as signs of impending collapse."

"I will take note of that, sir. Now if I may conclude. We are in much better shape than we were immediately after the Dunkirk evacuation. The re-structuring of units, their re-equipment, and the changes in deployment are all going well. Morale is high. There is a mood of quiet determination to defend the country and to avenge the defeat in France. I am confident that the Army, with of course the assistance of the Navy and RAF, is strong enough to deal with enemy forces of up to a dozen or more divisions that may be thrown upon our shores."

Churchill stayed quiet, nodding almost imperceptibly. Encouraging as Brooke's report was, he was still not completely won over, but he did not want to show any signs of dissatisfaction with the progress now being made. He knew the manpower losses were being replaced and that re-equipment was well underway, but he remained sceptical about the quality of leadership that the Army had shown in the conflict thus far. Brooke had been in the job for just a few weeks, and was clearly moving things in the right direction. *The question was whether he had enough time…*

After a brief lunch, the meeting moved on to the air situation. Churchill called on Air Chief Marshall Dowding for his report.

"Prime Minister, the Luftwaffe remains a tough adversary. They have perhaps twice as many aircraft as the RAF, but, as you know from the regular briefings, they've finally met their match. We are shooting down two or three German aircraft for every plane that we lose. Furthermore, many of our shot-down pilots are able to bale out and return safely to their units, so the advantage is even greater than the raw numbers suggest."

The battle was being reviewed on a daily basis, and Dowding had kept his introduction short.

"How are the men holding up?"

"They're in good spirit, sir, although it has to be said that they are tired, extremely tired. The constant pressure is taking its toll – of both pilots and ground crew. I'm doing my best to keep our operational capability up by rotating squadrons from the front line to quieter sectors before their efficiency drops."

"Good. Are you getting the aircraft you need?"

"For the moment, yes, sir. We're seeing the results of the increased production rate and have even been able to build some reserves in the holding units. The Spitfire has proven itself the best fighter aircraft in the world; better than the Messerschmitt 109 and far better than anything else the Germans possess – we know from prisoners of war that even the enemy accepts this."

Churchill was slightly irritated. "That's all very well about the Spitfires, Air Marshall. Pray tell me how the Hurricanes are doing." He was well aware that most of the RAF's fighters were not the glamorous Spitfires, but the workhorse Hurricanes – and that four hundred of them had been lost in the Battle of France.

"They're doing quite satisfactorily, sir. The aircraft is not as good as the Me109 in some respects, but we have improved it considerably since the early days in France – high octane fuel, advanced new propellers, and more armour protection for both pilot and machine. With these modifications the Hurricanes can just about hold their own against the 109s, and are more than a match for anything else the Germans possess."

"That is reassuring. Our pilots deserve no less. Now tell me, if, as it seems, the Luftwaffe is not having things its own way at present, what do you think it will try next? Night bombing? London?"

"Both would seem to be strong possibilities. I expect that at some stage they'll turn their attention to the capital, as they did at Warsaw and Rotterdam, using terror raids to try to break down civilian morale. That might well involve a switch to night raids – which are not accurate enough to use against military targets, but can inflict great damage on a large conurbation. That would be tough on civilians, but might give my fighter boys some respite."

Churchill was stoic. "London can take it, and what's more, Berlin will get some back. Now let's look for a moment at the battle from the other side. Are there any cracks appearing in the Luftwaffe's facade as their assault progresses?"

"Indeed there are, sir; several, in fact. They have a real problem providing full fighter cover for their bombers. As I said, the Me109 is a good fighter, bettered only by the Spitfire – but it's very short on range. When operating from across the Channel, it has limited ability to stay with the fight in our skies before it has to turn for home, leaving the bombers unprotected and vulnerable. The bomber crew POWs that we interrogate are very angry about this. It seems reasonable to assume that similar opinions are being voiced at their bases, which can't be good for morale."

"They have even more problems with the rest of their equipment. Their twin-engined fighter, the Messerschmitt 110, has a long range and quite good performance for a fairly large plane, but just can't survive in combat with single-engined aircraft, even our Hurricanes. It looks as if they've been withdrawn from the battle due to the level of losses suffered, as have the Stuka dive-bombers. As a result the Luftwaffe's effective front line strength has been reduced by several hundred aircraft. And of course they also have a big problem with aircrew. Most times they lose an aircraft, they lose the crew as well.

So even though they started the battle with more airmen than us, their losses, particularly of pilots, must be starting to hurt."

Churchill nodded. "That is encouraging. Do you think they've any other tricks up their sleeves, ready to spring on us?"

"None that we're aware of; at least not in the immediate future. As far as we can determine, their plan at present just seems to be to keep sending over the bombers until we crack – which, as you know, sir, we have no intention of doing. However, looking out to the medium term, it's a real concern that they'll equip their fighters with jettisonable fuel tanks. That would extend their maximum range as far as the Midlands, or double their endurance over London, which would give us serious problems. A few 109s have been modified to carry small bombs, but not, so far, drop tanks."

"That seems an unusual lapse on their part. Do we know why?"

"It's something of a mystery, sir. They used them during the Spanish Civil War on some older fighters, so there's nothing new in the idea. It may be due to the amount of engineering work needed to plumb them in to the 109 airframe, which is quite small. Or perhaps they simply failed to anticipate the need. In any event we think it will be a few months before they can introduce them – hopefully too late for the current phase of the battle, though it could bring us a real headache next year. Meantime, with any luck at all, the Germans will run out of aircraft and crew before we run out of fighters."

Churchill grunted. "You mentioned 'luck'. It leaves me somewhat nervous to be dependent on luck, unless I am in control of that elusive substance."

"I apologise, Prime Minister. That was perhaps the wrong expression to use. There are a number of factors not totally within our control which could have a serious impact. I've already mentioned the aircraft factories, which could become the object of intense attack, and must be protected at all costs. The same applies to the engine factories – the entire production of Merlins for the Spitfires and Hurricanes comes from just two engine plants, in Derby and

Crewe. If either were to be destroyed, we would face an immediate problem."

"I thought that we had a dispersal programme well underway?" Churchill queried impatiently.

"We have, sir. It's being implemented with great urgency, and I acknowledge the role that the Minister is playing," he nodded at Beaverbrook, "but we are very exposed until it's completed. I've also mentioned the radar stations, which are very vulnerable to low level attack. On occasion the Germans have knocked out individual stations, leaving a gap until we get it repaired or replaced. A concentrated attack on them could leave us seriously blinded. To guard against that, we are developing mobile stations to fill any gaps in the chain. The first few are already in service."

"Thank you for the clarification, Air Marshall," Churchill muttered dryly. "Your overall report is moderately reassuring. Also your comments about your concerns and exposures are taken on board. General Brooke, will you please ensure that anti-aircraft defences are reviewed with regard to the aircraft factories and radar sites. It would also seem prudent to increase the ground defence forces assigned to them, to protect against commando raids. Might this, perhaps, be a suitable mission for some of our better-equipped Home Guard units? Please consider that. Now let us move on to the Royal Navy."

Admiral Pound opened the folder in front of him. With a lifetime of service in the Royal Navy he was an intelligent and determined leader, though now in his '60s and looking somewhat frail under the bunker's harsh lights. He spoke quietly but confidently.

"Prime Minister, as a fighting force the Royal Navy is undiminished since war began. Our Home Fleet remains by far the most powerful battle fleet in the world. We have, of course, suffered some serious losses, most recently HMS *Glorious*. However, to set against that, we have added many new ships since the war began, including two new battleships and two aircraft carriers. And we have inflicted considerable losses on the Germans. We've sunk the pocket battleship *Graf Spee* and the cruiser *Konigsberg*. Also, the gallant

Norwegians did us a big favour by sinking the German's most modern cruiser, the *Blucher*, during the attack on Oslo. Even more important, in the context of defending against an invasion, we sank at least ten of their destroyers in Norway – about half their total fleet."

Churchill grimaced. "At least something good came out of that debacle. Please continue, Admiral."

"Paradoxically, despite the success there, my biggest concern is the pressure on our own destroyer fleet. We've suffered some thirty sunk, and as many again damaged, between Norway, Dunkirk and other theatres. Out of that much-reduced number of destroyers I have to provide resources for many different tasks: defence against invasion, escort duty for the Home Fleet, convoy protection, and a range of tasks in the Mediterranean now that we have the Italians to contend with. That's to say nothing of what may happen in the Far East with Japan's ongoing expansion. I can think of no higher priority than to convince the Americans to lend us the fifty destroyers that we've asked for."

Churchill nodded. "I am optimistic that there will be a positive response soon from the United States in that regard. Now another question. Would it help if we could persuade the Irish government to let us use the Treaty ports that we relinquished, rather foolhardily, eighteen months ago?"

Chamberlain looked stonily ahead, and stayed silent. He had negotiated the agreement to return the ports with the Irish Prime Minister, over Churchill's vehement objections at the time.

Pound responded, "There would be some advantage if it was done with the active co-operation of the Irish. But not as much as before France was occupied. Even if we regained access to the ports in Cork and Bantry Bay, the German bases are so close that we still couldn't route convoys through the south-western approaches."

"And if we didn't have their co-operation?"

"It would be quite counterproductive, Prime Minister."

Churchill looked sourly at Pound. "We will return to that issue at some later stage. Please continue."

"Prime Minister, I would like to conclude on a positive note. While identifying the challenges we face, and in particular the problem of prioritising the many demands upon us, I must be absolutely clear on one thing. The Royal Navy is in determined shape, and stands ready to repel any attempt at invasion."

Pound's report had been concise and reassuring, and Churchill acknowledged the contribution in an even voice. Inwardly, however, he felt a great sense of relief. There was no equivocation in Pound's report, but neither was there any fake optimism. The Royal Navy would simply continue to do the job it had been doing successfully for hundreds of years – defending the island against all-comers. For the first time in this series of meetings he began to feel a degree of satisfaction, even comfort, with the reports from all three Services.

That evening Churchill sat with General Ismay and Jock Colville, drafting a further message to Roosevelt. He needed to complete the negotiations for the old destroyers, but the Americans were driving a hard bargain in terms of access to British bases. For all the focus on the war, there were other matters of state to address. Bracken wanted to see him about the appointment of bishops for some vacant Church of England sees, and came across at the agreed time. He put his head through the door, and saw Churchill just finishing his dictation to one of the typists, who sat at a table close-by. Quietly he intruded. "Went the day well?" he asked, thinking it a reasonably neutral opening as he waited to judge the Prime Minister's mood.

Churchill responded briefly, "As well as could be expected, possibly somewhat better."

He started to review the typed letter.

Ismay was standing aside from the final editing work and acknowledged Bracken's arrival. "Hello, Brendan. Yes, it was a good meeting. Certainly the Chiefs are becoming more confident."

Before he could say any more, Churchill interrupted, somewhat tetchily, as he scribbled a correction. "So were the French generals, Ismay, behind the Maginot Line. We'd better not fall into the same trap."

The words were somewhat at odds with what he had just been saying, perhaps because, with the letter still in progress, he was only half-focused on the conversation. Ismay was slightly peeved, and made a somewhat tart response. "Fortunately there's no way around the Channel, Prime Minister," reminding him of the fatal flaw in the French fortifications.

Churchill looked up at him again. "No, but there is a way across it, and there is a way over it."

"And that's where the Navy and RAF come into play, not just the Army," said Ismay, taking control of the drifting conversation, well aware that the Prime Minister and he had a shared opinion about the capabilities of the different Services.

There was no argument back. Churchill knew that Ismay's interjections were valid, and glanced up. "No bad thing at that. The Navy hasn't suffered a major defeat in hundreds of years – a few close-run things, mind you, but never defeated, and the RAF is beginning to show the same never-say-die attitude. Also they have the right equipment, which perhaps the Army lacked in France. And as for leadership..."

The typist handed over the final version for approval, then left, followed a few minutes later by Colville and Ismay. Churchill went through to his small office with Bracken, and poured them each a whisky and soda. He sat down on a metal frame chair and began to relax in the company of his old friend, picking up the conversation with Bracken's original question.

"To be fair, Brendan, I was wrong to sound so negative. The way things are going, I'm beginning to feel increasingly confident that we can hold them off – at least for the time being."

Though not in the Cabinet, Bracken had been keeping his ear to the ground. He had detected the subtle changes in mood over the last few weeks, and had been anticipating the more positive sentiment that Churchill now expressed. His politically-acute brain had already begun to mull over the ramifications of a possible military stand-off.

"So where does that leave us, Winston? If they can't invade us, and we certainly can't invade them, what then? Do we wait for a few years for things to settle down, and then start sending each other postcards?"

Churchill chuckled at the thought. "Certainly not saying '*Wish you were here*'."

As he spoke the air raid warning sounded. The Luftwaffe was now coming over southern Britain by night as well as day, keeping the pressure on the RAF and the civilian population. Churchill refused to head down into the deeper shelter unless bombs were heard close-by, and he barely stirred at the wailing sound of the siren. He continued to address Bracken, now with a distinct change in his tone, and looked him directly in the eye.

"Brendan, you have raised a question of the utmost importance, the answer to which may well determine the course of this war." He paused, looked away for a moment, and sighed deeply. "However, as of this evening, and with so many immediate issues to resolve, I am not ready to take the discussion any further."

He relaxed again. "Now let us examine the first of these immediate issues, the selection of the new bishops."

He picked up the file from his desk, where Bracken had placed it, and began to scan the entries, two names beside each of the vacancies. As Prime Minister of a country with an established church, he had the archaic responsibility of making the final recommendations on church appointments to the King.

"In truth, I do not feel best qualified to make the choices, whether based on the theological or the other episcopal qualities of the contenders."

He looked again at the list. "However I console myself that at least my intentions are honourable – certainly better than one of my potential successors in this role."

"Halifax?" said Bracken, slightly confused.

"No," growled the Prime Minister, "Hitler."

CHAPTER SEVEN

In Berlin, on a fine early August morning, the mood was relaxed. After almost a year of war, and despite occasional inconveniences, the city still looked much as it had the previous summer. The private and public buildings were clean; the parks and gardens tidy; tramcars and motor traffic moved freely on the well-maintained streets. Seven years of Nazi rule had brought great prosperity to the city, for seventy years the capital of a united Germany and now the capital of the Greater German Reich. From the Sudetenland to the Rhineland, from Danzig to Vienna, the Germanic people were at last united, the country's opponents in disarray. The most deep-seated fear of the population, another long war, had been assuaged and a new *Pax Germanica* imposed on Europe.

Two weeks previously the triumphal parades had processed through the streets; the soldiers receiving wild acclaim from the crowds and the Fuehrer's name, adulation. Well might the red flags with their swastika emblem fly in celebration.

Even the weather on this Sunday morning was benevolent. Despite the earliness of the hour it was already getting warm, and it looked as if was going to be another sweltering day. The early risers were out enjoying themselves before it got too hot. Well-dressed families with young children strolled along the pavements or stood by tram stops, some perhaps going to church, others heading for the

Tiergarten to enjoy the gardens or visit the zoo, still open despite the occasional small air raid.

As the military cars bearing the General Staff officers swept through the quiet streets, the occupants could feel entitled to look out at the relaxed scene and enjoy a certain sense of achievement. They were, after all, the men responsible for the repose that the Berliners were enjoying. They had led the German forces to victory in Poland and the West, defeating the old enemy, France, in just six weeks of lightning warfare. Some of the officers, perhaps remembering their own youth, could look benignly at the young soldiers on leave, walking with pretty frauleins on their way to, or perhaps from, a lovers' rendezvous. In the pavement cafes some older folk were sitting, drinking their coffee and reading newspapers as they might have done a year ago. Only the coffee, now ersatz, was different. The one discordant sign that a detached observer might have noticed was the small number of teenagers around. The missing schoolchildren were out helping with the harvest, or being trained at Hitler Youth camps.

For all the sense of serenity around, the officers had much to be concerned about as they headed to the conference in Wilhelmstrasse. These men were the senior members of the *Oberkommando der Wehrmacht,* Hitler's General Staff, and were well aware that despite the victory over France and the parades through Berlin, there was unfinished business in the West. They knew that defeating England would not be an easy task. Although the British were clearly smarting from their defeat in France, they remained defiant and did not seem willing to accept that the war was lost. Churchill, alcoholic and anachronistic warlord that he was, had managed to stem the English peace movement which had started to bud in May. It looked as if he had succeeded in silencing the voices – some even inside his government – that recognised the inevitability of German victory and had been angling for negotiations. Instead he now seemed to be steadily hardening his position.

But there was an even deeper concern. In late July Field Marshal Wilhelm Keitel, head of the OKW, and General Alfred Jodl, his deputy, had been informed by the Fuehrer of his strategic intent. He was going to direct his armies to their real enemy, in the East, as soon as the long Russian winter ended. It seemed as if the painful lessons from the First World War had been forgotten, and that the OKW would be forced to plan for war on two fronts, unless the situation in the West could be resolved swiftly.

A few weeks later the plan had been brought to the rest of the High Command. The generals found themselves in a very difficult position. Though several of them remained unhappy at being directed by an upstart corporal, they had to accept, however reluctantly, that the Fuehrer had shown a military genius that belied his lack of staff training. Throughout the French campaign he had prodded them continually to push far beyond what they thought prudent, and he had been proven correct. Now all resistance to his leadership had quiesced. No one was brave enough, or foolish enough, to challenge his new directives. For his part, too, the Fuehrer was willing to put aside the old tensions with the generals, and welcome the professionalism with which they were executing his master plan. He knew now that they would not resist or procrastinate as he set about his goal of a new order in Europe.

Keen to move ahead with his crusade in the East, Hitler was getting frustrated with the British. He had given them adequate time and opportunity to seek terms, but so far without result. A number of tentative messages had been exchanged via Sweden in the previous weeks with senior figures in the British Foreign Office, assumed to be Lord Halifax, or Butler, his deputy. That link had gone quiet, and Hitler was conscious that he had only six or eight weeks left before deteriorating weather would make a Channel crossing impossible. He had decided to increase the military pressure further, to bring them to their senses. Doenitz's U-boats and Goering's Luftwaffe had been first to respond, and were achieving much success, but still Britain showed no sign of crumbling. It was beginning to look that, unless they went ahead with the planned invasion in the autumn, the confrontation could last indefinitely. Such a stand-off was unacceptable. It would require the continued commitment of front-line air and ground forces on the Channel coast that would be much better employed in Russia. Somewhat reluctantly, he ordered the OKW to set about the next stage of the plan for the invasion of Britain, now codenamed 'Sea Lion'. He had spoken to Keitel and issued a new directive to him, demanding a resolution.

Now, on this bright Sunday morning, Keitel began to address the group gathered in the Reich Air Ministry building on Wilhelmstrasse.

"Despite recurring reports that there are some in Britain who want to negotiate a peace agreement, it is becoming clear that the war faction led by Churchill is not prepared to countenance this. It appears that an invasion may be the only way to secure our western front ahead of our planned expansion in the East. Fuehrer Directive 17 now instructs us to scale up the air offensive and destroy the British air force in preparation for this invasion. I repeat, *in preparation for*. To be absolutely clear, our responsibility is to prepare the way, and be ready to execute at short notice if and when the Fuehrer decides. Each of you has the responsibility of addressing the challenges in your own command and also of meeting the requirements placed upon you by the other Services. The Fuehrer requires our final report within one week. When we present to him, you will each have to confirm that you are ready to carry out the tasks assigned to you or, if not, to be ready to answer to him in person."

General Franz Halder, the Chief of Staff of the German army, the Heer, was called upon to begin the discussion, and moved across to a large wall map of the Channel and southern England. One of the old Prussian military elite, Halder was far from pleased with the path on which Hitler was taking his beloved Germany. But as a professional soldier he did not let any sign of discontent mar his presentation as he began to discuss the army's preparedness.

"Herr Feldmarschall, the Heer will be ready. At this point we have twenty-nine divisions assigned in western France, and two in Norway, over and above the troops needed for garrison purposes."

He moved over from the table to a large wall chart of the area and, using a long pointer, began to identify the main infantry and panzer units. From each encampment area, dotted lines reached out showing the transit routes to their ports of embarkation for England.

"The main formations on the Channel front are Army Group A, assembled between the Belgian coast and Le Havre, and Army Group B, based in Brittany. The component divisions and their base areas are as shown here."

He tapped the map with the pointer.

"The men are rested, fully equipped and ready to carry out their orders. They are all, officers and soldiers alike, confident of victory. The Heer has already demonstrated its superiority to the best divisions that the British possess. As many of you have seen for yourselves, the Tommies fled out of France leaving behind, on the beaches of Dunkirk, enough material for an entire army! The divisions that are now reforming in Britain are of much lower quality: undertrained, underequipped and, one can reasonably assume, low on morale. Once our troops and equipment are conveyed across the Channel, and the supply lines established, we will defeat the British once again."

He paused. "And this time they will have nowhere to run to."

Field Marshal Keitel was impressed with Halder's approach. He portrayed just the right balance of professional military competence and allegiance to the Fuehrer's requirements. He also set a good example for the others, particularly the navy. The latter certainly had concerns, but should, he felt, spend more time discussing the contribution they would make, rather than their problems.

"That is most encouraging, General. The sea-crossing will be addressed shortly by Grossadmiral Raeder. For now, can you proceed to describe the planned operation once ashore?"

"Certainly. The plan of attack is extensive, but quite straightforward." Halder turned again to the wall map, moving over to its western region, and pointing out several areas of the Kent and Sussex coastline.

"The initial assault will be carried out by units of Army Group A: six divisions from the 9th Army on the beaches between Folkestone and Eastbourne and four divisions from the 16th Army on the beaches south east of Brighton. The seaborne units will make simultaneous landings at the locations shown and secure the beachheads. Parachute and glider troops will assist with landings behind the enemy's defences on the flanks of the assault, here and here, taking out gun emplacements from behind, and capturing several key strongpoints in the Folkestone area. Within 48 hours we will seize at least one of the Channel ports, allowing the Kriegsmarine to bring in the second and third waves and establish our vital supply lines. Over a seven day period we will land more than 200,000 men, with 300 tanks and a full complement of artillery and flak guns."

General Halder continued to lead the discussion on the landings for a further hour, looking in detail at the assault waves, the build-up of forces, and the securing of the bridgehead in preparation for the breakout.

"The breakout phase will see us advance to the initial objective line, from Rochester in Kent to Portsmouth by Day 5, bringing a number of ports and airfields under our control. At this stage we will have established a solid foothold in England, a springboard in fact, ready for the advance on London."

He paused a moment and took a couple of steps to his left, raising his pointer towards an area on the south coast of England.

"However before proceeding with the breakout, we will carry out a follow-up landing here, in the Dorset area, with four divisions from Army Group B. These troops will push rapidly in a northwest direction to reach the River Severn at Bristol. This will secure our western flank, and force the British defences to face both ways. As you know from previous discussions, the Heer would have preferred to carry out this secondary landing at the same time as the main one in Kent, in order to split the British defences from Day 1. However we accept the Kriegsmarine position that it cannot simultaneously protect two invasion lines across the Channel."

Raeder nodded very deliberately. He had eventually achieved concession on this issue, though the debate had gone to the Fuehrer before it was resolved. He chose to say nothing as Halder continued. "In the third phase, our forces in Kent will continue to push west towards London. Meanwhile, those from the Dorset landing will swing around from the head of the Severn estuary and drive east, staying well to the north of the capital, until they reach the North Sea at the Wash. This will leave the main body of the British army corralled into an ever-decreasing perimeter around London. The British will be placed in an impossible situation, their capital completely surrounded. At that point we will comply with the Fuehrer's instructions, either to lay siege to London and wait for the British to surrender as they run out of supplies, or reduce the city by direct assault, to rubble if necessary."

The presentation had been brief and precise. Without mentioning the term 'river crossing' which had been used dismissively in some earlier briefings, Halder had not laid any great stress on the difficulties which might be faced in the crossing of the Channel. Two thousand years ago Julius Caesar had managed it, and he didn't see any great reason why the modern German army couldn't.

It was time to move on to the naval operation, and Keitel turned to the head of the Kriegsmarine, Grand Admiral Erich Raeder. The Kriegsmarine was the service most worried about the entire Sea Lion operation. Raeder had argued long and hard with Hitler about the alternative of bringing Britain to its knees by cutting off its supplies of food, oil and munitions. But blockades took time, and Hitler was in a hurry. Once again, at the risk of irritating the others present, Raeder started by discussing the naval issues.

"At our previous meetings, Herr Feldmarschall, I identified the challenges that we face in meeting the requirements of the Heer, as set out by General Halder. I must avoid any perception that the Kriegsmarine is not fully supportive of Sea Lion, but I need to start by reminding the group about the reality of our naval capabilities. Since 1933 the development of the navy has been based on two specific requirements which, I must stress, were formally agreed with the Fuehrer. First, to build a surface fleet powerful enough to confront the Royal Navy in our northern waters and so prevent a blockade of our ports – as was catastrophic in the Great War. The second was to create a powerful U-boat force, to impose our own blockade on Britain, stopping their supply of armaments, oil and food from across the Atlantic and from their Empire."

Keitel thought some praise would help. "Admiral, you are being quite modest. We saw in Norway that the Kriegsmarine has developed many capabilities beyond the roles initially assigned."

"That is correct. We were able to demonstrate what a flexible naval force can achieve, even when assigned a role that has not been specifically planned for. We carried out a major seaborne landing and achieved strategic success. However this success, I must stress, was within the particular operational environment which existed there – the most important factor being that the Luftwaffe had complete control of the air. And despite this superiority we suffered serious losses, almost all to the British navy. As you will see later, this now demands the concentration of our naval forces into a single area of assault in Sea Lion."

Keitel was frustrated by Raeder's continued reversion to issues that had already been agreed. "Admiral, the Fuehrer accepts that air superiority is a pre-requisite to the Sea Lion crossing."

"I am conscious of, and grateful for the Fuehrer's support. To continue: for the Channel crossing the same requirement for air superiority exists as in Norway, but becomes even more critical due to the size of the operation and the location. We'll be engaging a still-powerful enemy in their home waters, with all the advantages that gives them in terms of logistics."

Keitel had heard it all before. Although he shared some of Raeder's worries, in Nazi Germany one did not let such doubt become visible in public. "Admiral, we all understand the difficulties that you face, and are confident that you will overcome them. Now let us proceed with our review of the naval operation."

"Certainly. As per the Fuehrer's instructions." Raeder's words could have been interpreted in many ways, but the safest was to regard them as simply a statement of compliance. But he had been determined to give his position, the same one as he had presented, bravely, to Hitler some weeks previously. He continued, moving from Halder's map to a larger-scale chart of the crossing area.

"For the initial landing we've gathered together over two hundred steamships and nearly two thousand barges, each capable of transporting some eighty troops or about forty horses. These barges have been mainly requisitioned from the Rhine fleets, and include Dutch, Belgian and French craft as well as German. A major limitation is that only about one third of them are self-propelled. We are compensating as best we can by modifying several hundred more to use an aircraft engine and propeller, mounted on an external gantry. The remaining, unpowered, vessels will be towed across by tugs. These river barges have a shallow draught, and can bring the troops close inshore before allowing them to disembark into the surf, or into small assault boats. Work is also underway to modify more than a hundred barges with bow doors and ramps, to handle heavier weapons. Each will be able to carry two or three Panzers, Mark IIIs or IVs, which can be driven straight onto the beaches, or alternatively a battery of field guns. We are also giving many of the barges some self-defence capability, mainly flak guns, to defend against low-flying aircraft."

Keitel was aware that a huge effort was underway to provide the capacity that the Heer had demanded. He also knew how exposed the troops would be during the crossing. "We are all conscious of the effort being made in the ports and shipyards, Admiral. If extra labour is required, I have been assured that it can be made available."

Admiral Raeder knew what was implied, and wanted nothing to do with forced labour. Surly, unskilled, and half-starved men from Poland or the newly conquered countries in the West were not what he wanted near his vessels. "I will bear that offer in mind, Herr Feldmarschall. As it is, my requirement is for skilled workers, shipwrights, metal workers and so on. I've been assured that all labour with the required level of experience has now been assigned. There isn't time to absorb unskilled workers, from whatever source, into the shipyards."

Keitel grunted. He knew that Raeder had not yet fully adjusted to the harsh reality of this new type of war, but now was not the time for an argument. He decided to return to the main issue. "How is work proceeding on naval protection for the transport fleet?"

"That is our major task at present. We have only eight destroyers available to protect the fleet, plus about a dozen smaller escorts and twenty fast torpedo boats. To supplement this inadequate number we're modifying several hundred small craft – fishing boats and so on – with machine guns and cannon, to act as auxiliaries. Outside the immediate invasion routes we will establish dense minefields, their positions as shown here." He pointed on the map to the long lines stretching from the mid-Channel banks to the English coast.

"Beyond that, the outer layer of protection will comprise U-boats. These will be assigned a defensive role in the North Sea, where they'll shield the fleet against any intervention by the British Home Fleet, and an offensive role in the south to seal off Portsmouth and Plymouth." Again he used a pointer to indicate the position of the two U-boat lines.

"While we're working hard to increase the overall number of escorts, it should be remembered that the Royal Navy possesses over fifty cruisers, nearly two hundred destroyers, and some four hundred minesweepers and coastal craft. They also have more than twenty battleships and six aircraft carriers, though it is unlikely that they will use those large ships in the narrow waters of the Channel."

Jodl interrupted, gruffly. "The British have many other commitments, in the Atlantic and the Mediterranean, as well as the Far East."

"That is true, Herr General. Not all of the forces I've mentioned will oppose us in the invasion area. However, for all that, more than half their fleet remains in their home waters, and even that represents a powerful force. It is absolutely essential that we counter that superiority by means of our air power. We must ensure that each and every attempt by the British navy to bring their forces into the combat zone is totally rebuffed by the Luftwaffe. Let me stress again. *The success of the invasion depends on us achieving total aerial superiority over the sea area from Harwich to Plymouth.*"

He paused for a moment to make sure that the message was clear, then continued.

"Even after the landings are achieved, it will be vital to maintain this air superiority for many weeks, to ensure an uninterrupted supply line – though I recognise that this will become easier when we can base our own aircraft in England, and push the British further away from the Channel coast."

With his stall firmly set out on the issue of air cover, Admiral Raeder proceeded to describe the routes that the fleet would take and the numbers of troops that could be transported in the first and subsequent waves. He had to explain yet again why the crossing would take up to eighteen hours, even though at its closest the coast of England lay just thirty kilometres from France... *the distance from the embarkation ports to the assault areas.... the dangerous banks that had to be avoided... the significant effect of currents on slow moving craft.*

He continued, "In regard to the actual landings, the final selection of landing beaches is now complete, as well as the loading schedule and the assignment of escorts and transport craft to the various fleets. We will finalise the remaining details by September 1st. But, as I said earlier, it's important that no one underestimates the scale of the task that we face."

It would all be straightforward, he thought to himself grimly, as long as the weather gods co-operated... *and the British!*

Keitel thanked him quite cordially, anxious to maintain a good working relationship, and then called on General Jeschonnek, the

Luftwaffe Chief of Staff. Since its foundation in 1935, the Luftwaffe had been the service most closely aligned with the Nazi Party's spirit. Jeschonnek was a staunch supporter of the Third Reich, assiduously carrying out his duties as Chief of Staff despite frequent interference from his boss, Reichsmarschall Goering. As the Fuehrer's deputy, Goering spent much of his time in Hitler's headquarters but he also continued as overall chief of the Luftwaffe, involving himself when it suited. Jeschonnek was very different in character from the bombastic Goering, but he still addressed the meeting with confidence and enthusiasm. Perhaps the main difference was his brevity.

"We have received our orders, and our preparations are almost complete. The first phase of the operation will be an all-out assault to destroy the British air defences. It will start on *Eagle Day*, August 13th, and will take three weeks."

He sat down, not needing to elaborate. The group already knew the Luftwaffe's ability to support the Heer's land offensives and to sink any British warships that tried to interfere with naval operations..

Field Marshal Keitel continued to chair the meeting for another hour. The plan was well understood, though, as the discussion continued, one new concern emerged. At previous meetings the planning had not gone further than the Battle of London, and Jeschonnek was concerned about the next stage. The Luftwaffe might have to support a battle which was getting further and further away from its bases in France.

"Clearly London will be the critical battle," he commented, "but we also have to consider the possibility of continued resistance after its fall, as Churchill is now proclaiming to be the British strategy. We have to prepare a plan for the capture of the airfields needed to support our drive north, and work out the supply lines to them. The shape of the country means it will be much more complicated than France. Does the High Command have an estimate of the time it's likely to take?"

General Jodl responded, "We still hope for a British surrender once London falls. If not, our advance as far as the north of Scotland may take some time, several weeks perhaps. There are no military obstacles of significance to cause us serious problems, though, inevitably, we will suffer casualties from British rearguard actions. However, I agree, we must set up a group to prepare a detailed plan."

Admiral Raeder was still trying to curb the enthusiasm of the others, and saw an opportunity to try a new tack. "What's the latest assessment of the risk of American intervention if our advance northwards is delayed?"

That very issue had been the subject of a recent discussion between Hitler and the German military intelligence section, the Abwehr, and Jodl continued, unfazed.

"According to the Abwehr's intelligence, the earliest that the Americans could mount a landing is in three months' time, even assuming their political establishment could make a fast decision – which seems unlikely with a presidential election coming up before year end. If they did want to intervene, they would need access to fully secured and operational ports to land their forces. To eliminate this possibility, we must ensure that we have the entire island of Britain, and of course Ireland, under our control well within that timeframe. As a specific safeguard, once London falls, key objectives in our breakout plan will be Liverpool, Glasgow and Cork. Those ports are the ones which would be most suitable for an Americans expeditionary force, in consequence of their location and the dock facilities available."

The mention of Ireland, and Cork, caused a small stir. There had been no previous discussion about an invasion of neutral Eire. Not that neutrality gave any protection in this war, as other countries had already discovered.

After another hour's discussion the meeting concluded, and the attendees said their farewells, only one or two giving a Hitler salute. The generals headed back through the streets to their homes, glad of the chance to spend a few hours with their families.

CHAPTER EIGHT

By the middle of August the Luftwaffe's attack had reached a crescendo over the ports and airfields of southern England. It was clear that they were determined to break down the RAF before the great assault by sea could begin, but the British pilots were proving resolute in defence of their homeland. On August 15th, the day of the heaviest battle so far, Churchill was in Dover Castle and watched for himself the fierce action in the sky, becoming elated at the bravery and success of the fighters.

Returned to Whitehall, he talked vividly to his staff about what he had seen, expressing his intense admiration for the achievements of the young pilots. Bracken however noticed that his talk was very much of the moment, with little embellishment about winning the battle or even looking forward to sweeping victories in the future. As he listened, he recalled his pregnant discussion with the Prime Minister a fortnight earlier. Nothing more had been said since, but Bracken decided it was time to see whether the Prime Minister was ready to expand on the cryptic comments made then. He followed Churchill into his small office, continuing the discussion about the Dover air battle.

As the conversation about the day's fighting wound down, he decided to leave an opening for Churchill, to see if he was ready to elaborate.

"Winston, if the RAF can keep it up for another month or two the Germans will run out of time. Not even Hitler would send his army across in the winter gales. We'll have won this round."

Churchill looked at his friend. Bracken thought it a strange look. It combined great trust and affection, tempered with uncertainty. He motioned to him to close the door and sat there for a moment, looking down at his desk, paused in thought. He began to speak in a very subdued voice. "I think you are right, Brendan, and thank God for it. It's starting to look as if we could stop the man if he were to attack, perhaps even inflict a heavy defeat on him. That in itself would not bring victory in this war – but it is a damned sight better than what we faced two months ago."

He hesitated for a moment, then took a deep breath and exhaled slowly, before continuing.

"However I am worried, desperately worried, about the longer term; about next year and the year after that. We stand alone, except for the countries of the Empire, thousands of miles away across U-boat infested seas. We're getting desperately-needed supplies of arms and munitions from the United States, but we have to pay for them in dollars, and our reserves are running low. In the First World War it took three long years before the Americans entered. I don't believe we have that time available to us now. To add to which they also have the Pacific to worry about."

He paused for a moment.

"Our current predicament may be difficult, but it is, perhaps, as good as it's going to be for a very long time."

Bracken picked up the nuance in his words and responded after a few seconds, in a very quiet voice.

"Winston, do I hear what I think I'm hearing? Are you implying that you would actually welcome the battle now?"

"The country is preparing itself with such energy and enthusiasm as I have never seen before. I believe we would prevail." Churchill seemed reluctant to give a straight answer to the question, but, after their long years of friendship, Bracken knew how to interpret his language.

"You *would* welcome it. Even, perhaps, to the point of provoking it?"

There was no reply for a long period. Churchill sat quietly, his eyes staring into the corner of the small room. It was the first time that he would verbalise the thoughts that had been gestating for several weeks.

"That, Brendan, is perhaps the unavoidable conclusion of my analysis. An invasion now, before they've properly prepared for it, might give us our best chance of victory. Lead them on... deceive them about our true strength... hit them with everything we've got as they struggle across in their tramp steamers and barges, and let the Channel swallow them up as the Red Sea did the Egyptians."

He paused. Bracken thought he saw a small tear in his eye, perhaps as he contemplated the enormity of what he was saying. Then his voice grew stronger.

"With such a victory achieved we could build our strength here on this fortress island. Then in the fullness of time, with the support of the Empire and, I pray, the United States of America, we would take the fight to the enemy and destroy the monster in his lair."

He paused again, took a deep breath and looked directly at his old friend who stood there ashen-faced.

"Such a vision is, I grant you, almost biblical in scope. The fruits of such a project would be immense... but the risks, I fear, are commensurate." Again he stared at the blank wall of his office and sat silent, his face hard-set. Bracken said nothing, waiting for him to continue. Churchill looked at his old friend, and saw the concern in his demeanour.

"Ah, Brendan, do not get alarmed prematurely. Before indulging in even the slightest further consideration, I would most certainly need to argue the case in Cabinet. Indeed it would be essential to do so. I would require absolute affirmation from the Chiefs that we do indeed have the ability to defeat the Huns."

Bracken had listened speechless as his hero spelled out the audacious plan in powerful language. Eventually he broke his stunned silence, moving from shock to cautious association with the idea.

"If that's your thinking, Winston, you'll need more than affirmation of their ability. You will need the total and unquestioning commitment of every man jack there. When the Nazis head for our shores we will need to show the strength of lions, from you and the Chiefs down to the rawest private or sailor. No doubts, no equivocation. And that absolutely starts at the top. Any plan must start with that."

Churchill knew Bracken was right. It wasn't enough for him to think through a plan and present it to the War Cabinet for approval, and to the Chiefs of Staff for execution. He needed to involve them now to win, first, their understanding, and then their commitment. More than that, he would need all their skill and experience to validate and improve the plan. There was no room for error or misjudgement, not with Hitler's stormtroopers heading towards England.

"That is wise counsel, Brendan. Any such strategy would have to be built absolutely on what the Chiefs are saying to me – their facts, their analyses, their opinions. It must be their plan, not just mine. In any event, only if they gave their unanimous support from a military perspective could I possibly ask the Cabinet for approval. Otherwise there could be a complete schism. It had been my intention to mull this over in private for some time yet, but now that I've verbalised it, I must move forward. Every day we delay reduces the chance of achieving the result I crave. So, rather than procrastinate, let me start the process tomorrow. At the end of the meeting I will ask each of the Chiefs for their personal assessment of our position, and to confirm their level of confidence. In fact, that should really be no more than formal consolidation of what I heard today."

"And not just these last few days, Winston. They've been moving steadily in this direction over the last two or three weeks." Bracken had been conscious of the gradual change in mood.

"That's true, Brendan, and it's one of the reasons for my growing confidence. What I see, what I sense, is the opposite of what was apparent with the French commanders in June. I see commitment, determination, and quiet confidence. Without that I would never have entertained these thoughts that I'm sharing with you. So tomorrow, after canvassing their opinions on the current military balance I will move on. I will allude to the strategic calculations that I have just presented to you; the emerging change in the balance of production as the Germans begin to harness munitions factories and forced labour all over Europe. I will also address the impending financial crisis – the fact that we have to pay for all these arms is a consideration that military men tend to overlook. I will then move to share with them the tentative conclusion that I've reached – and gauge the considerable reaction that it's sure to provoke!"

Bracken came in again, his political brain already hard at work. "That's the only possible approach, Winston, but you'll need to be extremely sensitive in your choice of words. They'll be shocked. Some of them, maybe all, will need time to think through what you're saying, and why. It would be a mistake to push for agreement there and then. Give them time and space."

"Hmm. Yes, that's good advice. I must give them the opportunity to consider and respond – a few days perhaps, certainly no more. I'm convinced they'll come to the same conclusion as I have... unless the window on our readiness that they've been presenting has been, shall we say, rose-tinted. My great concern is that the recent discussions around the Cabinet table about our capabilities may have been somewhat abstract. The Chiefs may have been hiding behind hopes, or assumptions, or caveats. If they know this is going to be for real I can anticipate a much greater level of honesty, both about their own preparedness and that of the other Services – on whom they depend."

Bracken was already planning ahead. "A further thought, Winston. You'll have to speak to the King – before Halifax poisons the royal well."

"Ah yes. Again, Brendan, you are right. The timing of that visit will be critical; the outcome equally so. No Prime Minister has ever brought such tidings to his sovereign."

He looked at him, sombrely, for a few moments, and then brought the discussion to a close. "Brendan, I have shared my deepest thoughts with you. I know I can rely on you for your support... and of course your discretion. Now leave me, I have some important work to do."

The Cabinet meeting resumed at 0930 in the morning. After a brief discussion on the previous day's air battles, they moved on to the second part of the naval review, an update on the Battle of the Atlantic. A senior naval officer presented charts showing how shipping losses were continuing to increase. Extrapolating from the raw numbers, he showed the projected future impact on imports and on oil inventories. It was clear that the situation would soon become critical. Unless the U-boat threat was defeated there would be a tonnage crisis within a matter of months. Then would come the hard choices about the allocation of the remaining shipping capacity – munitions or food? But, for the time-being, weapons, food and raw materials were getting through in sufficient quantity to keep the country supplied. Most critical of all, oil stocks remained adequate.

By mid-morning the presentations were complete and Churchill could feel his own sense of quiet confidence beginning to percolate to the rest of the Cabinet. He waited for the various staff officers and secretaries to depart, but asked the Chiefs of Staff and Beaverbrook to stay behind.

It was time. He was ready to share his almost heretical thoughts with them. Taking a deep breath, he sat forward in his chair. "The reports yesterday and this morning have been comprehensive, and indeed reassuring. Taking them all together, would anyone disagree with a summary of our position as follows? We are prepared. If Hitler were to try an invasion now we would inflict severe losses on his forces at sea and in the air; even heavier losses as they stumble ashore, and finally sweep them up a few miles inland as they run out of supplies."

The Chiefs of Staff looked squarely at him, and General Dill spoke on their behalf.

"That is a concise summary of our position, Prime Minister, and accurate. Having given us time to recover after France, Hitler would be a fool to try to invade us now."

For the first time at these meetings there was an understated, but palpable feeling of confidence round the table. There was no voice objecting to the analysis, but neither was there any show of bravado. The group was quiet, determined, and aware that avoiding an invasion was just the first step in the long and arduous journey ahead.

Churchill was reassured. He knew that the Chiefs of Staff had positioned themselves as he had hoped, making it possible for him to spring his dramatic plan. He spoke quietly, slowly, and with great solemnity.

"He would indeed be a fool to invade us now." He hesitated for a full five seconds, to ensure maximum impact on his audience.

"Unless we invite him."

Chapter Nine

There was a stunned silence in the room as the Cabinet members and the Chiefs of Staff struggled to absorb the Prime Minister's words. Beaverbrook was a few pages ahead of the rest, but chose to say nothing, leaving space for the others to come to terms with the startling suggestion. After perhaps half a minute of confused looks being exchanged across the table, Antony Eden was first to speak. The elegant, cultured old Etonian expressed his utter astonishment at Churchill's suggestion with classic British understatement.

"I beg your pardon, Prime Minister?"

Churchill sat grim-faced, well aware of the shock and confusion that his words had caused. He knew he would have to explain his seemingly outrageous suggestion most carefully to ensure that he brought the Cabinet with him, or at least stopped furious dissent. He had prepared his words as carefully as for any of his public speeches.

"Gentlemen, the future of our nation, indeed its very existence, lie in the epic battle ahead; in the decisions we take over the next few days, and the bravery, skill and determination with which our men carry them out. We all understand most clearly that if Hitler succeeds in defeating and occupying our country, there is no hope. His Gestapo and SS will sweep the nation like a new Black Death, imprisoning and executing all they do not like; squashing not just physical resistance, but all forms and expressions of freedom in Britain, as they have already done in Poland and now begin in France.

"While the bravery of our pilots is winning the day in the battle above our heads, let us consider our strategic position. It is undoubtedly most difficult. Hitler's military success has brought him to our front door. Through the miracle of Dunkirk we saved many of our soldiers, but lost almost all their equipment, which we now scramble to replace. Hitler, on the other hand, has been preparing single-mindedly for this conflict for seven years, training his soldiers and gearing all of Germany's vast productive capacity for war. Now they are further capitalised by the armament industries of Czechoslovakia, Belgium, Holland and France, which the Nazis will shortly harness in support of their war effort.

"If we turn to the geographical and political environs, our situation is equally precarious. Hitler has positioned his war machine around us in an arc from Norway to Biscay. He has covered his rear by means of his devilish pact with Stalin. He has secured his oil supplies from a pliant Romania. With our defeat in Norway, he has preserved the channel to Sweden for his iron ore. He has obtained the support of the vainglorious Mussolini, greedy for gains in the Mediterranean. Soon, perhaps, General Franco may align Spain with the Nazis, putting Gibraltar at risk and threatening to choke off the Mediterranean completely.

"Against that behemoth, let us now review dispassionately our own resources. We have the loyal support of the Empire, but they are thousands of miles away, except of course for our neighbours in Eire, who remain unmoved by our plight. In America we have President Roosevelt's moral support, but he is constrained from assisting us in a more direct manner by difficulties and delays in Congress. I hope and pray that the great American nation will eventually come to our aid, but can we survive until their democratic processes complete? In the meanwhile, all the military equipment that we source from the United States must be paid for in dollars from our rapidly dwindling reserves, and must then run the gauntlet of U-boats to be brought to our shore.

"So, I ask you solemnly, even if we hold Hitler off for the present, as now seems probable thanks to the gallantry of our pilots, how much more difficult will our situation be in six, or twelve, or eighteen months time? I doubt not the courage of our people, but will we still have the weapons, the fuel, even the food we need to persevere in the fight? Should we not instead tackle him now, in mid-Channel, where we are at our strongest and he is at his weakest? Before our strength is eroded, while he builds his? Could we bring him on to us like a small judo fighter who faces a larger opponent, but wins by turning adroitly and using the enemy's weight against him?

"Could we inflict on him a defeat which, while perhaps not fatal for his evil regime, would shatter his image of invincibility, and move our own people to persevere with the struggle? That would convince our American cousins that all is not lost in Europe? That would cause some of those still neutral... Spain... Turkey... Russia... to pause, and determine not to align themselves with the Nazis?

"I have thought long and hard about this painful question. It does appear to me most clear that the best prospect of sustaining our Kingdom and Empire is to have the fateful battle now. Have it now, before we are further weakened. Have it now, before the enemy becomes overwhelmingly powerful. Have it now, before he chooses the opportune day and hour to launch his assault upon us."

The faces around the table were white with concentration as the import of Churchill's words sank in. After an interval General Dill spoke, very quietly.

"Prime Minister, your suggestion comes as a great shock to us all. In our discussions yesterday and this morning we advised you that we believe the country could withstand an invasion attempt by the Germans over the coming weeks. We base our conclusion on the knowledge that the Armed Forces are moderately well re-equipped and that our people will fight to the death to defend our country and our way of life. There was no exaggeration in our words. We were not rashly presenting the most optimistic outlook. It was a solemn and calculated statement, knowing full well that there is an alternative, however unpalatable, of seeking negotiations with the enemy.

"However when we conclude that we can prevail against an invasion, we must also recognise that there are risks. The tide of war is never completely predictable. We would most certainly suffer high casualties, both military and civilian. You now suggest that we should, as you say, 'invite' such a situation. While we hear your powerful reasoning why we must consider such a course, I really must insist, and I think I speak on behalf of my military colleagues, that we are given time to review our previous conclusions. In particular, each of the Services must be allowed to confirm with the others the various assumptions that have been made. We must also estimate the number of casualties we might incur."

Admiral Pound added his view. "I agree with General Dill, Prime Minister. The picture that you put in front of us is indeed most worrying, even as we grow in confidence that we will survive the current battle. As you say, our focus has been on the immediate crisis. We have spent little time looking further ahead. You now force us to confront the narrow range of options that exist, and have suggested a dramatic alternative. But you must allow us time to absorb what you are saying, to analyse it, and then revert to you. We will do this most urgently."

Halifax had become increasingly angry and frustrated as he saw the Chiefs respond guardedly to Churchill's wild plan, rather than rejecting it out of hand. Finally he could contain himself no longer.

"Prime Minister, this suggestion is outlandish. We cannot possibly take such a huge gamble with the future of the nation. At best, we might achieve a marginal victory at a fearful cost in human lives At worst, we risk total disaster."

There was a tense silence, but no one raised their voice in support of Halifax. There were, instead, some discreet signs of agreement with Dill's more measured comments.

Attlee had been listening intently to the debate, and now spoke.

"Prime Minister, this has come as a great surprise, indeed shock, to us all. It is imperative that you allow the Chiefs of Staff the time to do what they suggest. We could only envisage taking the radical course you suggest if there is complete unanimity on the military side before. And while not quite agreeing with the Foreign Secretary's remarks, I do have concerns, and one question. As the fortunes begin to move in our favour in the current battle, to the point that we are increasingly confident that we can repel an invasion, will that not also be apparent to Hitler? What then would lead him to proceed now, when, as you say, time appears to be on his side?"

Churchill had chosen to ignore Halifax's outburst, but was conscious that Attlee had raised a valid issue. He addressed his reply to the group.

"That, gentlemen, is the great conundrum. It is where I need your help, to consider how it might be possible to reconcile the inconsistency. What I do know is that even great decisions of state are often made based on the perception of facts, rather than on the reality. So perhaps we can manage Herr Hitler's perceptions. At the same time as we build our strength to ensure that the decisive battle will most assuredly go in our favour, can we, by sleight of hand, portray such apparent weakness that he will proceed to engage us prematurely? Let me add that we know to our cost the ability of the German military leaders, who would certainly counsel careful preparation. But we also know that patience is not one of Hitler's virtues, if indeed he has any. By using all our skill and guile we may be able to exploit the unnatural alliance between the professional German soldiers and the Nazi thugs that rule their country."

He stood up.

"Let us meet again in three days' time with your response."

Beaverbrook came over to the prime minister's quarters shortly before midnight. Churchill was lying propped up on his bed in his silk pyjamas, nursing a whisky and reviewing the draft of a planned radio address.

"Well, Max, what did you think of the reaction?" he grunted, barely looking up from the paper.

"Very measured, Winston," he replied. "They were surprised of course – some of them quite stunned – but they listened intently. Your approach was absolutely the right one. If this strategy is right, and certainly your logic is powerful, it's vital you have their full support – in ways they never envisioned!"

Churchill put down the draft. "I must have that, absolutely. They'll have to commit themselves totally, one hundred per cent – unless they find insurmountable difficulties. And if they do find such difficulties, we must hear them now, and consider them in an open way. It is possible that there are military things I've overlooked that invalidate all my ideas or conclusions. If that is the reality, we'd better find out about it now, rather than in a month's time, or we could all end up against a wall enjoying our last cigars."

"And, in the worst case, if they do find that it's impossible?"

"In the worst case, we go back to Plan A, and keep beating the wolf back from our door. We can just hope and pray that the Americans, or even the Russians, come to our aid before the man uses his growing strength to overwhelm us."

For the next seventy-two hours frenzied analyses and discussions took place in the headquarters of the three Services. None of the staff officers could be told the reason for the sudden emergency, but by the nature of the tasks assigned, and from the urgency with which answers were demanded, there could be but one conclusion. *The invasion was imminent.*

In the Foreign Office, Halifax was distraught. This was Churchill at his maddest... *Gallipoli all over again.* He made a few half-hearted attempts to raise his concern with Cabinet colleagues, but was rebuffed. Only Chamberlain showed some slight sympathy, but it was clear that his strength was failing, and with it any appetite for rebellion against the Prime Minister. Halifax had only one option. He would speak to the King.

As instructed, the group reconvened three days later. General Ismay had co-ordinated the military input, but they had agreed that General Dill would be their spokesman.

"Prime Minister, on Friday you presented us with a radical suggestion. We asked for time to consider the issues raised, and we can now present our response. In respect of the first two questions, whether we are confident of defeating an invasion, and what level of casualties we might expect to suffer, we present our conclusions. On the third question, about differentiating between our actual capability and that perceived by the enemy, we have made some progress. But this is not solely a military matter. There are many aspects of a deception plan that need further work, with the involvement of a wide range of intelligence and political resources, before we could present a plausible picture to the enemy."

He paused for a few moments to see if there was any reaction from the Prime Minister. There was none and he continued, "Let me start by looking at the naval operations." He nodded in Admiral Pound's direction, but in a display of cross-service co-operation, which pleased Churchill, he continued the presentation himself.

"The armada of transport craft that the Germans are assembling has, in theory, sufficient capacity for the task of invasion. But, clearly, that fleet can only cross under the protection of their air force and navy. We can look at the implications of this. First, their navy. It's only a fraction of ours in size, just one tenth as big, and much depleted after their losses in Norway. In fact they're down to a score or so of destroyers and escorts. This leaves them desperately vulnerable to the Royal Navy. However, in partial compensation they can be expected to make maximum use of minefields and, perhaps, some U-boats on the flanks."

"Just 'some' U-boats?" interrupted Churchill, looking at Admiral Pound. "Why would they not use their entire fleet? If they were to send them all into the Channel, would that not create a great barrier to our ships?"

"Such a move is unlikely," answered Pound. "The waters of the

Channel are confined and shallow, and submarines lose their major advantage – stealthiness. The more they send into the Channel, the more our destroyers and coastal aircraft will detect and sink."

General Dill continued. "So we don't see them as a determining factor in the invasion battle. Unfortunately, the corollary is that the real menace from submarines will continue to be in the Atlantic, and so our convoy defences cannot slacken."

"So, something of a curate's egg. Good in parts. What about their mine barriers? Might they stop our ships penetrating the cordon?"

"We will certainly suffer losses from their mines, particularly the new magnetic type. However, as has been discussed here before, no minefield is impregnable to a determined fleet. A mine can only stop one ship; the rest of the squadron sails though the gap created."

"So your conclusion is that their U-boats will not be effective, nor their minefields, and they only have a fraction of the size of surface fleet that would be required to clear a passage. That only seems to leave their air force?"

"Yes, Prime Minister. The Luftwaffe can be expected to launch fierce attacks on our ships and ports to try to stop the Navy intervening. We have discussed this with you previously, and we reach the same conclusion as before. As long as we maintain air superiority, *or at a minimum prevent the Germans achieving the same over us*," he stressed each word for emphasis, "the Navy will prevail."

His words were emphatic. He let them linger for a few moments before continuing. "Our ships will undoubtedly suffer losses, perhaps severe losses, to the Luftwaffe, no matter how assiduous our pilots are in their defence. However, despite these losses, the Royal Navy will prevail. It will maul the invasion fleet as it crosses and tries to land. Subsequent to that, as our naval reinforcements begin to arrive from the north, we will stem all movement of reinforcements and supplies across the Channel. In a matter of two or three days we will have complete control of the seaways. Our ships will then turn their weapons onto the invasion beaches, and provide naval gunfire support on an immense scale to the defenders onshore, until we finally throttle the invaders."

Churchill had been listening carefully and asked another pertinent question. "General... or perhaps Admiral Pound, you might prefer to answer... what portion of our fleet will we need to commit, and at what stage, to achieve this? Are our destroyers and small craft sufficient, or do we need to employ – and so inevitably put at risk – the Home Fleet's major warships?"

Pound responded. "Prime Minister, the simple answer is that we will commit as much as is necessary, when it is necessary. We will start with the local units, destroyers and motor torpedo boats, and then bring in larger ships, starting with the cruiser squadrons, as and when required. We believe that this step-by-step approach is consistent with the plan not just to see off the German forces, but to smash them. The Army's new strategy of mobile, flexible defence gives us the time to do this. It won't be a question of the Nazis suddenly achieving a breakthrough and charging towards London. However, as I said, the one caveat is that we must maintain air superiority over the Channel and its approaches. If we lose that, we risk losing the Navy and, after that, the country."

That sombre warning brought the review on seamlessly to the air situation, and Dill continued. "At this point let's move on to the air battle. We are confident that over England itself – including the beaches and the landing grounds – the RAF will maintain air superiority. Over the Channel we will, at a minimum, prevent the Germans achieving superiority. This battle is already underway, and we are winning. So it will continue. There is again one caveat. In France, the Germans showed great skill in getting their air forces close to the front line, in support of their advancing troops. They took over French airfields and had aircraft based there within a few hours of capture. Should they succeed in getting forces ashore in England, it will be critical that we stop them capturing or establishing an airfield here. All potential targets in the invasion area will be defended tooth and nail – the orders have already gone out. Airfield facilities are being mined and booby-trapped. Fuel stores, in particular, will be guarded by dedicated men who understand the necessity, and are sworn to destroy them, whatever the cost."

The Prime Minister nodded. "They will need to be the bravest of the brave. This would seem to be the most critical directive to give our stay-behinds – that it is far more important to destroy any threatened airfield than to defend it."

Dill signalled his agreement and moved on. "Apart from protecting our ships, the other main role for the RAF will be direct attacks upon the enemy invasion forces. However, we recognise that sending in our day bombers, unprotected, to attack their fleet would be suicidal. On the other hand, if we were to try to protect them using our fighters, that would simply dilute the defensive air cover that we must provide over the Royal Navy's ships. So our only aerial attacks will be at night, using torpedo-carrying aircraft. By day we will concentrate all the RAF's resources on protecting our own ships, leaving the attack on the invasion fleet to the Navy."

"Can I assume that this policy will change once enemy forces are ashore?" interrupted Churchill.

"Indeed it will, sir. As they try to consolidate their positions in the landing areas we will hurl continuous air attacks on them. We've made significant changes to our tactics as a result of hard-earned experience in France, where our light bombers, Blenheims and Battles, suffered heavy losses to fighters and to their light flak, which is quite deadly. We are rushing new aircraft into production to replace them – fast, cannon-armed Beaufighters and Whirlwinds. We'll have at least fifty in service within a month, and we expect that they'll be devastatingly effective against lightly-protected troops. Our bombers will be reserved for gas attacks, should we need to resort to that."

Several members of the group shuffled uneasily, particularly those who had seen the effects of the hideous weapons at first hand in the First World War. Churchill sensed the mood, and spoke quietly but assertively. It wasn't the time for a discussion on the ethics or efficacy of using gas. "Let me reaffirm the government position: those weapons will only be used as a last resort. Let me also be clear that their deployment can only be authorised by me, or should it be thus, my successor as Prime Minister."

His choice of words was ominous. Even Dill hesitated for a moment, clearing his throat before continuing, "That brings us on to the Army."

Again Churchill interrupted. "Before we move on to the Army, General... you talked a few moments ago about the ships we will employ in the Channel, and the risk of air attack on them. Do we have any actual data about the effectiveness of aircraft against large warships?"

This time Dill called on Admiral Pound to respond. The Admiral reached into his briefcase and extracted a paper.

"We have some, sir... but, perhaps fortunately, not a great deal. We've gradually been building our understanding of the risks since war began. Professor Lindemann has helped with a scientific analysis of the data. If you will allow me, I will read some extracts from his report."

"Proceed," said the Prime Minister. He was confident that any report produced by Prof, his Chief Scientific Advisor, would be dependable. Pound opened the document at a tag and began to read.

'In the mid-1920s the Americans carried out a series of bombing tests against obsolete battleships. The ships were at anchor and unmanned, but nonetheless the experiment proved that it is possible to sink battleships from the air. As regards modern battleships, at sea and well-defended, there is little data. HMS Rodney was hit by a 1000lb bomb which penetrated the deck armour, but did not explode. It is reasonable to assume that if it had done so, there would have been serious damage to the ship, possibly immobilising it completely.'

Pound looked up. He didn't need to spell out the consequences of a British battleship lying adrift and undefended in the middle of the North Sea. He continued to read.

'For cruisers and other ships we have more data. Our Fleet Air Arm Skua dive-bombers attacked the German cruiser Koningsberg in Norway,

when she was alongside. Sixteen aircraft attacked, each with a 500lb bomb. They achieved two or three hits and sank her. In respect of Royal Navy cruisers, the Sheffield and Suffolk were attacked in separate engagements by about twenty German dive-bombers. They each suffered two or three hits – again we think of about 500lb – and were almost lost.'

"This is the most complete report we have, sir," said Pound, as he shuffled through the report to find another tag. "Professor Lindemann summarises the situation as follows."

'From this data we have calculated that an undisturbed attack by a typical formation of fifteen or twenty aircraft is likely to score one to three hits; enough to sink a destroyer; seriously damage, or worse, a cruiser; or cause significant damage to a battleship.'

Pound turned to Churchill and continued. "We believe that the key word there is *'undisturbed'*. That's why we're so insistent on the need for air protection, to break up the German formations before they get into position for accurate bombing runs."

Churchill asked to look at the paper and shuffled though the pages, skimming the content, before commenting, "I assume this all relates to daylight attacks?"

"Yes. By night, we are confident that the only possible attacks would be by torpedo aircraft, not bombers. Our own Swordfish practise night attacks regularly, but we haven't seen much evidence of German torpedo aircraft. The Italians have some capability, but we don't think that they have the skills to launch night attacks, even if their aircraft were deployed to the Channel."

Churchill nodded, and tapped the report with his hands, indicating his acceptance of its content. "So I think it's clear. By night our ships are reasonably safe from air attack. By day it becomes the number one priority of the Royal Air Force to protect them.

"Now let us move on to the Army."

Dill continued with his presentation. "At the risk of some repetition from last week's discussion, in May the Germans might have had a chance of quick victory, if they had carried out a landing while our forces were still in disarray after the withdrawal from France.

But not now. The construction of defence lines is well underway across the country. The army is re-equipped to an adequate level, and each division has a very clear understanding of its responsibilities in the event of invasion. The twenty-six infantry divisions are almost fully equipped as far as small arms and light support weapons go. Six of them are mechanised with transport and light armour. You have the charts in front of you, sir."

Churchill looked at the list placed in front of him. A block diagram showed the manpower and key equipment levels for each division. Dill waited a moment, but there were no questions, and he moved on.

"The two armoured divisions will soon be up to strength in tanks, and should be sufficient to match the small number of panzers that the Germans can hope to get ashore. The quality of our tanks is adequate for the task in hand. Our Matildas are much slower than the German tanks, but they have better armour. That makes them well suited to a defensive battle, particularly in a tight corner of England, where the Germans will not have the room for manoeuvre that they had in France."

The Prime Minister interrupted again, somewhat impatiently. "What about the artillery regiments? Is their re-equipment on schedule? What about the anti-aircraft units?"

"The shipment of field guns from the United States has been distributed to the regiments, more than replacing the losses suffered in France. We are mounting some of them on flat-bed lorries, which gives a degree of mobile artillery support for our tanks. You also ask about our anti-aircraft defences. Regrettably, there the situation is not nearly as good. Our main weapons are both excellent, the 3.7in high level gun and the Bofors, but we simply don't have sufficient numbers to cover all the likely targets. As with the Navy, the Army will be mainly reliant on the RAF to stop the Luftwaffe, particularly the Stukas, getting through."

Dill finished and closed his folder.

"Thank you, General. Your report is very reassuring. It is clear that we continue to make significant progress. Now let us move on to the other side of the equation that I asked you to consider, namely the enemy's weaknesses, and how we might exploit them."

"Yes, Prime Minister. I would like to hand over to Admiral Pound, as we will be talking mainly about naval issues"

Pound opened the folder lying on the table and began.

"Prime Minister, we all recognise the extent to which the German fleet is inferior to the Royal Navy, and I won't labour that any further. But an even bigger weakness is their lack of understanding, up to the highest level, of naval and amphibious operations. They've had to assemble an invasion fleet under great time pressure and, it would seem, with little forewarning. Three quarters of their transport capacity is provided by Rhine barges, which are flat-bottomed, low-sided, and totally unsuitable for the task.

"The Channel can be treacherous with winds, currents and sandbanks all providing serious problems. Even if they get a period of clear weather for the crossing, that will inevitably break within a matter of days, as they try to bring in reinforcements, giving them huge problems. There is a real possibility that the beach landings would be a disaster even if unopposed by the Royal Navy and RAF. There is not the slightest doubt that the Germans will suffer serious losses on each wave of their assault, and on each resupply mission. We know from Gallipoli in 1915 just how difficult it is to sustain a major assault over a beachhead."

Churchill, the architect of the disaster in the Dardanelles, said nothing, and Pound continued.

"In fact, as this study progressed, it became even clearer how much more serious the situation would be if they were to capture a port, whether though direct assault - from the sea or by parachute, or by encirclement from behind if they manage a successful beach landing close-by. The distance across the Channel is short, and they might be able to maintain a supply line with a relatively small number of fast cargo ships. In this context I have re-emphasised the orders to prepare all ports in the area with block ships, ready to sink. As well as that, demolition charges are being set on key items of infrastructure – cranes, locks and so on – all wired for immediate destruction. Just as important, I have ensured that precise orders have been issued, right down to Petty Officer level, leaving them in no doubt about their responsibility to execute the demolition orders at the first sign of enemy forces in their vicinity."

Again Churchill showed his approval. "That is prudent. Perhaps General Brooke will be able to provide some regular or Home Guard troops to reinforce the naval defenders."

Dill took over again from Pound. "Moving on to the air battle, we find their second great weakness. Not their men or equipment, which are good, but their capacity for self-delusion. They seem to believe that they've eroded the RAF's strength by about half since the Battle of Britain began, whereas in fact we have as many fighters now as when it started. Goering continues to boast that he has almost destroyed the RAF. That miscalculation represents a critical weakness in their planning which we may be able to exploit."

Churchill turned to Air Chief Marshall Dowding to follow up the point made by Dill. "Can you be sure that the success they boast of is not just fatuous propaganda, designed to bolster their own morale and undermine ours?"

Dowding responded "One might well come to that conclusion when listening to the wild claims that they're making. However our interrogations of POWs and recordings of their private discussions show that it's genuine. They believe that they're destroying our aircraft at a rate twice as fast as they actually are. They also seem to be totally unaware of the great increase in our fighter production – with the new Spitfire plant in Birmingham now in full operation – not to forget the excellent work of Lord Beaverbrook's repair organisation. It's quite remarkable how quickly local garages and workshops are now able to get damaged planes back into service."

"That all sounds very plausible. Please continue, General Dill."

"Moving on to a third critical weakness, it's clear they have a complete lack of understanding of the British character and morale.

They seem to believe that there is a substantial body of people in England ready to sue for peace, and thereby accept German dominance over continental Europe. On the ground, talking to our troops, and hearing from them what civilians are saying, I can tell you there is no such mood. Our fighting men will fight, and our people will support them."

Churchill indicated his assent. "I concur with that assessment. I have recently received a report from our mail censors, who continue to report a high level of morale among the civilian population. Long may it continue!"

"In summary, Prime Minister, if they come, we will savage their armada as it crosses the Channel, slay them in thousands as they land, and then sweep up the remnants in the first week or so as they try to push inland. There is consensus across the Army, Navy and Air Force that each service is fully able to carry out the tasks assigned, both direct and in support of the others. We can, and we will, destroy any attempt at invasion."

Churchill was pleased and relieved. The very structure of the presentation showed the Services working together in a most encouraging way. The information provided was detailed and consistent. He then took a deep breath before looking up.

"Gentlemen, I also asked for your estimates of casualties."

Dill shuffled the papers in front of him, though he was well aware of the answer they contained. He looked squarely at the Prime Minister. "Seventy five to one hundred thousand military casualties, sir, dead and wounded."

There was a murmur round the table. The number of military casualties envisioned was more than double what had been suffered in the Battle of France. Then Dill spoke again. "Perhaps the same number of civilians." The room went silent. The scale of casualties was appalling. This was the first war where the civilian population – men, women and children – were in the front line.

Churchill knew that he could not afford the discussion to focus solely on the potential casualty figures. The brutalities of this war would continue, one way or another, until Nazism was extinguished – or Britain itself.

"Gentlemen, your analysis of the military situation seems most thorough. Even with the caveats you describe, addressing which must be an essential element of our plan, you have confirmed the first part of our conjecture, that we can and will repulse a Nazi invasion. The casualty estimates are, of course, alarming. The military must do all they can to achieve victory with the minimum number of casualties. We will also need to do more, much more, on the civilian side: evacuations of towns and cities, shelters in public parks, slit trenches in open spaces and so on. I will ask the Home Secretary to get this in hand urgently and report to us at our next meeting."

He paused, and then moved to wind up the day's discussions.

"General, your summary of our readiness and of the enemy's weaknesses has been most valuable. It provides excellent input to the complex challenge of developing a deception plan. If I may frame that question for your consideration. *If we are so confident that a Nazi invasion will be an abject failure, how can we best disguise such likely outcome from the Germans? Why might they see it differently, and how could we encourage such a fatal misjudgement on their part?*

"I understand that work is underway on the military side of this. I encourage you to keep working on that. However I anticipate that the broad issue of political disinformation will involve even more subtle and complex discussions. So as work continues on the military aspects, I will ask a small group of colleagues to begin consideration of the political dimension."

CHAPTER TEN

Churchill wanted to have the first discussion about the military deception plan in private, well aware that certain elements were likely to prove contentious. He arranged to meet General Ismay in the Map Room to discuss progress. He was conscious that the redeployment of some forces away from the front line of defence was a potential issue, not to mention the consequences of any political moves and the impact on the civilian population. He would need to marshal his case carefully and be sure-footed with the War Cabinet to avoid the decision being delayed or even derailed, caught up in a quagmire of argument. When he came into the room, Ismay was seated at the table with three folders spread out in front of him. Even as he entered, he could see that one of the folders was quite substantial, the other two much less so. He cast his eyes purposefully on the array of papers, and grunted.

"I note the thickness of the various folders, General. Am I to assume that the problems you referred to yesterday are still manifest in the final report?"

"Yes, Prime Minister, I'm afraid that remains very much the case. We have a detailed and, I believe, effective plan with regards to the RAF." He put his hand on the thick folder in front of him. "Air assets are highly mobile. The very mobility that the Germans exploited so ruthlessly in their French offensive is just as valuable for us, when we now want to disguise our strength."

He laid his hands on the two smaller folders.

"It is much more difficult for the other two Services – particularly the Navy. Their operations and assets are effectively static, even ships unfortunately in the context of this new, fast-moving warfare. Efforts to hide them are most difficult, as they are continually subject to scrutiny from enemy reconnaissance aircraft. "

"And I don't suppose we can prevent that?"

"No sir. Even with our radar network it is not practicable to stop single high speed aircraft making quick dashes over Britain, any more than the Germans can stop us doing the same to them."

"Well, let us proceed with the RAF plan. Perhaps if it is sufficiently convincing we can build upon it to create the overall picture."

Ismay opened the thick folder and focussed on the summary page, switching to a more formal tone as he began to speak.

"The RAF confirms that it can respond to the requirement, namely to give the enemy the impression that it is a spent force, while at the same time preserving its strength for a decisive battle later. It is certain that the invasion will not take place unless the Nazis believe that they have achieved air superiority over the invasion area. To encourage this belief, the RAF will orchestrate an apparent reduction in strength, on a carefully planned basis, to lead the enemy to believe that they are wearing us down. Aircraft and ground equipment will be moved rapidly to deceive them – out of sight to give the impression of steadily declining strength, and then back into position to take the offensive at the precise time required."

He paused. "That's a summary of the report, sir. It then goes on in considerable detail to identify the sequence of movements and actions, right down to squadron and airfield level."

"That's more or less as expected, Pug, and all very positive. Though there is one thing that I've been mulling over. As we set about misleading them, we'll need to be very conscious not to overplay our hand. It could destroy the entire plan if the enemy's intelligence service were to become suspicious."

"Agreed, sir, and indeed the RAF Intelligence people have been giving that a lot of thought. They've come up with some good ideas. In particular they understand that it will be important to match the reduction in our strength with what the Germans expect to be happening."

"Have the Nazis been sharing their deliberations with us?"

"Not exactly, sir. But fortunately we are able to get a good idea of their state of mind from a range of sources – propaganda broadcasts, POW interrogations and other intelligence sources, particularly Ultra decrypts. For example, every day we hear from Berlin radio the claims they make about our aircraft losses. And while there's clearly some exaggeration for effect, it's not just idle propaganda. Our interrogations of downed Luftwaffe pilots confirm that the Germans genuinely believe that the RAF is down to its last few hundred fighters. In our deception plan we will adopt tactics to reinforce that view. Ultimately we want the Luftwaffe to aver to Hitler that they have achieved air supremacy over southern England. We'll then be ready to smash them as they move to take advantage of this supposed superiority."

Churchill pursed his lips. "Can we be sure that they're not just deliberately exaggerating their claims to maintain their own pilots' morale, while all the time being aware of the true picture?"

"That's something we've been considering, sir, and trying to get some evidence rather than just opinion. The Air Intelligence people have done some very good work. If you'll bear with me for a moment..."

He leafed through the folder and extracted a document. "What we have, and they don't, is access to the hard facts. For example, we are able to match the claims made by our own fighter squadrons against those physically verified. We've taken all the claim reports made in the last two months which were categorized as 'confirmed' by Fighter Command and compared them with actual crash sites on land, or independently witnessed at sea. There is a substantial discrepancy between the two. In fact we've been able to extract a fairly consistent ratio between claims 'confirmed' based on combat reports, and those actually evidenced."

Churchill interrupted him, very peremptorily. "Be more precise, General Ismay. Are you are saying there is a serious inconsistency between what the RAF is reporting to Cabinet on a regular basis, and what we are actually achieving?"

"Sir, for every German wreck that we can positively identify, there are about two kills rated as 'confirmed' by the squadrons. To be fair, there will be some additional German losses into the Channel and on their return to France, but not enough to explain the discrepancy."

Churchill glared at him. "That is extremely disturbing information, General, which I will come back to anon. For the moment we'd better see if can use it to our advantage."

Ismay had known how uncomfortable the news would be, but continued.

"Since we know *exactly* what our losses are, we can scale that up by the same factor of two and calculate roughly what the Luftwaffe is likely to be reporting to its masters."

"Double what we are in fact losing?"

"Yes sir, and that leads on to their likely calculation about our remaining strength. There are only three inputs to that equation: what we started with – which they more or less know, what they think we're building, and what they think we're losing. Then comes the clever bit. The RAF will gradually withdraw fighters from the front line in accord with what the German Intelligence people are likely to be calculating. The withdrawn fighters will be redeployed to secret bases in the north and west, and stored in camouflaged dispersal areas until they are needed."

Churchill set his chin square and looked at the weighty file, slowly nodding his head in approval.

"Ismay, despite the disturbing information about our victory claims, that is quite excellent work. Clearly, with the fight taking place over our heads, we have superior battlefield intelligence and

I'm delighted to see us make such scientific use of it. However I see one great problem. We may certainly be able to feign weakness by reducing the number of fighters in this controlled way. But can we avoid catastrophic damage and casualties as we do so?"

"That remains a real challenge, sir, and they're giving it a lot of thought. With a much smaller number of planes confronting the enemy raids, the RAF recognises that it has to change its priorities and tactics. So instead of simply trying to destroy the maximum number of raiders, the new tactics will focus on causing maximum disruption to their formations, trying to minimize damage and casualties on the ground.

"They go through this in quite a lot of detail in the report. As soon as a raid is detected approaching the coast, they'll send up a small number of fighters to attack the escorting 109s. The German top cover is always the killer for our fighters as they are trying to tackle the bombers lower down. So we'll engage the escorts in a fight early on, try to drive them away from the bombers and force them to use up fuel so they can't stay as long over Britain. With the escorts gone, even a small number of our fighters should be able to cause chaos in their bomber formations."

"Aren't we already trying to do that, and finding it difficult?"

"That's true, sir. Fortunately we have the new Spitfire Mark IIs just coming into service, which have much better performance at high altitude. These will be scrambled as early as possible and should be able to get up to the 109s in good time."

"Do we have enough of them to make a difference?"

"Just about, sir, for that one specific task. There are three squadrons equipped already and two more scheduled for next month."

"Does Beaverbrook know the importance of these aircraft?"

"He does, sir, and he's been very supportive, giving top in priority to their delivery. Now, once the new Spitfires have done their job distracting the escorts, we'll send in small numbers of fighters, mainly Hurricanes, against the bombers. A big change here is that we'll use head-on attacks. The German bombers with their glasshouse cockpits are very vulnerable from the front. We can certainly expect to score some victories, but, more importantly, we'll disrupt their bombing runs with the ferocity of our attacks. I should add that these tactics can be expected to lead, unfortunately, to a small number of head-on collisions. But even that is likely to reinforce the Germans' belief that the RAF is in desperation."

Churchill looked at Ismay and indicated his approval. "That will certainly make their day-trips less enjoyable. Will the approach still work if they change their target strategy, for example if they switch the focus of their attack to London?"

"Well, by day it wouldn't invalidate our tactics; probably just make the fighter boys even more determined to break them up. By night, the situation remains as it is at present, very painful for civilians, but almost irrelevant as far as an invasion is concerned. In any case, they're bound to turn their attention back to the ports and airfields as the date of the invasion approaches."

"Well I suppose that would help Fighter Command. I know that it's the continuous pressure that gives Dowding most concern."

"In fact, the new plan does help in that regard. We'll have run down the number of aircraft and men in the frontline airfields and at the same time increased the anti-aircraft defences as best we can. We're also planning to move in large numbers of obsolete aircraft as decoys. I should add that protecting the ports is just as much of a problem. With them we're going to increase the number of anti-aircraft guns and balloons, and we'll do as much as we can with smoke screens, decoy fires and so on."

"More balloons? Good. Keep the Stukas away from the ships, Pug. That's what we learned at Dunkirk. The level bombers don't do nearly as much damage."

"Yes sir. Everyone is conscious of that. There is one final twist in the RAF deception plan. They plan to gather together our remaining biplanes, the old Gladiators, from various second-line units and training squadrons, and throw them into the battle. This should reinforce the impression that the RAF is running out of first line fighters."

"That may be a worthy objective, Ismay, but we can't afford to throw away our most priceless assets, our brave young pilots!" growled Churchill.

"Sir, the Gladiators will be ordered to make a single pass at the bombers and then dive away. No heroics. The RAF is very aware that we must minimise pilot casualties. We just need a sufficient number of sorties to make sure that the bomber crews see the old planes. The old biplanes can actually climb quite high and are just about fast enough in a dive to be safe from the bombers' defensive fire. We'll keep them to the west of London, and hope that there won't too many 109s in the area."

"Make sure that Dowding's people understand that. You'll also have to find a way to get that message right down to the squadrons without compromising the secrecy of our plan. It won't be easy trying to dampen down the courage of those remarkable young men."

"I understand, sir."

"General, this is a well thought-out strategy. However it will, inevitably and regrettably, lead to increased damage and casualties on the ground, both military and civilian. We must take urgent action to minimise those. Nevertheless I am much taken by the proposals. We will hold the enemy's attention with these new tactics in the south-east corner of the country as we build a great reserve of fighters in the west. Then, at the chosen moment we will hit them with a tremendous blow. With the RAF keeping the Luftwaffe off the Royal Navy's back, our ships will be free to set about their unprotected armada. Yes, this has great promise."

He leafed through the rest of the report, being delighted with the comprehensive nature and the detail of the RAF planning. He closed the document and looked at Ismay. "For several reasons the calculation of the numbers of aircraft being left, week by week, to face the Luftwaffe is critical. Have you discussed this with Prof and Beaverbrook?"

"Yes sir. In considerable detail."

"Good, let's get them to join us after supper. I want to see actual numbers."

Prof Lindemann and Beaverbrook joined the meeting an hour later. As Beaverbrook knew the production figures and loss rates inside out, he had been deeply involved in the planning work. Lindemann had been brought in to make sure there was scientific validation of the assumptions made, and it was he who presented the statistics.

"We've been very rigorous in the calculations on how this should evolve. We know the Germans had reasonably accurate information about our strength at the beginning of the battle, and had a good idea what our production rates were, through commercial espionage. The information we are getting from POWs correlates moderately well with our theory about the ratio of claims to actual victories. We are quite sure that their High Command believes they are destroying about 250 of our fighters per week, and that we're building less than 100. That would result in them estimating our net attrition at about 150 aircraft every week."

"And the reality?"

Beaverbrook answered. "We're actually losing about 120, and building almost as many. Indeed some weeks we're building more than we're losing."

Churchill pursed his lips. "So, Herr Goering thinks we are weakening at a rate of 150 aircraft each week, against an actual decline of, maybe, ten or twenty?"

Beaverbrook nodded. "There or thereabouts, Prime Minister. We're pretty confident on the numbers. Even taking a conservative approach, we can certainly add more than 100 fighters every week to our reserve – a reserve the Germans will know nothing about."

Churchill looked to Ismay. "Will the dispersal operation not become visible to the enemy?"

"Unlikely, sir. There is a normal rotation of squadrons around airfields for tactical reasons. For the deception we will just rotate out from the frontline stations more than we rotate in, and then hide the withdrawn aircraft in remote bases. We've identified plenty of locations with woodland close-by. Once the fighters get to the remote airstrips, we just wheel them under cover. The pilots and ground crew will sleep rough for the few weeks necessary. The Hurricane squadrons, at least, got quite good at that in France."

Lindemann took over again. "One complication is that as we reduce the number of fighters we throw into the battle, the Germans will presumably make fewer claims. We have been through a number of iterations to compensate for that. Taking everything into account we calculate that in four weeks' time – which we took as the horizon, before they run out of suitable weather – they will calculate that we have less than a hundred fighters left, whereas we'll actually have four or five times that number."

"What about pilots, Ismay?"

"Pilot numbers remain critical, sir. We can replace planes easily enough, but we can't replace experienced pilots with novices. A major benefit of our new tactics is that as we reduce the level of engagement, the number of pilot casualties should reduce in parallel. It should also remain the case that we save about half the pilots from planes shot down. On the supply side, the RAF's training units are doing everything they can to build up the numbers. They are also bringing into the frontline some very experienced pilots from the conquered countries; Polish mainly, but also from Czechoslovakia, France and Belgium. They are experienced *and* aggressive. At times the problem is to curb their enthusiasm to have a go at the Jerries. There are also resources coming in from the Empire. The first Canadian squadron is already in action, and more are on the way. However, clearly that there is no point having 500 planes in reserve for the crunch battle if we don't have the men to fly them. I'm afraid that we'll have to call even further on Bomber and Coastal Commands and the Fleet Air Arm for trained pilots."

Churchill was decisive. "They won't like it, but needs must when the devil drives."

Beaverbrook and Lindemann finished their contribution and left, allowing Churchill and Ismay to continue their discussion into the evening.

"Ismay, this RAF plan is powerful and deeply thought out, for which I am most grateful. It is sufficiently convincing that it may well carry our entire strategy forward on its own. But you'd better also tell me what you have come up with on the Army and Navy side."

"The situation is somewhat different with the Army, sir. Like the RAF, they are able to hide a lot of their equipment, except for the big coastal guns and so on. But that isn't actually the issue. We are probably manufacturing somewhat more, and importing a lot more weaponry than the Germans imagine, but again not enough to affect their conclusions radically. The difference is that they clearly believe they have the beating of our Army. They've already done so twice, in Norway and France, and are probably even wondering about our soldiers' morale. The good news arising from this lack of concern is that we can just go on, hell for leather, re-equipping the divisions as fast as we can."

Churchill now understood why the portfolio on the Army was so slim, and accepted the conclusion. Then it was time to tackle the tough one, the Royal Navy. Ismay had been talking for most of the evening, and his voice was getting raspy. He also seemed slightly on edge, which was rare for him. Churchill went over to his whisky decanter and poured a drink for himself. He offered one to Ismay, who refused politely, and just asked for some water. After the short break Ismay continued.

"Sir, the naval plan is the real challenge. The tactic of redeploying our assets and hiding them away, which works so well with aircraft, just doesn't apply when you are considering naval vessels – not to mention port facilities. It might just be possible to secrete a number of smaller Royal Navy ships in remote anchorages, but that isn't very satisfactory when we want to bring them back into battle. In any event it couldn't be done with the bigger ships."

From Churchill's time in the Admiralty he knew the problem.

"I understand. As well as which, if the enemy were to spot what we were about it could potentially expose our entire strategy."

"Quite, sir. And even if we were able to hide them, it would be almost impossible to manipulate the Germans' calculations of our actual strength. They know what the Royal Navy's order of battle was at the start of the war, and they have reasonably accurate knowledge of our losses and acquisitions since then. We might try to use decoy fires and smoke canisters on ships which come under attack to give an illusion of a higher level of losses than actually suffered, but it's marginal. Taking an overall view, there are considerable problems in trying to disguise the immense capability of the Royal Navy."

Ismay paused, to allow his comments to be absorbed.

"So, in terms of the Army, nothing needs to be done, and in terms of the Navy, nothing can be done. Am I summarising correctly?" Churchill was at his most succinct.

"Almost, but not quite, sir. I would like to ask for your consideration of a somewhat different approach, being fully conscious that the Royal Navy is presumably Hitler's biggest worry... and rightly so! Some of our brightest young staff officers have been tossing this issue around, and have come up with an interesting hypothesis. The Germans don't fear our Army because they believe it *cannot* fight. Perhaps they wouldn't be so fearful of the Royal Navy if they thought it *will* not fight."

"Explain!"

"I will, sir, and beg your indulgence if I stray too far beyond my military brief. The thesis that they've come up with is that it might be possible to use a different deception approach for the Navy. They suggest that it might be possible to achieve the desired result by manipulating the impression, not of its capacity to fight, but of its willingness to do so. It may be possible to create a question mark over the Navy's loyalty. Our sources tell us – indeed Hitler himself has stated – that he has no desire to interfere with the Empire. He doesn't know the British character, and he may be of a mind to believe that this will strike a chord with the Navy – the people charged with maintaining the Empire as well as protecting Britain. It might be possible to create the illusion that the Royal Navy sees no point in being sacrificed to the Luftwaffe's bombers, in what appears to be a futile attempt to repel an invasion; that the Navy, or at least a large part of it, will seek to preserve itself for its traditional role in the seaways of the Empire – whatever the dispensation of the government here."

Churchill looked at Ismay, and for a few moments Ismay wasn't sure whether he was about to be fired. Finally he spoke. "As you say, Pug, you have gone well beyond your strict military brief. I commend you for that. How far have you taken your thinking on how this might be achieved?"

"Not far, sir. We wanted to gauge your reaction first."

"It's devious... quite excellent, in fact! It could be the key to the whole strategy... But it will require a whole new set of thinking about how we go about it... It's not just a military pageant; there are subtle political overtones as well... I know who I'll get to help. Bracken! It's right up his street, actually.

"You've done good work, Pug. Now it's time to take it to the Cabinet; time to involve them in what may be the most momentous decision ever taken by a British government."

At the Cabinet next morning, Ismay gave the same presentation, beginning with the RAF deception plan. After he finished, Churchill summarised the report with great gusto. "In just a few short weeks the RAF will build a great reserve of aircraft, ready to deliver a fierce rebuff to the Luftwaffe. It will maintain a great aluminium umbrella above our ships, protecting them as they set about the Nazi armada, and then fall upon the surviving troops as they try to land."

The presentation of the RAF plan had been so intense and compelling that there had been little interruption from the audience. Finally Attlee spoke. "General Ismay, you have provided a precise and thoughtful plan, which we much appreciate. However I have great concern that, given greater freedom of the skies over England, the Luftwaffe will cause immense damage to our cities, ports, aircraft factories and invasion defences – not to mention causing a huge number of civilian casualties."

It was difficult to phrase a reply that did not sound callous. Attlee had put his finger on the issue that was at the core of the decision they faced. After a noticeable hesitation Ismay responded, "Deputy Prime Minister, we are deeply conscious of that. Second only to deceiving the enemy, the focus of this new plan will be on disrupting the raids, with the specific aim of reducing damage and, of course, casualties. But, I accept, it's a difficult balance."

"Can we do anything else on the military side?" Antony Eden added his concern.

"One area we're still refining is the deployment of our anti-aircraft artillery," Ismay continued. "We have already done that to a certain extent, but can go further – bring almost all our heavy guns into London, and move the low-level weapons to the airfields and ports. That means almost denuding the provincial cities of guns, but we might be able to compensate to some extent by using some more fighters. Even though we have to disguise the fact that we have a large number of aircraft secreted away, we might still be able to release a small number – enough to give a moderate level of protection."

The meeting continued with a discussion of the measures to be taken to reduce civilian casualties. There was agreement on evacuation of the major cities, and the rapid building of trenches and other simple shelters for the civilians that remained. Fortunately such a reaction to the increased risk of attack was consistent with the message they wanted to convey to the enemy; that Britain was sinking fast.

There followed a brief report on the Army, presenting and clarifying the conclusion the planners had reached. It was accepted by all that there was no need for a deception plan.

Finally it was time for the contentious part; the radical idea regarding the Navy. Admiral Pound had been briefed to a certain extent, enough to avoid a major flare-up at the Cabinet table, and sat quietly as Ismay opened. As on the previous evening, he began by describing the difficulty of trying to disguise the Navy's strength, and how it might be possible, instead, to create the impression that it was not fully committed to the struggle. To make it less contentious, the Prime Minister had agreed to take over as the discussion moved into the political arena.

"It is clear that Hitler believes there is considerable support in England for negotiations. In his speech to the Reichstag last month he was still offering us terms. His most recent communication via the King of Sweden conveyed the same message. It may be possible to build a clever political deception around this, leading him to believe that there is a growing tide of opinion here in favour of a settlement; that the will to resist is collapsing; that there is even, perhaps, the possibility of a coup d'état in the train of a German landing. Signs of such defeatism in the country at large would align well with an apparent lack of stomach for the fight within the Royal Navy."

He looked around the table.

"To achieve this, we will need the support, witting or unwitting, of a number of influential people. Some of these were, shall we say, late converts to our policy of total resistance to the Nazis."

If Halifax felt uncomfortable, he said nothing.

"We will build a make-believe world of a Britain in turmoil. We will feed information through the growing number of agents that we've turned, one way or another, getting them to report on supposed peace rallies and so on. We will arrange some press coverage of labour disputes, where indeed some of the left-wing unions have been a bit discommoded by Stalin's pact with Hitler. We will create the mirage of a Britain on the point of capitulation as a result of our heavy losses and internal dissension – just as happened in France. We will offer this merry potion of disinformation to a thirsty Mr Hitler. Let us hope it will be sufficient temptation for him to imbibe, throw caution to the wind, and launch his ill-prepared, and doomed, invasion."

Late in the afternoon Brigadier Stewart Menzies came over to Churchill's room to give the daily intelligence briefing. As head of MI6, traditionally masked from public view with the cover name 'C', he was the person holding the deepest of Britain's secrets. Amongst these, the breaking of Germany's encrypted Enigma communications network and the resulting stream of intelligence, codenamed Ultra, was by far the most important. All information from the source was communicated, in person, to the Prime Minister alone. After Menzies had finished his report, the Prime Minister decided it was time to inform him about the strategy that was developing, and the great deception plan that would be part of it.

"C, I want to talk to you about a most important exercise that we are involved in. You are the first person outside the War Cabinet to be briefed – but I expect that you, of all people, can keep a secret!"

As he proceeded, Menzies listened intently. He was impressed that no hint of the plan had reached him beforehand, and followed Churchill's exposition closely, indicating his understanding at various key points. He asked a few questions to clarify the area where the Intelligence Services would be most intimately involved, particularly the use of captured German spies. Finally, as the discussion wound down he commented quietly. "There is a related aspect to this, Prime Minister, which I had been planning to discuss with you at the appropriate time. It involves some extremely sensitive information. May I continue?"

Churchill grunted, which Menzies took as assent. Before proceeding, he stood up and went over to the door. The procedure for the Ultra meetings involved a strict quarantine zone around Churchill's private quarters, but Menzies checked again to make sure that the exclusion area was being respected. He came back into the room, and began speaking in a quiet voice.

"Sir, the information involves the Duke of Windsor. We have reason to believe that not all contact between his household and the Nazis has ceased."

Churchill looked at Menzies directly, somewhat stunned. He was aware, of course, of the Duke of Windsor's pre-war meetings with, and admiration for Hitler. But since the abdication there had been no hint of disloyalty to the country. His recent despatch from Lisbon across the Atlantic to act as Governor of the Bahamas had been a pragmatic decision to keep him out of Nazi hands, while also avoiding any possible deflection of the nation's loyalty from King George VI.

"The Duke of Windsor is not a traitor," he said, both in genuine disbelief of the apparent allegation, and perhaps slightly embarrassed in view of his support for the Duke, the erstwhile King Edward VIII, before his abdication.

"Not the Duke, sir. But there is someone close to him, someone who is deeply indignant at the course of events that has occurred, and who has no national loyalty to this country."

Churchill snorted. "Do you have any evidence of this?" He had never liked her very much, but that did not make it any easier to accept the allegation.

"Not enough to have brought it to you attention earlier. We're still not sure whether it's deliberate or whether she is just being extremely loose-lipped with some very unsavoury characters. In view of the limited potential for damage with them in their present location, we were happy to keep a watching brief until either more evidence appeared or the risk increased. Things may now be evolving to the point where we might regard the situation as increasingly risky, but also perhaps having some potential to be used to our advantage."

"What are you suggesting, C? That we involve the Duke in some way? I know Windsor, and even in his present predicament he would not be a traitor to his country... or to his brother, the King!"

"Sir, I'm not suggesting for one moment that he would. But it might be possible to arrange events that would lend support to such an interpretation from, shall we say, an external perspective – without the conscious involvement of the Duke, and without alerting the other party."

"I'm still listening," growled Churchill.

"As an example, we could arrange his return to Lisbon, advising him that the country needs him closer at hand. That would play to his vanity of course, but if we managed it carefully we might be able to create the impression that it had been done without the prior agreement of the government. Perhaps we could use a Royal Navy ship, which would support the impression of divided loyalties with the Armed Forces."

Churchill mulled over the suggestion. The allegations were, perhaps, a shock, but not necessarily a huge surprise. It had been clear at the time of the Windsors' meetings with Hitler and others in Germany that they had been greatly impressed by the Nazis. It was not unlikely that Hitler would have responded to this attention with some reciprocal interest. It offered possibilities.

"Lisbon might be rather too proximate, but the idea has merit," he answered, then sat thinking for many seconds. "Any activity in this area will need the utmost sensitivity and discretion," he murmured. "Whatever we might endeavour to arrange must be open to benign interpretation, both now and long into the future. Anything that led to a suspicion of treason by such a senior Royal could damage the monarchy for decades, perhaps for generations to come. As such, it cannot be simply a political decision: the King will have to be briefed, and give his approval."

Since the first disturbing hints had begun to seep out from the Bahamas, Menzies had been pondering on just these complex issues. He knew where he stood.

"Sir, if this helps ensure that there is a monarchy in future decades, it will be worthwhile."

CHAPTER ELEVEN

Churchill was satisfied that a powerful strategy for military deception was taking shape, and that General Ismay would see it refined until complete. The political side would be the challenge: putting together a sophisticated and subtle confection that would stand scrutiny by German intelligence, yet would not cause consternation for the ordinary civilian or soldier at home. The complexity of Menzies' intriguing about the Windsors was just the first indication as to how tricky it was all going to be. He decided to turn again to his old partners in conspiracy, Beaverbrook and Bracken. The unusual set of skills that they had deployed over the years in his parliamentary battles would now be deployed on a much more important stage.

As the Prime Minister outlined the requirement to them Bracken's brain began to bubble. He was in his element. He was no expert in military intelligence or diplomatic machinations, but as the idea was gradually unveiled it became clear that an immense political intrigue would be integral to it. He warmed to the challenge. All his skills as a schemer and his excellent contacts with the press would have to be brought to bear. He began to develop the outline of a plan, thinking aloud.

"We'll need to warm up those contacts from early in the year – Sweden, Spain, maybe even Italy. The Swedish channel still seems to be open. Spain is complicated: too many agendas. Italy is even trickier, now that they are in the war – although Ciano was one of the most active people trying to find a compromise beforehand, so we might find a way to get to him – maybe the Vatican would help?

He continued, in soliloquy mode.

"Are our RC bishops still in contact with Head Office? Must find out how. And some of our senior dukes – Wellington, Kent, Hamilton – said enough warm things about the Nazis to be a bit embarrassed now, so we may be able to entreat them to get back in touch with their old contacts... Goering, Hess and co., perhaps through Sweden again, or Switzerland. And of course we mustn't forget the King – over the water."

Churchill chuckled to himself as he listened. Bracken had often lifted his spirits even in the darkest days with his irreverent sense of humour, and now his deliberate misuse of the ancient Scottish toast to an exiled Jacobite king was the *bon mot* in the circumstances. He looked down at the whisky glass in his hand, but didn't raise a toast.

"Brendan, let us leave aside the Duke and Duchess for the time being. We should limit ourselves to traditional subterfuge for now. The possible use of our royal resource, 'over the water' as you say, will have to be most subtle, and deniable long into the future. Any contribution must be a subliminal one, generated within the devious mind of Herr Hitler, perhaps through some carefully orchestrated events and coincidences that lead him to believe what he wants to believe. Now let's return to consideration of the main message that we wish to impart to the enemy, and its timing, then we can elaborate."

The pressman in Bracken began to compose a note aloud.

"*This war has gone far enough. Neither Germany nor Britain wants to sacrifice its young... the flower of its manhood again.*" He paused for a moment, his hand circling as he searched for the words. "*We...* No... *Some of us have heard the message that Germany has no designs on the Empire if left alone in Europe. However the warmonger Churchill* – apologies, Winston! – *will not listen to reason. There are many of us who feel this way, and the number continues to grow. We are realistic*

– That's a good word, we are not traitors or appeasers fighting old battles, we are simply 'realists' – *about the current situation and wish to...*

"Now let's think about what door such a malignant group would want to open. I can't see any of the appeasers actually asking for an invasion. Quite the reverse in fact. They've always wanted a quiet life. So what can they ask for that will sound logical... that Hitler will listen to, maybe even acknowledge, but then ignore and go down the path we want him to follow?"

"Perhaps a temporary armistice while a new *modus vivendi* is negotiated?" suggested Beaverbrook.

"Perhaps." Bracken developed the idea. "They might ask for a public offer from the Germans to suspend hostilities against England if we refrain from attacking them? Same thing, different language."

"Maybe suggest the League of Nations do something... anything," Beaverbrook shrugged.

"That would indeed be a sign of deep despair," Churchill scowled, conscious of the impotence of that organisation in the years leading up to the outbreak of war.

"What about an offer of a ceasefire and a prisoner of war exchange? They have many more of our men prisoners than we theirs, but it would still be emotive," Beaverbrook suggested.

"Yes, we must appear to be weakening," said Churchill, now entering the spirit of the discussion, "on the precipice of defeat, but still determined and, of course, still capable of doing considerable damage to a Nazi armada. An old bulldog, badly injured, but still growling away on the sands. These defeatists, or Realists if you prefer, must look as if they are willing to shackle the dog in return for some Nazi baubles."

Beaverbrook agreed. "It's vital that it doesn't appear that they're just playing for time – though it's not unlikely that Hitler will suspect that's the reason for the approach. We may have to back our weasel words with some actions early on."

Bracken began to look for a more sophisticated approach. "What about some hint of dissent at the highest level of government, as well as in the Armed Forces? Perhaps hinting at serious inter-service rivalry? It's logical that if the Royal Navy gets destroyed, Britain won't have the wherewithal to rule the waves or the Empire... so to ensure that the country can continue to do so, they ask Hitler nicely to lay off the Royal Navy and limit his attacks to the Army and the RAF."

"I can just imagine how that would play out with the Chiefs of Staff!" Churchill chortled. "But it is intriguing, nonetheless. It's consistent with the Nazi's view, now in apparent alignment these so-called Realists, as to how this brave new world will be divided. The Germans will rule mainland Europe and a neutered Britannia will rule the seas, and of course the Empire. It appears to recognise the obvious; that our army was seriously mauled in France, and now also the RAF, in the Battle of Britain – but not, so far, the Navy. Hitler knows that he has to either destroy or neutralise the Royal Navy before he invades. It's too powerful to be left to chance – the same issue we had with the French fleet. Yes, this is good. It even hints at dissension right up to Cabinet level... only my closest friends call me a *warmonger*!"

Bracken expanded. "Let's think about his likely reaction. Hitler doesn't have to respond to the suggestion of a ceasefire, why would he, when he thinks he's winning? But he likes the idea of some sort of Vichy-style arrangement here. He still needs to gain effective control of our naval bases, so he knows he has to invade at some stage. But the thought of a quid pro quo where he avoids serious attacks on the Royal Navy in return for the Navy not trying too hard to stop him... yes... might just be the sort of idea that would appeal."

"Even better, it fits in nicely with our idea of getting the Windsors to take a long sea trip back to Europe – on a Royal Navy warship," added Beaverbrook.

"With the Government appearing totally wrong-footed by his sudden departure... and the Navy's chain of command not keeping Downing Street informed." Churchill pulled his glasses forward on his nose and looked over the rim at his friends.

"Gentlemen – or are we perhaps now Players – this has great promise."

The Prime Minister was in ebullient mood as he opened the Cabinet meeting next morning.

"I am extremely pleased with the efforts to date. I had hoped that a scheme based on deceiving the enemy about our true strength would prove feasible, and your work over the last 48 hours seems to support this. I have also been thinking about the other side of the equation, namely leading the Nazis to believe that the spirit of the country has been hollowed out; that we have no stomach left for the battle. We intend to use our previous, though now tenuous, links to the enemy to implant that thought. We each need to understand the elements which underpin the approach, and also the way in which it supports the strategy. Here is the message we propose to send."

He put on his reading glasses and lifted the document.

"*This war has gone on long enough. Too much blood has already been spilt. Neither Germany nor Britain should sacrifice the flower of its manhood for the second time in a generation. Some of us have heard the message that Germany has no designs on the British Empire if the new position in Europe is accepted. However the war faction, led by Churchill, will not listen to reason. There are many of us who feel this way, and the number is growing all the time. We are realists about the current situation and wish to move towards an accommodation with the Third Reich, starting with a temporary ceasefire. We propose that there should be no new movements of troops on either side of the Channel; that the RAF and Luftwaffe should be limited to patrol activity over their own territory; and that the withdrawal should begin of all naval forces from the region. Within a week of this being achieved, a new British government would be ready to begin talks, with a view to achieving an early peace agreement and an exchange of prisoners. As an indication of intent, the Royal Navy is prepared to move three of its major warships from the south coast of*

England to Scotland. In return, we ask the Luftwaffe to cease the bomb-
ing of London for a three-day period."

"Wonderful! So the Navy scarpers just when we need them most," said General Brooke, who had not been briefed.

Churchill looked at Brooke and continued, with a small acknowledgement of the aside. "This will be the carrot put out to tempt Hitler. He sees the chance for a minor tactical victory in the area of naval strength, where he is most worried, while we reduce our civilian casualties despite having run down a good part of our fighter defences. We also create the impression that senior powers in the Navy – influential enough to move battleships – want an end to the war, on terms not inconsistent with Germany's vision. In this manner we tempt the Great Dictator to engage, to test the strength of this new anti-war faction. His record shows that he will demand more and more, and then spurn the chance of peace. He'll probably also ask for the Army and RAF to withdraw from their positions and airfields in the southeast."

At Churchill's nod, Ismay took over. "So we might prevaricate on this for some days, as if there is a power struggle going on... maybe even pretend to move a few squadrons back... we're already planning to abandon RAF Manston in Kent for tactical reasons. We can arrange a few other signs of weakness. But of course the Army doesn't move out of its fortified positions. We frustrate him for a week or two, as he fantasises more and more about the outcome. Then what does he do, when he realises that the country is not about to crumble after all? We know what usually come next with Hitler when he senses weakness – the full-scale assault, just as we've planned."

The debate on the political element of the deception plan continued in an increasingly positive tone for another hour before the Cabinet gave its support. There was agreement that the plan was strong, credible and consistent with the military deception that they had previously agreed upon.

Churchill then moved to wind up the meeting. "Gentlemen, your consensus on this is most reassuring. We will move forward with our plan to tempt, engage and then thrash Hitler's armies. Now we must give the plan a name which, should it leak out, will convey our apparent desperation about our unpreparedness. I have already chosen.

"Almost a thousand years ago, an English Saxon king faced invasion by the Danes. He was reluctant to mobilize the English army because of the effect it would have upon the harvest. The Danes duly invaded and conquered. That king's name was Ethelred, and he has gone down in history as Ethelred the Unready. Well it is now time to resurrect that name, and perhaps exonerate it for all time of its negative connotations. Our plan to ensnare Mr Hitler will be known as 'Operation Ethelred'.

"But this time... we will be ready."

CHAPTER TWELVE

On the short drive over to Buckingham Palace, Churchill was pensive. His driver and bodyguard knew there was something deep in his mind and refrained from their usual small talk, leaving him to concentrate on the matter at hand. This might indeed be a most difficult discussion, he thought, on both counts; the plan itself and the role that members of the Royal family would have to play in it. Until now, in his weekly Tuesday briefings with the King he had only shared the most general discussion about Ethelred, not even mentioned the code name. He had advised the King that the country was well prepared for an invasion, and that if it happened they would stop Hitler hard in his tracks.

"Some of us might even welcome the opportunity to do so, sir," was as far as the earlier conversations had developed. Now he had to share the unfolding plan in much greater detail than he would normally do in regard to a military operation. The King had the constitutional right to be consulted. It was unthinkable that a war strategy which would result in significant enemy forces landing in the realm be withheld from the sovereign. He would also have to inform the King that a central part of the plan was to mislead the Germans about Britain's strength and determination, and to alert him to the role that the King himself would be asked to play. He would use the word 'mislead', rather than 'deceive' the enemy. It sounded a bit

more military and above board. In strict etymological terms there wasn't much of a difference, but if the latter expression evolved to the word 'deceit', the King would find it difficult to be supportive, particularly as his own brother would be an important player in the charade. *Charade – that could be the word to use*, he thought grimly, knowing the Royal Family's enjoyment of the party game.

They arrived at the Palace, and Churchill walked up the steps and towards the ante-room to await the audience. Just a few minutes later the door was opened, and he was ushered into the King's presence. After a few moments of small talk, which seemed tenser than usual, Churchill began his discourse.

"Your Majesty, at our last meeting I advised you that the Cabinet was moving towards the conclusion that our best chance of ensuring the country's survival was to encourage the enemy to mount a premature invasion, and to destroy the Nazi hordes mid-Channel. I have to inform you that a considerable amount of discussion and planning regarding this has taken place, and that we are now in the final stages of preparing a most elaborate trap for the enemy."

Churchill had already stretched well beyond what he had previously communicated, and the King listened intently, his face growing pale with the enormity of what was being laid out by the Prime Minister. Although Halifax had already briefed him in a private meeting, the plan sounded all the more desperate coming from the lips of his Prime Minister. For months now the threat of invasion had been real. His own bodyguard had been tripled to forestall any attempt at a *coup de main* by German storm-troopers; the trees along the Mall had been uprooted to provide an emergency take-off strip if the Royal Family had to be evacuated, like their distant cousins in the Netherlands and Norway. Until now the hope had been that, with the growing strength of the nation's defences, an invasion would be avoided. But now, contrary to that budding hope, here was his Prime Minister saying that he planned a great gambit to initiate the very invasion he thought they had been working to avoid. He swallowed hard, thinking about the devastation the plan would bring to the country – even if successful. As for the consequences if it were to fail! He thought about the nation... its values... its institutions... He thought about Elizabeth and the two young princesses.

As a constitutional monarch, even if he was diametrically opposed to the plan, the King knew he had little authority as long as Parliament supported the Government in its decision. Apart from his right to warn, he would only have power to act in the matter if there was a split in Parliament which threatened to bring down the Government. But he was desperately worried. Much as he had grown to like Churchill, and respect him as the only man who could have stopped the tide of Nazism after Dunkirk, he knew Churchill's reputation for wild flights of fancy. As First Lord of the Admiralty he had been the champion of the disastrous landings in the Dardanelles in 1917, where tens of thousands of British and Anzac troops had died in a fruitless venture. Indeed in the current conflict, although the defeat had in Norway had quickly been subsumed in a much greater disaster stretching across Europe, he knew that Churchill had been one of the leading figures pushing for that failed pre-emptive invasion.

"Is there complete support for this action in my c-c-Cabinet?" He stuttered slightly under the stress. His question was partly for information, but was also a warning shot, hinting at the one situation where the King could exercise authority. And he knew that Halifax, and possibly others, were opposed.

"Your Majesty," Churchill began using the formal address, "The War Cabinet has considered the various options that are available to us for the progression of this struggle. It would be fair to say that there was initially a reluctance to contemplate the course I now present to you – until we examined dispassionately the inevitable consequences of the alternative, that is, of not taking this decisive action. It is the case that the approach now decided upon has the unanimous backing of the Cabinet and the Chiefs of Staff, and, if they were asked, I am quite certain, the vast majority of the House of Commons."

There was no conceivable way in which such a top secret plan could be discussed in Parliament, not even in a secret session. But he had understood, and responded to, the nuances in the King's questioning. He continued on to the even more difficult part of the conversation. "You are well aware, sire, of the great strides that we have made in preparing this country to repel an invasion. If the Nazis knew our actual strength they would be mad to attempt such a course. In consequence, a central element of our plan is to mislead them in that respect; to portray the country as weaker militarily than it actually is, and to have our political establishment appear riven with self-doubt.

"In respect of the military arrangements, each of the Services is preparing detailed plans as to how they will encourage this erroneous perception by the enemy. I am more than willing to arrange a detailed briefing for you, sire, should you desire. However at this point I would like to advise you, and indeed seek your advice in regard to the other vital element in our ploy, which lies in the political arena."

Without receiving any feedback from the King, he proceeded.

"We intend to encourage Hitler towards the belief that the unity of purpose in Britain is waning; that there is a growing faction in the country, in the establishment and in the Armed Services, that is ready for compromise. Such a faction would require leaders, in the Services and in the political domain of course, but also in the matter of the state itself. For the government, an apparent Quisling can no doubt be fingered – not an appetising role for any of us, I can assure you, sir.

"In respect of the state, it is necessary to convey the impression that there is a potential sovereign-in-waiting who could at least be portrayed as having legitimacy in a constitutional sense, but who would be seen as amenable to the Nazis' will."

Churchill waited for a comment, having introduced the subject in the most tangential way he could. Halifax had not been made aware of this subplot, and the King, unalerted, was greatly shocked.

"Should I infer that you see such a role being assumed by the d-d-Duke of Windsor?" he queried, his stutter becoming more pronounced.

"Sir, through his meetings with Hitler in 1937, the Duke has put himself in a position where he may be able to render a very great service to his country," Churchill replied adroitly.

"By allowing himself to be perceived as a Nazi stooge?" The King raised his voice, both out of a latent sense of family loyalty, and a deep concern that any popular anger towards his brother might well overspill onto himself.

"This is indeed a vexed problem, and I have given it much thought. It is my considered view that we can encourage Hitler to believe that the opportunity for such a felicitous outcome from a Nazi point of view is developing, without this being attributable to any direct, or indeed indirect, actions of the Duke."

There was another, more difficult, element to come in the discussion, but Churchill remained focused on winning the first phase of the argument. The King remained unconvinced and interrupted tersely.

"Please explain, Prime Minister."

"Sir, when we discussed the Duke's assignment to the Bahamas some weeks ago, there were many factors taken into account. It was imperative that he did not fall into the hands of the Nazis, either in France or in Portugal. It was also important that he did not in any way cause a stirring of the unfortunate passions from his abdication in 1936. His subsequent meetings with Hitler, and their possible misinterpretation, were further reasons for the decision, which was taken, as I was indeed most grateful, with your full support. None of this rationale was discussed in public, and the Duke's military service in France and subsequent appointment as Governor in the Bahamas showed him responding appropriately to the nation's needs. We believe that a similar approach in this current situation would have an equally benign outcome."

The King was silent for a few seconds. He was fully aware that Churchill had been a strong supporter of the monarchy both in 1936, admittedly in a somewhat convoluted manner, and since. He had managed to be both supportive of his brother in his initial reluctance to abdicate, and later to become a firm and loyal supporter of the new King once the inevitability of abdication became clear.

"What precisely would you have me ask the Duke to do?" he asked, now fully prepared to hear out the Prime Minister. For Churchill, however, it brought him to the most challenging part of the discussion.

"Sir, it is our intention that the Duke will relocate from his current residence in an irregular manner; a manner that will be interpreted by the enemy as him getting ready to support a defeatist faction within the United Kingdom. In normal circumstances the execution of this arrangement would be reasonably straightforward. We would ask you to issue the Duke with an order instructing him to leave the Bahamas, immediately and without fanfare. This would be arranged in a way to cause the enemy to suspect that this was at the behest of some shadowy group. However there is a great difficulty with this approach."

He paused and took a deep breath.

"We have reason to believe that certain information is escaping from the Duke's household to the enemy."

The King looked directly at Churchill, startled, but neither commenting nor showing dissent. He was well aware of the gossip about the Duchess's relationship with the German Ambassador, von Ribbentrop, before the war, and the suspicions that still surrounded that topic.

Churchill continued. "We are most concerned about the security of all communications in regard to this critical operation, both while in the process of conveying the mandate to the Duke and, subsequently, after it has been delivered to him."

"How then do you wish to proceed, if you are proposing that I do not communicate directly with the Duke? Do you seriously envisage him leaving his post without receiving an order, or indeed permission, from myself?"

"Sir, if it were to become apparent to the Duke's household, and subsequently, let us say, to foreign powers that the instruction has come from you, that very information would undermine the interpretation that we wish the enemy to make. The precise means by which we communicate the message, and its timing, are very much complicated by the risk of leakage. I would ask you, sir, to trust me to arrange this with all consideration for the immediate and long term consequences."

Now the King was even more alarmed. "I trust that you are not suggesting that the Duke be inveigled in some underhand way into joining this plot, this artificially created plot, involving supposedly disloyal elements. I can assure you that he would not be party to such behaviour."

That very possibility had indeed been considered by the committee, but discarded at Churchill's instruction, in so far as it could well cause damage to the monarchy itself in the long term.

"That is indeed a real difficulty, sir. For the reasons I have mentioned, the Duke cannot be informed that his transfer is at the request of the sovereign and his government, at least not in advance. We intend to do so at the very last minute, by presenting him with a letter from you, sir. It is vital to the security of this plan, and indeed the nation itself, that any information which does, er, leak out about the relocation must imply that forces other than official ones are at work. In consequence, from the time that the Duke becomes aware that the action is by your direct command we will need to quarantine him and his household, for a period of at least one week."

"How precisely do you intend to achieve that, Prime Minister?"

"A Royal Navy warship will be made available, and the Duke and Duchess conveyed to an appropriate new location, perhaps Canada, or perhaps back to Nassau after a certain time at sea. There will be no public announcement, at least not to begin with, as their disappearance must appear to be unauthorised. At some later stage an appropriate statement can be issued, possibly referring to urgent medical treatment needed by one or other of the couple."

The King sensed a further problem. "How much of this information do you intend to share with the Duke and Duchess, and at what time?"

"Once the couple are on board a Royal Navy ship, and at sea, the requirement for confidentiality is assured. I believe it will be appropriate to share much of the information with the Royal couple, though our concern about leakage of information means it will have to be handled in a circumspect way. The real challenge is prior to that; to stop any message being passed outside the household, by whatever means, telephone, oral or written, that would indicate that this sudden movement is at the command of you or your government. From the moment this quarantine is assured, the Duke will be informed. We think that will be best handled through presentation of a letter from Your Majesty. Such letter will need to be quite specific that the Duke and everyone in his household must submit themselves from that moment to the precise commands conveyed therein."

The King had listened, in a considerable degree of shock, despite the forewarning from Halifax. "Prime Minister, this is a most grave situation, both the overall plan, and the direct role that you ask me to play. You must give me time to consider, and consult to the extent that is possible. Clearly from a constitutional point of view you are the leader of my government, and it is not for me to determine government policy. At the same time I am deeply disquieted by this discussion. I did not ever envisage that a situation could emerge where I would empathise with the dilemma faced by my brother before his abdication – and realise the very limited range of options that a monarch has available to him."

This time it was Churchill who blanched at the King's unspoken threat. Quite abruptly, the audience was over. An equerry opened the door and ushered Churchill out.

The following afternoon a small meeting took place in the Palace. For centuries the role of the Privy Council had been to brief the monarch on matters of state when he or she needed advice. In attendance were Churchill, Attlee, Eden – and Halifax. Also present, unusually for a political discussion, was General Dill, representing the Chiefs of Staff. The discussion was controlled and unemotional. Each of the men, in their role as advisors to the King, stated their position, and their recommendation. Churchill deliberately left Halifax to last. The Foreign Secretary was in a difficult position. He again raised the concerns that had already been discussed and addressed in Cabinet, but it was clear that he had no support to call upon, or even to refer to. Though he had spoken to the King in private about his alarm, he now found himself out-manoeuvred. There was consensus among the other Privy Counsellors in support of the plan, and there was nothing he could do but relent.

The King realised that, if not a complete consensus, there was formal government agreement, and that he had no option but to accept their decision. He had one final, difficult question. "What will happen if the Duke refuses, for whatever reason, to comply with the instructions given?"

Churchill took a deep breath, but did not shy from the answer. "Sir, the Duke is a serving officer of the Crown. If he refuses a direct order from his sovereign he will be subject to the normal sanction for such behaviour, namely arrest. I am optimistic that if this reality should need to be pointed out to him, any further thought of disobedience will be dispelled immediately."

The King looked at his Prime Minister quite coldly, then stood up and faced the group. "Privy Counsellors, this whole episode has come as a great shock to me, both as King and as the brother of one who is to be involved in an involuntary and very disturbing manner. Having heard from you, I now realise the depth of thought that has gone into this, and the necessity for the actions that the Prime Minister relayed to me yesterday. I give my consent, and will have the letter prepared as has been requested. Please convey to all involved my urging that, within the complex circumstances that pertain, the maximum possible civility will be shown to the Duke, and to the Duchess."

On his return to Whitehall, Churchill immediately reconvened with the small group he had appointed to run the Bahamas operation: Menzies, Bracken and Pound.

"We will now proceed with the plan for the operation in Nassau," he began, careful to avoid any indication of the tone or substance of his discussion with the King. The others were careful not to enquire.

Admiral Pound began, "Prime Minister, the relocation will largely be a naval affair, both the evacuation itself and the subsequent transfer of the royal party to whatever destination is decided upon – as a working assumption we have assumed Canada. We have a small number of suitable ships in the South Atlantic, which could be in position in five to six days, the most appropriate being one of the cruisers, HMS *Cumberland* or HMAS *Australia*".

"Not *Australia*," interrupted Churchill abruptly. "It is essential that the enemy interprets these event as an indication of political turmoil here in Britain, rather than further afield in the Empire. We must use a British ship rather than a colonial." He looked at Pound.

"I understand, Prime Minister. *Cumberland* it is. It will take a day longer to get there. If any problems emerge regarding its availability we will use a British destroyer instead. A bit less comfortable for the Royal party, but it will achieve the same purpose."

Menzies took over, "As you advised us yesterday, we have no evidence to suggest that the Duke would co-operate with this plan if he believed that it was being orchestrated by the enemy or by a disloyal group within the government or the Services..."

Churchill interrupted to agree, perhaps somewhat disingenuously. "Even if that were a remote possibility, the whole perception of such an event in years to come could cause great damage to the monarchy."

Menzies understood. "Yes sir, we understand that the evacuation must take place in accordance with an order received from the King. The risk is that if we do present him with such a direct order, that fact will become known to, ah, other parties and then, via whatever route, to the enemy. Needless to say, if the Germans were to perceive this aspect of Ethelred to be a subterfuge, it's likely that the whole plan could be compromised, with calamitous results. We have something of a dilemma there, and the solution seems to come down to timing."

Bracken joined in, quite enthusiastically. Planting stories came easily to the experienced intriguer. "As long as the physical transfer is handled discreetly it shouldn't be too difficult to manage the external perception. Knowing the social milieu that they move in, we can easily seed in advance the idea that the Duke's return to the throne is a natural part of an overall settlement with Germany. Knowing the regular contact they have with visitors from the United States we can be quite sure that news of his disappearance will become known to the American press very quickly. We can certainly help stir a heady brew of conspiracy theories and false trails with the people that we already have in situ."

Menzies agreed, "I agree, Brendan. We can create such a spider's web of rumour and counter-rumour that the unheralded arrival of a Royal Navy ship in the dead of night and the couple's sudden departure won't come as a total bombshell."

Churchill turned to Menzies. "Short of physically press-ganging the Duke and Duchess, how will you achieve the transfer from their residence without disclosing that the operation is, in fact, authorised?"

"That's the nub of the problem, sir. Some aspects of the operation are quite routine, for example isolating the villa in the late evening after any entertaining there has finished. We simply cut all the telephone lines and make sure that there are no radio transmissions emanating from the villa. Physical quarantine is not a problem either. Their security guards work for us and, as you know, sir, they have very specific orders in respect of various contingencies. The tricky part is the removal itself, bearing in mind the conflicting objectives of not letting them know in advance that it is by order of the King, while at the same time showing our authorisation in a way that will ensure the Duke's compliance."

Churchill added, with emphasis, "And will allow a benign interpretation of the event in the future."

Menzies nodded. "We have not found any absolutely dependable way of doing this other than by, effectively, serving a warrant. The team assigned will include a senior naval officer, in uniform, and a King's Messenger. Both of these will be personally known to the Duke, to give him some degree of comfort with the events as they unfold. We will also have one or two female officers to accompany the Duchess. The messenger will advise the Duke that he has a letter from a high authority – unspecified to begin with – stating that he and the Duchess are to accompany them forthwith for reasons of their personal security. From that point, the Duchess will be accompanied to her room to collect personal belongings. At no time will she be out of sight of a female officer. Once she has left the room, the letter from the King will be given to the Duke. The couple will be given one hour to pack. They will each be accompanied at all times, and kept apart as far as possible; certainly they will not be allowed to be alone together. Any room that they move through in that period will be thoroughly searched afterwards."

"What about the servants? What will they be told?"

"A message will be left for the house servants that the Duke and Duchess have moved at short notice for reasons of their personal safety. Of course, next morning the remaining staff, including those of our people remaining in the residence, will be subject to intensive questioning by the authorities there. We can expect, or arrange if necessary, a flurry of radio and telegraph communications from Nassau, which will certainly be detected, and possibly decoded, by the enemy's wireless listening service."

Churchill accepted the plan, although he looked somewhat down. "That is more or less what I expected. It's clear that the precise sequence and timing of events are critical."

Menzies now looked directly at Churchill. "There remains one difficult question, Prime Minister. What are our orders if either, or both, refuse to comply with the orders given?"

Churchill sat glum-faced. He had known the Duke since he was a boy, and even with all the difficulties that surrounded the abdication, had always liked him. He answered, in a grave voice. "This operation affects the fate of our great nation, the lives of hundreds of thousands of our people, the future of our constitutional monarchy. The personal wishes of a small number of people, however exalted, will not be allowed to put at risk its success."

He hesitated, wincing as he thought of the King's final admonition.

"Make sure the party is comprised of physically strong individuals... And have them armed."

CHAPTER THIRTEEN

Early next morning a meeting began in the Music Room at Admiralty House. It was the Ethelred political steering group, come together for the first time. Most unusually, rather than a minister, Brendan Bracken was in the chair. With so many intricate and interwoven threads to be played, Churchill wanted someone with a deft political touch in control, and had overruled objections to his selection from several Cabinet colleagues.

Although the group was nominally political in its remit, the *realpolitik* of wartime meant a strong interplay between the civilian and military operations, and several of the members came from the Services. As much of the elaborate subterfuge would involve the Royal Navy, Admiral Pound had decided to attend in person. He was conscious that there were some sensitive naval topics on the table for discussion, and he had brought along Captain McIntosh, one of his brightest staff officers, and Commander Hughes, a signals officer. The two branches of the Security Services were well represented. From MI6, responsible for overseas intelligence, came Brigadier Menzies and one of his senior staff officers, who chose not to introduce himself. Two officers were in attendance from MI5, the equivalent agency for domestic intelligence. They were coyly introduced as Colonel W and Major K. The Army and RAF were each represented by a middle-ranking officer attending in a liaison role, as those Services were expected to be only marginally involved in the plan.

The ten members sat down in a distinctly edgy atmosphere. Although they had a shared, well-defined objective, some of the serving officers were uneasy. Having the spooks there was bad enough, but Bracken was not their kind of chap at all. Knowing his closeness to Churchill they chose not to show any open signs of discomfort – a decision quickly confirmed as wise when Bracken opened the meeting.

"The Prime Minister has asked me to chair this group. In view of the urgency of the task and the need for a consistent message from our work, it is essential that our activities are totally co-ordinated. If any of you disagree with decisions made here, he has issued a simple edict. You will proceed without delay to set in hand any tasks assigned. Only after those preparations are underway may you, if you choose, make representations to the P.M. In view of the importance of the task entrusted to us and the clear instructions he has given me, I would counsel you to use such channel of escalation most reluctantly."

The naval staff officers looked uneasily at each other. Menzies and the other intelligence people were less concerned. They probably had enough on Bracken to ensure that no unacceptable decisions would be forced through.

Bracken continued. "First, I have some announcements to make. Mr Chamberlain is seriously ill, and will be resigning from the government shortly. Also, Lord Halifax will be resigning in a matter of weeks. At a later stage he will be taking up an important post outside Britain, but the timing of his resignation can be used in support of any scenario that we wish to create. Furthermore it has been decided that the Duke of Windsor will be required to absent himself from his post in the Bahamas for a period, at the appropriate time, in a manner that will appear not to be have been approved by H.M. Government."

There were more looks across the table. Clearly there was some heavy hitting going on already. Pound commented, "That is sad news about Mr Chamberlain. I've noticed how poorly he's been looking recently. As regards the Duke of Windsor, we are already actively involved in that situation."

The intelligence people were aware of all of this and, indeed, much more about the various figures mentioned. They also knew that since the leaks out of the American Embassy had been stopped with the arrest of a junior clerk there, it now seemed that there was no sensitive material getting to the Germans other than through channels controlled by the British. Thanks to Ultra, they were able to decrypt enough supposedly secret German communications to verify what the enemy really believed.

Bracken continued with his preamble. "To start with, let's remind ourselves about the basic impression that we want to convey. It is as follows: Britain is weakening; a powerful group of politicians and military commanders, many of them senior Royal Navy officers, want a negotiated settlement. This group – calling itself the Realists – wants an accommodation between the powers, with Britain and Germany recognizing each other's sphere of influence. Their intention is to replace the current government with one amenable to such a peaceful solution. That government will pledge allegiance to King Edward VIII."

He looked across the table to the MI5 representative. "We should begin by discussing the channels that are available to transmit this message. Colonel W…"

The senior MI5 man began, "Chairman, we have identified three main conduits which we can use to feed appropriate misinformation to the enemy. The first is a side-channel to the official communications still in progress with Sweden, the second is using our contacts in the Vatican to pass messages to Ciano, and the third, well… we have obtained the services of a number of captured enemy agents who have – shall we say – *chosen* to work for us."

Bracken nodded. "Excellent, let's start with those. We know the content of the message – the one read to the War Cabinet two days ago. It should be relatively straightforward to have Butler pass it on via the Swedish embassy. He meets the Ambassador regularly, and he would be expected to be a leading member of a defeatist government."

'Rab' Butler had worked as Halifax's deputy in the Foreign Office in the years when appeasement had been the main plank of Britain's policy towards the Nazis. While the Foreign Secretary had distanced himself to some extent from the failed policy, there was still some doubt about Butler's resolve. It was also well known that Churchill and he had had a mutual dislike of each other, bordering on loathing. Butler's profile seemed to fit him well for the planned role.

The MI6 staff officer took over. "The same information can go out via the Vatican, through the good offices of our envoy there and his contacts in the Roman Catholic church." The two intelligence agencies didn't always see eye to eye, and Bracken was relieved that they were in alignment about the ways to use the communications channels. The details could be sorted out later.

He moved on to the third conduit, turning to the senior MI5 officer. "Colonel, about our uninvited German tourists, you know most about their *modus operandi*. Can you suggest how we might best use them?"

"Yes, Chairman. The agents are not a very impressive bunch, quite low-level actually. So obviously they couldn't be expected to have access to the high level of intelligence that the other channels are passing. I suggest that the best way to use them is for passing on selected background material that is supportive of the overall theme."

"That seems sensible." agreed Bracken. "Now let's focus on the precise wording of the communication. On reconsideration the original version was perhaps rather too long, and somewhat over-elaborate for an opening gambit. We need to split it into two or three separate messages, the first being a gentle feeler. I'll make sure that the P.M. is happy with that. By the way, Admiral, regarding the offer to withdraw ships from bases on the south coast, is that part of the plan still operative? Have you identified the ones you will send to Scotland if we get a positive response from the Germans?"

"Yes, Chairman, HMS *Queen Elizabeth's* move from Portsmouth to the Clyde was already planned. She's one of our oldest battle-ships, and is in the middle of a major refurbishment. She still needs a lot of fitting-out, and we want to get her out of harm's way as soon as she is able to sail. Also, several of our cruisers are wanted in Greenock for refit; radar, anti-aircraft guns and so on, so there will be no problem choosing a couple at the appropriate time."

There was nodding around the table. Bracken continued, not see-ing any need to be diplomatic. "Now let's talk about some visible signs of discontentment in the Navy. Admiral, what would you ex-pect to happen if the government was concerned about a mutiny developing?"

Pound was not amused that such a scenario had been decided upon, but had accepted the decision and knew the reason for the Chairman's question. "With the clear understanding that such an event is extremely unlikely, were it to occur it would undoubtedly cause a split in the Navy. In consequence of that I would expect to see significant movements of personnel, and perhaps ships, by one of the groups, trying to forestall action by the other."

Bracken listened. "So, transfers of navy personnel, and Royal Marines perhaps, heading to the affected ports to confront the mu-tineers? How would they be transported? By ship... train... road?"

"Probably all of those, same as happened after the mutiny at In-vergordon in 1931 – though of course we weren't at war then."

Bracken probed further. "And what would be the likeliest place for this 'extremely unlikely' event to occur?"

"If anywhere, I would expect the Mersey or the Clyde. There is a fairly strong Red influence in both ports, which might be assumed to be lukewarm about the war since the German-Russian pact was signed. For our purposes I don't think the Nazis will be too apprecia-tive of the differences between sailors, shipyard workers and dockers."

The schemer inside Bracken was already hard at work. "The only problem with a mutiny is that it's not very visible. Might be easier to stir things onshore and link it to a supposed mutiny on the ships – our very own 'Battleship *Potemkin*'!"

"That makes sense," said Colonel W. "We can use one of our turned agents to leak information which supports that interpretation."

"Excellent. Now let's think about the timing," Bracken continued. "Pity we missed the twelfth of July. Not too difficult to start a riot in Glasgow on Orangemen's Day – and maybe even Liverpool too. Is there anything happening in mid-August that we could use as a catalyst?"

Menzies responded. "Well grouse season starts – probably not too relevant for Merseyside dockers!"

One of the naval officers, Captain MacIntosh, was Scottish, and joined in with a more useful suggestion. "What about a disturbance at a soccer match? The football leagues are cancelled, but aren't there still some local matches being arranged? Are Glasgow Rangers and Celtic playing soon? Shouldn't be too difficult to arrange a riot there, perhaps using a few *agent provocateurs* in the crowd – though I hasten to add that it's not my field of expertise, nor indeed my sport. I'm a rugby man."

Menzies chipped in, approvingly, "A riot linked to a mutiny on the Red Clyde? Interesting idea, Captain. It could certainly be arranged easily enough... and perhaps something similar in Liverpool too. A small fracas in a stadium... maybe arrange for a few spectators to attack the referee after a disputed decision... the match abandoned... some heavy-handed policing. That might just do the trick, with a bit of stirring to help it along. Later on, a few bonfires down near the docks... rumours of sabotage etc. to justify a heavy police and troop cordon around the area."

Bracken smiled. "That's a good suggestion. Even better, we have a perfect way of getting the information to Berlin. We can arrange the disturbances for late afternoon, just before the evening mail boats head off to Belfast and Dublin. Delay the ships for an hour or two. Hundreds of passengers held up... some fires and smoke... an explosion or two... crowds milling around the docks... large numbers of police and troops. That information should be picked up in a day or two by the German embassy in Dublin. I could even call in a few favours and get the Irish papers to mention the disturbances."

The junior MI5 officer, Major K, voiced some concern.

"That's fine about the Irish press, Chairman, but it will be tricky to manage the media coverage at home. Obviously the press here wouldn't want to, or indeed be allowed to cover disturbances or anti-government riots in the middle of a war."

Bracken was nonplussed.

"That's probably not a huge issue, Major. The very fact that the Irish papers cover it while the British press studiously ignores it will probably look significant to the enemy. It all lends weight to the conclusion that we want them to draw, that the government is trying to hush it up."

Menzies was impressed with the ingenuity being shown and now entered the full spirit of the discussion.

"We could issue a notice cancelling police leave in those areas. 'Preventing sabotage in the docks' would be a perfect cover story. That would lend further support to the interpretation. There are quite a few Irish-born policemen in the two cities, and word will get back to Dublin quickly enough, through relatives and so on."

Mackintosh came back to his soccer theme.

"What about stopping all radio coverage of football matches in Liverpool and Glasgow – maybe even cancelling future matches? That might be noticed. I wonder does their wireless monitoring service have time to listen to football?"

Commander Hughes, the naval signals officer, joined in. "As far as getting the riots noticed, it would be easy enough to supplement all the physical commotion with a sudden increase in wireless traffic about troop and ship movements around the two ports. We can be sure that the Germans monitor the number of transmissions emanating from different sources, and they probably have a good idea who's sending them, as we do theirs. They may or may not be able to understand the actual content of the messages, so we'd better play safe by assuming they can, and use real orders, followed by actual movements. Actually, we can probably use the sabotage story... and perhaps arrange some military exercise to generate the stuff that we need."

Bracken was very satisfied that a compelling story was being created.

"I think we have enough to be going on with regarding the civilian unrest. We'll need to get a message out via one of our German visitors, a day or so after the 'riots'. That should encourage the Luftwaffe to come over and have a look. We'll have to keep the pot boiling for a few days – the fires and so on."

Captain MacIntosh spoke again, emphasising the importance of the military dimension.

"Chairman, the Clyde and Mersey are all very well, but there really needs to be an agenda around Scapa Flow – that's the base the enemy will be most concerned about. If we could create some signs of disloyalty there..."

Bracken knew he was right. The Home Fleet's main base, in the Orkney Islands just north of Scotland, would be the main focus of the Germans' attention.

"I agree, Captain. Scapa will be key. If it looks as if the Fleet is not of a mind to tackle the invasion that would be huge encouragement for the Germans. Can you take that idea forward for us? What would happen next?"

"Well, presumably if the government was concerned that the fleet in Scapa was showing signs of disloyalty, it would want to defuse the situation as quickly as possible. Probably send in troops or marines to take over the shore facilities there, especially the coastal batteries. Then follow that up with loyal officers and crews to take over the ships."

"You think probably just men to start with?"

"Yes, Chairman, they wouldn't want to risk a confrontation by sending warships up from Rosyth. In fact they probably wouldn't send the men by sea for the same reason. The Navy rebels wouldn't allow them passage – there could be blood – so they'd have to send them by air. Come to think of it, the rebels would want to pre-empt such a move... maybe taking over the army facilities in Orkney and blocking the runways on Kirkwall airfield."

Bracken was getting enthusiastic. "There is a very persuasive story coming together here. Big navy blue trucks spread across the airfield. The Germans fly over Scapa Flow frequently, so they'd soon spot that!"

Pound was impressed by the imagination that his two staff officers were showing, but concerned that the discussion was getting over-elaborate. He moved to dampen down the enthusiasm.

"It's going to be difficult to do all that without causing a lot of confusion within the Forces."

Commander Hughes was proving a useful addition to the planning group. He responded to the reservation expressed by Admiral Pound without, perhaps, detecting the nuance in it.

"We could use much the same approach as Liverpool, sir. Send orders to the Army and Navy commanders in Orkney that, in view of the strategic importance of Scapa, the Royal Navy is to be given prime responsibility for manning the island's defences. That justifies the movements of sailors and marines to various sites around the island. It would have to be sent by courier – no radio. Then another alert – again by courier – saying there are intelligence reports about a planned German airborne assault to seize the airfield. So the runways have to be blocked. After that, lots and lots of wireless traffic about the status of the airfield defences; enquiries about ship movements, supply levels and so on. Eventually the naval personnel get ordered back to barracks, but we leave some uncertainty about whether they are obeying. We'll have to put some of our own men in charge of wireless communications. Each message will need to be carefully vetted."

It was a powerful, intelligent contribution, but Pound made a mental note to speak to Hughes later on the subject of taking a lead from his superiors.

The plans for the use of the Swedish link and the military subterfuge were coming together nicely. Bracken then moved on the third conduit.

"What about the Italian connection? Presumably the hierarchy here is still in touch with the Vatican, via Spain or the U.S. or whatever, and there are plenty of high-ranking naval officers who are Roman Catholic. We'll need to find one to act as a channel."

Menzies came in again. "No problem doing that. But it won't be enough to just pass on a diplomatic memorandum; we'll have to factor in something more specific on the military side. After all, the Mediterranean is one of the busiest theatres for the Royal Navy. It seems plausible that an appeaser or even a Fascist sympathiser in the Navy might pass on information about warship movements, which would also eventually get to the Italian intelligence service... and Ciano."

Pound was still uneasy about any slight on the Navy's honour. "A few who were enamoured with appeasement perhaps, but I don't think the Nazis or Italians would believe we have actual traitors in the Royal Navy."

Hughes offered his boss a way out of his discomfort. "Probably better if a leak of military information can be made to look inadvertent. There is bound to be a large amount of interesting stuff floating around there at any time, some of which is likely to be filtering across to the enemy. We can dolly that up to suit our own purposes."

The MI5 officer, Major K, was well aware of the MI5 surveillance reports on the subject, and supported Hughes. "Certainly we know that some of the sailors in Malta have Italian-born girlfriends, and we suspect that at least a few of them are working for Italian intelligence. It should be easy enough to get information about movements to some likely go-betweens. It's all beginning to fit together quite naturally. Some of our sailors let it slip out in pillow talk that they won't be around for a month or two... that part of the Mediterranean Fleet, let's say several cruisers, is urgently needed in Britain and will be leaving shortly for the Clyde."

Bracken was pleased. "That is very subtle, Major! Taken together with the reports about disturbances in the fleet here, it casts even more doubt on the loyalty of the home naval squadrons – to the extent that we have to weaken the Mediterranean fleet to reinforce home waters."

Pound jumped in to the debate, grimacing. "We have to be careful here and watch the timing of those transfers – we can handle ships moving from Portsmouth to Scotland, but we can't afford to strip the Mediterranean Fleet bare."

Hughes offered an answer, addressing himself to his senior officer. "Sir, we could arrange it so that the ships don't go far past Gibraltar. From there on, we could generate dummy signals traffic from other small ships or submarines to simulate their journey north."

The discussion continued between the three naval officers, with MacIntosh coming in again, also addressing the Admiral.

"Sir, if we are going to withdraw some ships from the Mediterranean, and are going to make sure that the enemy finds out about it, had we better be alert to the possibility of an Italian sortie, trying to take advantage of the situation?"

Admiral Pound took over, "Indeed we had, Captain! But better still, we might be able to pre-empt it. Absolutely within these walls, we are in the final stages of planning a carrier strike on their main base at Taranto. We should be able to pull that forward by a week or two and give the Italians something else to worry about."

Bracken was now in expansive form, and began to summarise.

"This is all very positive. There's a remarkably consistent message coming together. Military and civilian unrest at home... signs of mutiny in the same navy bases... political divisions opening up... Britain beginning to crack. Yes, these are the seeds that we will start planting over the next week or so, in parallel with the RAF beginning its run-down. As a sign of the Realists' good faith and influence, we'll offer to withdraw the three ships from Portsmouth. Hopefully Hitler responds by stopping the bombing for a few days, and then – whether he does or doesn't – we start the disturbances in the ports. After that comes the 'rum' news from the Bahamas about the Duke of Windsor disappearing! Hitler gets all excited about everything building up to an easy victory and then... and then..."

Bracken stopped in mid-sentence.

"And then what? We've sent in the teasers, and the old mare Britannia seems willing. But who's going to do the business?"

"You mean will Hitler be up for it, or will he just sit there expectantly, waiting for a British champion to emerge?" said Menzies, continuing the theme.

Admiral Pound pulled a face. "I think the metaphors are getting a bit mixed, but I can see the problem. Clearly it's not feasible to take the teasing-up, as you call it, much further. Too difficult to sustain... and we couldn't have large actual movements on the military side or indeed an obvious schism in the Cabinet without genuinely affecting our capability."

"Not to mention confusing the hell out of people," added Menzies.

Bracken was still musing. "So his legions will be all set to roll, but we still have to find the trigger. And we can't really offer him much more by way of encouragement."

Captain McIntosh came in again. "If I may modify that statement slightly, Chairman? We *can* offer much more. We may not be able to *do* much more. But towards the end of the deception we can offer what we like, as long as we don't have to follow though by actually doing it!"

"That's smart thinking, Captain," said Menzies. "We can't go any further with an actual build-up for the reasons discussed. On the other hand, we can't just cease and desist. So it's got to be a switchback."

"Can you explain, Brigadier?" queried Bracken.

"Yes, Chairman. We allow, in fact, we encourage the enemy to build up momentum in a certain direction, and then at the last moment we make a sharp change in course, and hope that his momentum will take him over the edge."

"I think I see." said Bracken, beginning to appreciate Menzies' suggestion. "So, we might send one or two further communications from the Realists offering, say, a major withdrawal on the naval side, in return for something or other. Adolf and his buddies get all excited, but just before it comes to making the actual withdrawal, or whatever, we do this switchback. Is that it? Let's say, announce that a plot has been discovered and broken-up. Hitler will have been building his hopes for an effortless victory, and now we tweak his nose."

"Of course he may suspect that it's been a deception all along," said Pound.

"It doesn't really matter whether he does or not," countered Menzies. "He's been gingering up his own generals for action, and now he faces a huge loss of face if he backs down."

Bracken was persuaded that Menzies' approach was as good as they would come up with.

"Yes, C, I think that's got to be it. We lead him along for a few more moves, then dash his hopes. Communications from the Realists stops. There is an announcement that Mr. Chamberlain and Lord Halifax have resigned from the Cabinet. The Prime Minister speaks to the nation. And then we can only hope that Hitler, Goering and the others have committed themselves to such an extent that they have to go ahead. It's quite devious, actually. I can just imagine him fuming at his generals and intelligence people – very hard for him to walk away. If he does, he looks like a loser for the first time. That might even cause his own generals to see him as less than a god."

Bracken brought the discussion to a close.

"Gentlemen, I think we have the bones of a plan. I will talk to the P.M. tomorrow."

Bracken went over to Downing Street in mid-afternoon, at Churchill's suggestion, and they went for a walk in the garden. On the previous evening, there had been an air-raid on London for the first time, and smoke could still be seen rising in various directions. At least that meant a heavy raid was unlikely today. Even the Germans needed to rest up from time to time. He started to go through his thoughts about the deception plan with the Prime Minister, but was stopped immediately as he described the plan of approach via the Swedish embassy.

"Not Butler," snapped Churchill.

Bracken was quite surprised at the vehemence of the reaction.

"Sorry, Winston, we thought that in view of past events he would be a natural man for the rather, shall we say, heretical communications that we wish to send.

"No, no, no. He doesn't know about Ethelred, and must not find out. I've already been clear to Halifax about that. We must have absolute confidence that the messages and signals that are sent out are those that the Cabinet has decided upon. There must be no risk of the messenger adding his own spin to the ball."

Bracken didn't argue. "I understand. The other suggestion was the Duke of Hamilton."

Churchill was happier. "That makes more sense. Friendly towards the Nazis before the war, but now a loyal Brit, committed to the fight. He had a lot of contact with them pre-war, including von Ribbentrop and Hess. I believe he even met Hitler in 1937. But he's lost too many colleagues in the RAF to have any sympathy with the Boche now."

"He doesn't have any link to the Swedes, though."

"No? Then let us create one. There are a number of British airmen interned in Sweden, are there not? Well, we would like them back. Put Wing Commander Hamilton in charge of the negotiations. That will get him into a position where he can act as our courier at the appropriate time."

Late in the evening Churchill headed down to his country residence in Chequers. He didn't like leaving London, now the battlefront, but he needed a few hours away to charge his batteries, and make sure of his perspective on things. The preparations were going well but he was still troubled by doubts, not about the plan's feasibility, but as to whether the General Staff were willing to take it to its ultimate conclusion. The damage and the casualties from the previous day's raid on the city had brought home the reality of modern warfare and the likely consequences of the decisions they were taking. He needed to make sure that there was alignment in their thinking, and he had asked General Ismay to come down and stay the night. After dinner the two men retired to his study.

"Pug, I want to talk to you, openly and candidly, about Ethelred. I can sense the enthusiasm that's building in the team, which is most encouraging. However enthusiasm's only part of the story. I need to be sure that there is absolute understanding among the Chiefs about our objectives. We must be crystal-clear in our think-ing. We're preparing a rat-trap, a most sophisticated rat-trap, and are getting ready to spring it. We have to make sure that we catch the biggest rat possible. Now, remind me again of the numbers ex-pected in the various waves of the Nazi attack."

Ismay thought for a moment. "In the first wave, we expect eighty to a hundred thousand men landing by sea, and perhaps ten thou-sand parachutists. They may be able to make some small reinforce-ment the next day, using their fast ships, but the bulk of the sec-ond wave – up to another eighty thousand or so on barges and slow steamers – can't come until two, maybe three days later. One would expect the third wave, on day four or five, to be somewhat smaller, with maybe half that number of troops. By that time they'll be suf-fering quite badly from losses of barges and landing craft, and they'll also need to allocate a lot of their reduced shipping capacity to sup-plies for the troops already on shore. Food, ammunition, and all the other accoutrements of an army on the move... vehicles... field kitchens... pack horses... medical stations and so on. The only thing that could change that schedule radically would be if they succeed in capturing a usable port."

Ismay was precise on the numbers, but once again raised the biggest risk to the British plan, the loss of a port.

Churchill listened. "So, two hundred thousand or more of their best troops for the initial invasion? Twenty or so divisions, with presumably more being conveyed across later in second-line echelons. If we were just to fling back the first wave from the beaches, how many would we expect to kill or capture?"

Ismay thought for a moment. "It depends where we stop them. If we let the entire first wave land before springing the trap we might get the lot – perhaps eighty thousand. On the other hand if we break up the armada as it crosses, or drive them back so that they abort the whole thing, a lot of them may be able to turn round and straggle back to France. So we might get, maybe, half that number... or less."

"Thirty, perhaps forty thousand? That would be a fine propaganda success, certainly in contrast to what's gone on hitherto. But for Hitler, in the context of his master plan, no more than an inconvenience. Remember how grateful we were to have limited our own casualties to such numbers in France? If we defeat him too quickly we may have just stirred up the hornet's nest, and forewarned him so that he comes better prepared next time."

"That's a real possibility, Prime Minister."

"Pug, this is our first chance for a resounding success in this war. We have to delay springing the trap until the second, even the third wave has landed. Then the prize will be all the greater, although the risks, I'm conscious, increase in parallel. And yet... unfortunately... the further we let go, the higher our own casualties will be. You can see the dilemma."

"To be frank, sir, I don't see it as a dilemma at all. I can assure you that the only option we are planning for is the larger engagement. That is the strategic objective that you have set out, and we have embraced. It's the only military plan that we are considering... draw them in... increase the RAF's response gradually rather than unleashing all our reserves as soon as the battle starts... engage them with a layered defence on the ground... commit the naval reserves on a phased basis and so on. That's also been the basis for the calculation of our likely casualties and the measures being put in place to mitigate them. Be in no doubt, sir, all our planning is focused on achieving a ringing victory over Hitler, not just embarrassing him."

"I'm pleased to hear that, Pug. The navy, the beach defences, the inland defence lines; together these will form the great sausage machine into which the Nazi legions will be fed. We must start grinding them down from the time their fleet first appears, but also leave them sufficient hope that they continue with the later waves, so we can keep grinding away. It's not good enough just to send the rotten meat back to the butcher. It's going to take a very fine balance in terms of managing our military response."

Ismay responded, "The Chiefs recognise that, sir. It will take fine judgment. Letting the first two waves get ashore, though bashing them about heavily as they do so, means a great number of their men will be in our clutches. We'll then hit the third wave with everything we've got, especially the cruiser squadrons, to smash the remainder of their assault force. There's no need – in fact it would be counter-productive – to let the third wave land. We must hit it hard while it's still mid-Channel, even though that means some of their troops might be able to swim back to France in their underpants."

"That is imperative, Pug... but one question. We talk about the first, second and third waves. In the fog of war can you be confident that we'll be able to distinguish between them – particularly if there are feints, mock landings and so on?"

"That, actually, is a very perceptive question, sir. It's possible that we've been a bit too structured in our thinking. I will talk to the staff officers. It may be good insurance to monitor the number of first-line troops still remaining in the embarkation areas. If there is any difficulty in distinguishing between the assault waves then we have, at least, an alternative benchmark we can use. Once we see that the last major formations of their troops are on the way, we can unleash our full response. And just as important, we must sever their supply lines as soon as that happens. That'll make things impossible for the troops already ashore, forcing them into an early surrender."

The Prime Minister was still listening intently. "Ah yes, their supply lines, the Achilles' heel in their entire operation. They may be able to fight for a while without food, living off the land, but their panzers won't go far without fuel, and their troops won't do much damage without ammunition!"

He looked at Ismay.

"Pug, you've given me considerable reassurance. God knows we would only embark on this plan in pursuit of a crushing success. Two hundred thousand of the Huns dead or in our prison camps. That would be a victory to cherish!"

Ismay took over. "Not to mention sinking the rest of their surface navy, and destroying most of the Luftwaffe, which they will presumably throw in as the situation on the ground worsens. As an aside, we'll also end up sinking maybe half of the entire continental barge fleet, which will bugger up a lot of the German war industry."

"We'll have to bugger up more than their industry before this foul war is over, Pug. But our goal is clear; a victory to stop that man in his tracks; a victory to match Trafalgar or Waterloo."

"Prime Minister," he said, reverting to a more formal tone, "we are looking for a victory that will match Trafalgar and Waterloo combined."

Churchill hesitated for a moment, looking straight into Ismay's eyes and smiled.

"Thank you, General, for confirming the brilliance of my plan with such stunning imagery," he said, with only the slightest hint of friendly sarcasm. "But you have summarised it well. There is no middle way, no other option. This is the battle that will turn the tide of the war."

CHAPTER FOURTEEN

Two days later the War Cabinet and the Chiefs continued the discussions. They debated a suggestion that as part of the strategy to draw in the second and third waves, the powerful cruiser squadrons should be held back and not launched against the first wave of the assault. The hesitation should reinforce the perception that the Royal Navy was not totally committed to the struggle. Admiral Pound voiced his deep reservations. He didn't have an issue with the concept or the intent, but was increasingly worried about the demands on his destroyer resources and the lack of operational flexibility that could result from the decision. While eventually acquiescing in principle, he asked to see Churchill later to discuss some points in more detail.

The Prime Minister was not particularly happy about a meeting outside the formal Cabinet structure, where everyone could have their say, but he had a high regard for Pound and was prepared to listen to him. The Admiral came straight to the point. "Prime Minister, this morning's decision to leave the cruisers in quarantine as part of the Ethelred deception gives me great difficulty. We are desperately short of destroyers, and the cruisers represent my only reserve. As you know I did raise my concern, but didn't want to object too strongly there and then. I realise there are many trade-offs, some of them complex, and I wanted to discuss them with you in person."

"Proceed, Admiral." He gave his permission rather than encouragement.

"Sir, you know the challenge I'm faced with day upon day; spreading the inadequate number of ships I've got across the various battlefronts. Let me look at the numbers. Obviously the highest priority is the Channel. Here I've got about forty destroyers, plus a similar number of smaller craft, in bases along the coast between the Humber and Plymouth. In theory that gives me a superiority of two or three to one over the German Navy – but if we were to suffer serious losses to the Luftwaffe, that margin could quickly be eroded. Until now, our strategy has been based on getting reinforcements from the ports further up the east and west coasts, particularly the cruiser squadrons. But if we're now going to hold those back as part of the Ethelred deception, I begin to get very concerned."

Churchill bristled. "That's not the complete story, Admiral. The cruiser squadrons are to be held back only until the trap is sprung. They will then, most assuredly, be committed to the battle!"

"I accept that, sir, but none of our plans envisage the Germans having complete naval control of the Channel at any stage."

Churchill was listening. "That is true, but is it really a possibility? Have you no more destroyers that you can find to act as a reserve if our initial losses are heavier than expected?"

"Is it really a possibility, sir? In war it's unwise to rule out anything as impossible. As for reserves, let's look again at my other commitments. I have to provide escorts for the Home Fleet. We still don't know if it will be needed to face the German battle fleet – perhaps trying to break out into the North Atlantic to attack the convoys, or coming across the North Sea towards Scotland as part of a second invasion force. The simple fact is that if the Home Fleet needs to be deployed – anywhere – it has to be supported by an adequate escort group to defend against U-boats. That means we can't reduce the number of destroyers assigned to it below the current, barely adequate, number... unless we're prepared to accept that the

Home Fleet is effectively immobilised."

Churchill accepted Pound's point, somewhat begrudgingly. "I suppose there's not much point in having a great fleet if it cannot put to sea."

With that point established, Pound continued, "The third task is convoy escort. You're familiar with the merchant ship losses, so you know the pressure we're under there, sir."

Churchill grunted. "I understand, but let's come back to a question we have discussed before. Is there any sign of U-boats being re-assigned to protect the German invasion fleet? Could we not re-deploy some of the convoy destroyers on a temporary basis to back up the anti-invasion group?"

"There's no sign of that, sir, and we're already under intense pressure from the Merchant Navy and the ship owners to increase the number of escorts protecting the convoys. Each Atlantic convoy really needs at least six escorts – usually two or three destroyers and about four corvettes, depending on availability and the perceived threat at the time. The little corvettes stay close to the convoy, to make it difficult for the U-boats to penetrate. There is no discussion about using them in the invasion battle. With their single gun they would be of minimal value in the Channel. Furthermore, at their top speed of twelve knots they couldn't even get there before it was all over. Unfortunately, by themselves they can't provide adequate protection for the convoys. The destroyers are key. They're the only ships with the speed to hunt down any Asdic contacts that we obtain – which often takes several hours – and then catch up with the convoy, or respond to a new contact. The problem is greatest in the air gap, outside the range of patrols from either side. That's where the wolf packs gather, and where the convoys are most vulnerable."

Churchill knew that Pound had not come just to complain. "Do you have any suggestions as to how we might resolve the issue, Admiral?"

"Sir, one possibility is that if the invasion battle is expected to be over in a week or two, we could consider turning back any convoys that hadn't reached mid-Atlantic, and so free up their destroyer escorts for the invasion battle."

He paused, waiting for the expected response from the Prime Minister.

"Admiral, I have no intention of trading defeat in the Atlantic for our victory in the Channel! In any event we need those convoys: the aircraft, weapons, fuel and ammunition – not to mention food. No, the convoys have to keep coming, but, I agree with your earlier comment, we should leave the corvettes where they are. Do you have any other suggestions?"

Pound took a deep breath. "Sir, give me back some of the cruisers that are now to be reserved outside the battle zone."

"You know why we're doing that!"

"I do, sir. But we've got to make sure we don't make just one more, small, improvement to the deception plan at the cost of greatly weakening the forces actually engaged in the battle – perhaps critically so. If we suffer heavier than expected losses to our destroyers in the opening battles, and there is then a delay getting reinforcements down to the scene of the fighting, the risk is that our naval forces in the invasion sector could be decimated."

"How many would you want?"

"Sir, give me back six of the light cruisers, three each for the northern and southern destroyer flotillas. That would beef up the two fleets in terms of firepower and anti-aircraft defences."

"You make a persuasive case, Admiral. All right, I will agree. You can have the cruisers you ask for as a reserve – just the ships, not the actual squadrons. Take the six ships, rebrand them as 'heavy destroyers' or 'flotilla leaders' or whatever, and assign them to the destroyer squadrons. Hold them as a reserve close to the Channel, for release only upon my command."

"Thank you, sir."

Next morning Bracken and Pound had arranged a further meeting on the naval deception plan. Bracken went straight to Pound's office and was greeted by a smiling Admiral as he went in.

"Morning, Brendan. Some good news for a change. The President has agreed to lease the destroyers in return for the West Indies bases. Confirmation came in overnight."

"That's excellent, Dudley, even if it has been a long time coming." said Bracken. "You must be relieved. I guess the odds in the convoy battle are starting to look a bit better."

"Well, yes and no. Medium term it's very good news. It replaces all our losses since the start of the war, and then some. Having said that, the ships are old, and won't be suitable for all purposes, but they'll certainly give us a lot more muscle in the Atlantic."

"What about Ethelred, Dudley? Any impact, one way or the other?"

"Not really. In fact, in the short term it hardly changes anything. The ships are all in mothballs; a lot of their equipment removed; engines full of preserving oil; things rusted and needing to be freed up... gunge everywhere... crews to be trained on U.S. equipment... boilers, guns, wireless..."

"So how long before they're ready?"

"Two to three months, even for the first of them; up to six months before we see them all." Pound was well aware of the work needed to get ships into commission.

"And the Germans will know that as well, presumably?"

"Unfortunately they will, Brendan. It's marine engineering, not voodoo."

"So, it doesn't affect the Channel battle one way or the other, for the time being – but if the Germans delay the invasion to next year, presumably it makes the odds a lot more challenging for them."

"That sums it up rather well. Come to think of it, it supports our overall strategy quite nicely – encouraging them to shoot off prematurely."

"That's always assuming that this one bit of good cheer doesn't affect Winston's decision to go ahead with Ethelred. What about the news itself, can we go public, or do we need to hold back for a while?"

"No reason not to announce. In any event it's going to leak out soon in the States. Hard to keep a secret there!"

"OK, I guess that makes sense. We'll give it a big splash for morale reasons at home... but the Nazis will know the reality. Right, Dudley, let's go and see the P.M."

Bracken and Pound walked over to the War Room and found Churchill and Beaverbrook deep in conversation, finishing up a review of the week's aircraft production figures. They had already heard the news about the American ships. Although reasonably satisfied with the deal he had done with Roosevelt, the Prime Minister was far from ecstatic.

"For a good friend, the President drove a hard bargain. Lucky he didn't want the Crown Jewels as well. Still it's good news. We need the ships desperately but, as you rightly say, Admiral, the transfer of these old destroyers doesn't change the entire military outlook. And there aren't any more bases or territory to barter away for the rest of the stuff that we are going to need ... planes... tanks... guns..."

Coming on the back of so many difficulties over the previous year, there was at least some cause to celebrate, and Bracken allowed a glimpse of his mischievous old self to show. "Well, we could always give back Canada," he said, *sotto voce*. Churchill glanced up and caught the twinkle in his eye.

"Oh, I'd forgotten about Canada!" came his quick riposte.

Still musing over the aircraft production reports, Beaverbrook had missed the sly looks across the table and, startled, rose to the bait. "I really must insist, Prime Minis..." before he realised that his leg was being pulled, and joined in the laughter for a moment. The tension was gone and there was quick agreement on the matter in hand. Bracken could give the deal the full publicity works at the appropriate time. But fifty destroyers didn't change the strategic balance.

Ethelred would go ahead.

CHAPTER FIFTEEN

Just over a week later, Air Chief Marshall Dowding was at his desk in Fighter Command's headquarters at Bentley Priory. The previous day had been the bloodiest yet in the battle. The RAF's fighters had inflicted considerable losses on the Luftwaffe, but at a high cost – 38 aircraft lost and 22 pilots killed or missing. In previous weeks this would have meant a full review of the battle. What had happened? How many Germans had been shot down? Were any mistakes made? Had the Luftwaffe changed their tactics? What could be improved before tomorrow's expected raids?

Today, however, instead of working on such issues he had other concerns on his mind. At 1300 the call came through from the Cabinet Offices. He sat upright in his chair listening to the voice on the line, then put the phone down and called his adjutant into his office. He issued the expected order with a single word: "*Ethelred.*"

The adjutant left immediately to get the operation underway. Since the battle had begun two months earlier, the regular rotation of exhausted squadrons away from the heart of the action to quieter areas had been a key element of Dowding's plan. It gave them the opportunity to rest and refit. With the staff work for these squadron moves well-practised, the execution of Ethelred moved ahead smoothly. At a high level, it was straightforward; for every two squadrons rotated out of the battle area, only one would be rotated in to fill the gap. Starting with 11 Group, facing the centre of the German assault, and then 10 and 12 Groups on the flanks, the transfer orders were issued.

First to go was 610 squadron from Biggin Hill. An hour after their Spitfires landed from the final sortie of the day, the tired pilots were briefed about the unexpected transfer. An advance party of ground crew would leave by road early in the morning to make preparations at the new base, a Training Command airfield in deepest Shropshire. The aircraft would go in the late afternoon, in sections of three or four at a time in case a prying German reconnaissance aircraft might spot the unusual activity. When the final aircraft had gone the rest of the squadron personnel would set off for the secluded airfield; to the tents and, for a lucky few, the farmhouse accommodation that waited.

The operational briefing for the pilots had been precise.

"Sections will take off at fifteen minute intervals, starting at 1800. As soon as you land at Ternhill, your aircraft will be moved under cover, in a wood a few hundred yards away. Ground crew will re-arm and refuel the aircraft there, and then camouflage them. Any engine testing or heavy maintenance work on the Spitfires will be done at night. While you're waiting to be recalled you can keep your hands in flying some of the trainers at the base."

The pilots left the meeting with mixed feelings: some with relief at the chance of a break from the grinding battle fatigue, others with a sense of frustration that they were being withdrawn from the battle at such a critical time. The Hurricane unit that was to remain behind at Biggin Hill, 32 squadron, was briefed on the reasons for the unwelcome reduction in station strength, and, more importantly, on the change in tactics now that they wouldn't have their Spitfire buddies to give them top cover. The rationale presented by the station commander was slightly opaque.

"We expect there'll be an increasing number of attacks on airfields in the invasion area, so a much greater degree of dispersal is necessary. Also, more rest and refit time is needed for squadrons, in preparation for the battle ahead. You'll get your turn soon. Some of the squadrons being withdrawn will be re-equipping with new models. I hear there is even a chance that the cannon-equipped aircraft will be appearing – at long last."

It was close enough to what was happening for it to be accepted at face value. There was some good news for them as well. As there wasn't a replacement squadron coming to replace 610 they would now have their choice of facilities in their airfields; the best protected revetments and hangars for the aircraft; the most comfortable billets for themselves. They were also pleased to hear that there would be some additional Bofors guns coming to the airfield, which should discourage the Luftwaffe's low-level attacks.

They were also briefed on the change now required in their tactics, for which the Wing Commander had a logical explanation.

"As you know, the battle is expected to last many months yet and the RAF needs to position itself for a long war of attrition. The powers-that-be have concluded that hit-and-run attacks on the Luftwaffe formations are giving a better success rate than mass attacks. Also, the change to head-on attacks is based on proven results. Our eight-gun firepower has a devastating effect on the Germans' glasshouse cockpits, and, as you know, their forward-facing defensive armament is weak, just one or two handheld guns. You may not enjoy it very much – just think how the Nazis will feel!"

The Hurricane pilots were somewhat vexed. Their planes were older than the Spitfires, yet it seemed that the Spit squadrons were to get new aircraft first. And they were even more uneasy about the new tactics. Head-on attacks had not featured in the RAF's manual of air tactics, yet this was what they were being asked to do – *and it was bloody dangerous*!

In developing the strategy, one serious concern for the RAF staff officers was that aircrew shot down across the Channel might give away the whole plan under interrogation. It was vital that no information leaked out which might compromise Ethelred. At every

Fighter Command base the message to the pilots was blunt. "This change in tactics is not to be discussed with anyone outside the squadron, not even with close friends or family who might be serving in other units. Furthermore, the standing instruction about pursuit of enemy aircraft is re-emphasised. No fighter aircraft is to go beyond the mid-point of the Channel, even if that means missing the opportunity to finish off a damaged opponent. Any breach of either of these orders will be a court-martial offence."

Two days later the new tactics were used for the first time. The result was far from perfect. It started well, with the radar stations doing their work and getting 66 squadron up in their new Spitfires in good time. Fifteen minutes later they had reached 28000ft and were attacking the 109 Staffel, whose pilots were unpleasantly surprised to find British fighters up so high. The Spitfires scored several kills in a swirling dogfight, in return for one loss. Several thousand feet below, however, the Hurricanes sent after the bombers found the new tactics difficult. Head-on attacks demanded split-second co-ordination between the sector controllers and the pilots, and only the experts of 1 squadron timed it right, knocking down six Heinkels and Junkers 88s. The other squadrons got it badly wrong as they tried to engage. Misjudging their high closing speed, they only got off a few ineffective bursts before they had passed through the German bomber formation, and were trying desperately to avoid the diving Me109s. To make it worse there had been three head-on collisions. Two pilots were killed but, miraculously, one pilot managed to escape as he accidentally took the tail off a Heinkel with his wingtip, and was then thrown clear as his Hurricane disintegrated.

While the British were not over-pleased about how the day had gone, for the German bomber crews it had been terrifying. They had seen more than thirty Hurricanes smash through their formation at a closing speed of over 800 kilometres per hour, with the escorting 109s too late to do anything about it. Fourteen bombers went down out of the three hundred on the raid, including a few to the unexpectedly heavy flak. The remainder dumped their bombs early, over the Isle of Sheppey rather than the London docklands. They were happy when it was time to turn for home.

In Luftwaffe headquarters, despite the vivid reports from the frightened bomber crews, the intelligence officers read the situation quite differently. They noted the ferocity of the RAF attacks and the reports from the still-shaken bomber pilots about suicide attacks. But the numbers were telling. Only eighteen losses in total out of more than five hundred aircraft committed. *Things were finally swinging in their favour.*

As the days went on, a further run down in the RAF's strength was orchestrated, in line with what the planners thought that the Luftwaffe would be calculating. Those squadrons which remained in the front line were further reduced in size, with each of their two flights now reduced from six to four aircraft and the spare aircraft spirited away to the reserve. This way of slimming down had the benefit that it could be reversed in a matter of hours, when the time came. With fewer aircraft now facing the enemy, even those RAF pilots who had been most uneasy about the new hit-and-run tactics accepted that there really was no choice. With a bit more experience and learning from the mistakes of the first days, they could still make the Luftwaffe pay a heavy price for its aggression.

Down at Roborough airfield, on the outskirts of Plymouth, the young pilots of 247 squadron were waiting around the dispersal area in the autumn sunshine. They were desperate to get involved in the great battle taking place over Kent and Sussex, just 200 miles away, but were limited instead to making uneventful patrols in their old Gladiators over the naval base, chasing away the occasional German reconnaissance aircraft. Squadron Leader Armitage understood their frustration, but was able to take a somewhat broader view of their situation. He knew that, while their old biplanes were a delight to fly and had achieved some success against unescorted bombers in France, they were no match for the Luftwaffe's modern fighters. They were a hundred miles per hour slower than the Me109s, and had only four Browning machine guns with which to face the 109s' cannon. Their only advantage was their manoeuvrability, being able to turn in much tighter circles than the German fighter. But even that was purely a defensive tactic; a 109 could climb, dive or just accelerate away from combat anytime it wanted. With the fast moving pace of aircraft technology, the Gladiators had gone from world class fighters to obsolescence in two years. No battle tactics, skilled piloting or *esprit de corps* could obviate that fact, and Armitage was quietly grateful that Fighter Command had assigned them to this quiet backwater until they were re-equipped. In the meantime he had to maintain a careful balancing act between keeping his squadron's morale high in case they should they be called into action, while pushing as hard as he could for the promised Hurricanes.

The call from the 12 Group headquarters that morning had left him confused. He was to prepare his squadron for a transfer to Northolt, just to the west of London, in twenty four hours' time – without receiving their Hurricanes. Group had said little, warning him against any speculation prior to a full briefing the next day, but inwardly he was very worried. The reports he had heard about the battle had been reassuring. They told how the RAF was knocking down German planes at a rate of three to one, and the mood of everyone he had talked to was one of quiet confidence.

So if we're winning, he asked himself, *and our losses are moderate, where are the bloody Hurricanes we've been promised; and why are we being thrown into the battle just before we get the equipment we need?*

He had paraphrased those questions in the call with Group, but their only response was that 247 was needed to act as a reserve squadron and to provide local airfield defence in the battle area. He would get a full briefing after the squadron arrived at its new base.

Armitage had his orders, and whatever concerns he might have, he was keenly aware of his responsibilities. He walked over to the

Operations Room where the full squadron had assembled.

"Good news, chaps. Group has just been on the phone. We're off to Northolt tomorrow."

A cheer went up from the young officers and sergeant pilots in the room.

"Will we be getting our Hurricanes when we get there, sir?" asked Pilot Officer Bill Jennings, at 19 one of the youngest and newest pilots assigned to the squadron.

"Not for a few weeks yet, men. They want to build up more reserves for the frontline folk before converting us. We'll be providing local protection for the airfield with our Gladiators. Should still give us the chance to see some action."

The excitement of getting into combat outweighed any concerns the men had about the adequacy of their aircraft. In good spirit they headed off to their quarters to start preparing for the move.

At Royal Naval Air Station Hatston, in Scotland, a similar process was underway. There, the pilots of 804 squadron were less enthusiastic. They had seen action in Norway against the Luftwaffe. They had suffered losses, and knew how poorly equipped they were with their Sea Gladiators. They had been hoping that the new American Grumman fighters now on their way would have arrived before they were called to action. They were even more concerned about their relocation to a Fighter Command airfield in the south east. They were carrier pilots, trained to provide air defence for the fleet, and versed in Royal Navy tactics. While dozens of Fleet Air Arm pilots had been seconded to fill the gaps in the Fighter Command squadrons, this was the first time that an entire squadron had been drafted. They had no experience of working in the different environment of Fighter Command. The tactics, radio communications and sector control were all completely different. Some fairly direct questioning of the C/O took place and after doing his best to deflect them, he eventually had to end the discussion quite curtly.

"Gentlemen, we have our orders... Dismissed!"

By next evening the two squadrons, with almost thirty aircraft, had assembled at Northolt and Hendon airfields. The squadron leaders were collected by car and brought to Group HQ to meet with the Group Captain. He spoke to the concerned officers quite bluntly.

"It may be difficult for you to accept that you've been posted at such short notice and pitched, as you may see it, with such unsuitable equipment into the heat of battle. I can give you some further information – but this must not be communicated to anyone else in your squadrons, not even your flight commanders, until you are given specific permission. The RAF is gathering all its resources for a mighty attack on the Luftwaffe, at a time and place of our choosing. In order to build up a reserve for this decisive battle, the squadrons that you are replacing have been withdrawn for refurbishment, and your two Gladiator squadrons are being deployed to fill the gap. We all recognize that the Gladiators are no match for the German fighters, but you can give a good account of yourselves against the bombers. For this reason you are being deployed to the western part of the London sector, where there are few 109s, and those that may occasionally appear have very little time to hang around or get involved in dogfights with nimble biplanes. I must stress that this is a short term assignment, no more than a week, I expect, perhaps two. Your role is to fill the gap in the frontline. We recognise that you cannot inflict significant losses on the enemy."

The squadron commanders looked at each other, unsure whether to raise objections, but the Group Captain continued without waiting for comments. "I need to make it absolutely clear that you are not here as sacrificial lambs. Your tactics will be – and this is a direct order – to make single diving attacks on the enemy formation and then get to hell out of it. I repeat, in case there is any misunderstanding, your Gladiators may be dispensable, your pilots are not. After one single attack you will dive away and recover to base. Engage with German fighters only if attacked and, in that event, circle inside them until they run low on fuel. Any significant damage to a plane and the pilot must bale out. No heroics, which might save an obsolete fighter but will certainly risk the life of a valuable pilot. Again I stress: this is a carefully considered deployment. It won't last long, and you have my promise that as soon as it's over your new equipment will be waiting for you at your home bases."

He looked directly at the two squadron leaders, both of them still distinctly uneasy.

"Make sure you bring your pilots back to fly them."

At 0800 next morning came the signal for 247 squadron to scramble. They rushed to their aircraft and took off, receiving their instructions from the fighter controller.

"Vector 090, Angels 24."

The directions were clear; head due east and climb to 24000ft. For the old Gladiators it meant a long, hard struggle, and it was almost twenty minutes later before the squadron had reached the assigned altitude. They were then instructed to orbit over Walthamstow, which they did for forty minutes until their fuel began to run low. They were then instructed to return to base. As they landed, 804 squadron received the call to scramble and headed off on patrol, though with the same negative result. In the afternoon it was the same story, two more sorties, but no sign of the enemy. The Germans weren't coming that day.

For the controllers at the sector stations, the tactics that they had been told to use with the Gladiator squadrons were extremely unusual. Normally the scramble signal was delayed until radar had picked up the clear signs of an impending raid. This helped reduce wear and tear on both fighters and pilots, and the Hurricanes and Spitfires could still climb fast enough to intercept the attackers. It was explained to them that different considerations applied to the Gladiators. They climbed more slowly than the monoplanes. Also, to compensate for their lower top speed it was vital that their attacks on the German formations be made in a dive, which meant they had to get well above them to start with. The decision had been taken to fly them off even before there was any radar warning. The

Luftwaffe was coming over regularly enough for the controllers to guess the approximate time of attacks, and with good judgement, get the aircraft in position.

The unspoken explanation was that considerations about minimizing wear and tear on the aircraft and pilots did not apply. The Gladiator squadrons would be gone within the week.

Two days later it did work as hoped for. After a quiet morning both squadrons were scrambled shortly after 1300 and were already climbing to altitude when the radar controllers detected an incoming raid. The German bombers were at 16000ft, and their fighter cover stretched up several thousand feet above. Quickly, the Gladiator squadrons were given a new heading, 110 degrees, directly towards the raiders, and an altitude of 22000ft. It was still a long way up to that height, but if they could get there in time they would have a reasonable chance of surviving, even against the 109s.

Fifteen minutes later, they spotted the formation. "Bandits at 1 o'clock low!" came the excited call from Squadron Leader Armitage. "Tally ho!"

The twelve planes of 247 squadron headed in a dive towards the raiders, working their speed up to about 300 mph. Finding the German fighter escort in the way, they had no choice but to engage them. The Sea Gladiators of 804 squadron were a bit slower due to the extra weight of their naval equipment, but managed to find a route though to the bombers.

Two minutes later they were almost in range.

"*Achtung! Britischen Jaeger!*" came the alarm call from the Gruppenkommander of the escorting 109s, straining his eyes to identify the approaching fighters. Not Hurricanes... what were they... biplanes! Gauntlets or Gladiat – yes Gladiators... closed cockpits. Christ, they're moving pretty fast for old timers. "Get after them, protect the bombers!"

Within another minute the tidy formations had tuned into a bedlam of diving attacks and twisting dog fights. A few of the 109s almost got caught napping by the Gladiators' surprise attack and had to make their escape by going into a steep climb. With their powerful engines they quickly outpaced the old planes. One or two made the mistake of trying to turn with the manoeuvrable biplanes, and collected a few bullet holes before realising their mistake and either diving or climbing away. The bombers suffered more in the attack. Two of the Heinkels were hit quite badly and started to drop out of the formation. A Dornier 17 caught fire and fell away, with the crew taking to their parachutes. The bombers' gunners were also putting up a stiff defence, and without armour protection or self-sealing tanks, several of the Gladiators were badly hit. Two pilots bailed out safely, but Sgt. Pilot Geoff Bailey was hit in the chest as he attacked another bomber. His last conscious action was to aim his crippled plane at the cockpit on the Heinkel, and fliers on both sides watched with horror as the planes collided and exploded. No parachutes emerged.

With their task achieved, the aircraft of the two squadrons dived away to the west. The pursuing 109s couldn't follow for long. After only a few minutes of tail chase they reached their low fuel point, and had to turn for home. Some of the younger pilots were very frustrated that they hadn't been able to open their score with an easy kill against an old Gladiator.

It hadn't been much more than a skirmish, but Group HQ was happy. Not only had the Gladiators got involved in a lively dogfight where they would have been spotted by hundreds of enemy flyers, they also had claimed four German bombers destroyed, and a few 109s damaged, for the loss of just three of the biplanes and, sadly, one pilot. The old-timers had done their part. A few more days like that and the Gladiator squadrons could be released, their job done.

By late evening the Luftwaffe intelligence specialists had completed their analysis of the combat reports and forwarded them to Goering's headquarters. Soon the Reichsmarschall was jumping around with excitement... and relief! He had been proven right! The RAF was almost out of fighters. Obsolete biplanes were now being thrown into the battle, even some old navy planes. It was just like Poland all over again. The Luftwaffe had suffered only ten losses, some to the early Spitfire attacks, and two or three to the Gladiators' suicide attacks. His fighters and bombers had shot down more than twenty-five British planes. This was what he had been predicting for the last month. They were victorious.

"Put me through to the Fuehrer, immediately" he trumpeted to his secretary.

In Whitehall the battle was also being discussed. Churchill called Dowding directly, and was much relieved to hear the outcome and the low number of RAF casualties. He had just put down the phone when Jock Colville came in, saying that Brigadier Menzies was outside and wanted to talk to him as soon as possible.

"Send him in," he replied.

Menzies was shown into the office, and the door was closed firmly behind him. He stood still for a minute, waiting for the quarantine area outside the office to be established, and then spoke, quietly and briefly.

"Canaris wants to meet, urgently."

The statement may have been short, but the import was immense. The head of the German military intelligence service, the Abwehr, was seeking a meeting with the head of MI6, Britain's Secret Intelligence Service. Churchill said nothing for a few moments, instead looking straight at Menzies as the message and its implications sank in.

"You? In person? When did this happen?"

"Yes me, sir, in person. A note was left in a drop-box for the Berne embassy yesterday."

"Where?"

"Sweden or Spain. My choice."

Another silence.

Churchill was still looking at Menzies. "Do you have any idea what he wants?"

"No sir. But I have to assume that it's of the highest importance. As you know, any information we've received from him in the past has been of exceptional quality... going right back to his warning about the attack on Poland, even though we were reluctant to believe him at the time. The same goes for his alert on the invasion of Norway."

"What about his alert on our naval ciphers? Have we seen any results yet from changing them?"

"It's still early days, sir. It took some time for the Admiralty to change them after he told us that they'd been broken. The new ciphers have only been in operation for about two weeks now, though it's beginning to look as if there's some reduction in U-boat attacks. If they don't know where our convoys are..."

"Has he ever shown interest in meeting before?"

"No sir, it's the first time. I must admit I was very surprised. Obviously such a step would be extremely risky for him."

"And also, perhaps, for us?"

Churchill was painfully aware of an incident in Holland early in the war, when two British agents had been captured in a German sting operation and great damage been done to the intelligence network on the Continent. It would be infinitely worse if C himself were to be taken. He looked directly at Menzies, waiting for his reply.

"That is a concern, sir. Though based on his record it seems unlikely he'd be a party to such a ploy, willing or unwilling. In any event we wouldn't be caught napping twice."

"I would sincerely hope not, C." Churchill looked hard at Menzies, before continuing in a more discursive way.

"The more I think about this approach, the more intriguing it becomes. What might he want, to be prepared to take such a risk? To share some extremely important information with us; so important that he doesn't want to use an intermediary... The date of the invasion perhaps? Or might he want to ask us for some very exceptional service... help with removing Hitler?"

"Those could both be possibilities."

"Defection?"

"Unlikely, sir, he doesn't need to meet me to do that."

"What about the Realists? Could Canaris have heard about them already? If so, he would probably try to warn us, even at great personal risk. He seems to hate Hitler nearly as much as we do, maybe more. You had better check with Pound and Bracken to see if any messages have gone out prematurely. "

"I already have, sir, on my way over. Absolutely nothing has been released yet. The first message is due to go out in three days' time."

"Then let us revert to the first two possibilities. We've no reason to think he knows about the remarkable insight we get from Ultra – but he must be aware that our reconnaissance and intelligence resources are watching their every move. And even if he does know the actual date, that doesn't really add a lot to what we can determine ourselves."

"That was my own conclusion, too, Prime Minister. In any event the date would still depend ultimately on the weather."

"As for bumping off dear Adolf... well I, for one, wouldn't miss him. But why would they need us? The German army is well able to do that without any assistance from us. And even if there were to be such a happy event, we are in no position to take military advantage, unfortunately."

Suddenly the colour drained from Churchill's face. "Unless they have discovered the whole Ethelred confection."

The thought was frightening. *Could the Germans have discovered the plan?* Only a dozen or so people knew of it, and there was a total ban on telephone or wireless discussion. *Good God, could there be a Judas in the inner circle? Could the Nazis now be planning their moves fully aware of the British deception? A huge double-bluff?*

After a brief pause Churchill gathered his thoughts.

"Is Ultra indicating any changes from what we were seeing before Operation Ethelred started, or indeed from what we would expect in the lead-up to an invasion?"

"None whatsoever, sir."

Churchill breathed a sigh of relief. "Thank God for that. Perhaps then, looking at it both from our side and theirs, a leak is unlikely. Nonetheless, without giving the slightest indication of my reasons, I will ask the group to consider the risk of leakage and to take account of it in future arrangements. That would be prudent. In fact, even if the Nazis come to suspect a deception, it may be that the worst consequence is simply that they decide not to invade. That would be disappointing after what we've invested in Ethelred... but we'd gladly have settled for such an outcome a few months ago."

Menzies continued listening, as Churchill came to his conclusion.

"Now, about Canaris, it does appear to me that the risks involved in meeting him at this stage far outweigh any possible benefits. We have a plan underway. Thanks to Ultra, we already have the means to check how successful our deception is being, and also the integrity of any assumptions that we've made. So let us continue on our current path. You will not agree to meet Canaris. When Ethelred is over and the Nazi war machine has suffered its first major defeat, then will be the time to engage with him or other brave Germans who might help put an end to this nightmare."

On the following Tuesday, the Duke of Hamilton walked along leafy Montagu Place, in the heart of London's embassy belt. In his brown briefcase were files of correspondence regarding the RAF internees detained in Sweden. In the pocket of his blue uniform jacket was a letter.

The formal meeting was civil, but not very productive. The Ambassador pointed out that there were very few British internees being held in their jurisdiction. They had many more internees of other nationalities, and any decision about release would have to be on an even-handed basis. "The numbers would not necessarily work in Britain's favour," he added, with a diplomatic smile.

After the inconclusive discussion on the interned airmen, Hamilton made his unexpected approach. He stated that he wished to make it known that, even at this late stage, some senior members of the government and Armed Forces were interested in pursuing opportunities for peace. He took the letter from his pocket and presented it, asking that it should be passed on to a representative of the German Foreign Office. The Ambassador was startled, but listened carefully, in a non-committal way. Acting as an intermediary to pass on official government communications was one thing, but handling clandestine messages was quite different. He was well aware of Hamilton's connections with the Nazis before the war, but had assumed that that was all in the past. He accepted the note, but advised that he would have to take guidance from Stockholm before he could promise that it would be passed on to the intended recipients.

Four days later they met again. Hamilton learned that the note had indeed been passed on and that a reply had been received from Berlin. Their response was cagey, just seeking more information. The very speed of the turnaround indicated that the initial message had not penetrated far into the German diplomatic channels. But at least the channel had been established.

Hamilton proceeded to deliver the second message. It revealed the existence of a group of politicians and senior officers, who regarded themselves as 'Realists', and wished to establish whether, even at this late hour, a peaceful solution to the conflict could be achieved. This time the ambassador was more confident that the message would be passed on.

The response to the second message took a few days longer to appear, which was certainly a positive sign. The reply, also, was more encouraging, seemingly trying to authenticate the status of the group. On the following day Hamilton passed over the third message. This time the stakes were raised. It offered to demonstrate the *bona fides* and the influence of the group by transferring three major warships from the invasion coast of England to Scotland, as a *quid pro quo* for a three-day cessation of the blitz on London.

As anticipated, there was now a break in the conversation.

Chapter Sixteen

At the daily Fuehrer Conference, Hitler met with his inner circle. These were the men he relied upon to execute his master plan; his close political associates and the senior OKW commanders. He listened to the briefing from Reichsmarschall Goering on the air war, and indicated his satisfaction with progress. Field Marshal Keitel provided the latest information on the Heer's invasion preparations. After that, Raeder gave a brief, non-contentious update on the naval situation. It was all very professional, quite similar to the meetings before Poland and France. But on this day there was a feeling of anticipation in the air. Word had got around that there had been another significant communication from the Realists on the previous evening.

With the formal agenda items completed, Hitler moved on to a favourite subject; whether it might still be possible to get the British to accept that they were beaten, and come to the negotiating table. He reminded the group that he had previously indicated that he would not be vindictive in the event of such negotiations. He was willing to reach a sensible agreement where each power would respect the other's area of influence. He acknowledged that he had been kept informed about the communications taking place over the previous ten days, and felt it was now time to discuss the implications.

"This morning I was shown the latest message from this group, these 'Realists', relayed via Sweden. Reichsminister, read it out for the group."

Von Ribbentrop drew a folder from a leather briefcase. It contained the original English version, with a translation attached. He read it aloud. There was a murmur as he highlighted the offer to withdraw three warships from the south coast of England in return for a pause in the bombing of London. After finishing the note he continued to speak.

"This is the third message received via the Swedish intermediary over the last ten days. As with the previous ones we can't be sure that it's genuine, or identify the originator. However this one is somewhat different. Just as in the earlier messages it suggests that there is a growing peace faction in England, at least in their navy. But, more importantly, this time it offers a way to validate the extent of their influence."

Hitler was somewhat cagey, reluctant to place too much trust on an unverified communication. He commented, "It would certainly be of great benefit to our Russian campaign if we could achieve a quick resolution in the West – and also minimise our losses there." He turned to Keitel. "Generalfeldmarschall, make sure that your senior staff are made aware of this possibility. Ensure that our plans retain the flexibility to respond quickly if a suitable opportunity presents itself."

"Yes, Fuehrer." Keitel would have been delighted to avoid the need for, and the cost of a heavily-contested invasion. He turned to von Ribbentrop. "Reichminister, do you have any indication at all about the source of the messages?"

"We have very little information to go on. All we've been told to date is that they are coming via a senior military contact – we believe it's the Duke of Hamilton – but it appears that he is not necessarily the originator."

Hess, the Deputy Fuehrer, was not deeply involved in the invasion planning, but was very familiar with the various groups in Britain which had been pro-German before the war. He added his opinion. "That could be significant. Hamilton was certainly friendly towards us in the past but, as far as we know, he's now on active service in the RAF – in an operational role in Scotland, not a staff position. Strange that he now pops up in London... And this latest message talks about transferring several warships out of the combat zone. If that happens it implies that whoever is originating the messages has considerable influence, or at least high-level supporters, within the British navy."

Goering took the telegram and looked at it again. "Certainly it does suggest that there are peace supporters in both their navy and air force – and none of us is too worried about their army! Are they finally showing some sense? Has it finally become clear to them that the Royal Navy, as well as the RAF, will be destroyed if Churchill persists in his defiance? If they hope to avoid that, it would make sense for them to look for a settlement now that would spare their navy and the remains of their air force."

Admiral Raeder was less enthusiastic. "Unfortunately what we can't tell is whether these Realists have the power to actually control the movement of ships, or whether they have just obtained information about some future planned moves."

Hitler knew Raeder was right and snapped at his generals. "We need that information quickly. If this new group does have the authority to order movements, it would be extremely significant... certainly more so than if they simply know about things that are going to happen anyway. Get the Abwehr to find out."

Keitel agreed at once. "Yes, Fuehrer. I will instruct them to check the pedigree of these reports. We will also obtain whatever information we can from our agents in Britain, and will try to find other ways to test the genuineness of these 'Realists'. As a quick test, Fuehrer, perhaps we could increase the stakes. We could offer a four-day lull in the bombing in return for four ships being transferred north!"

"That's a good idea, Keitel. Do it. Let's see if they can step up to the mark."

Hitler turned back to the assembled staff group and continued discussions on the Sea Lion preparations. There was no further reference to the British messages, but it did seem to several of the participants that there was there a jauntier tone about the rest of their discussions.

After the meeting ended, Keitel went across to see Canaris. He gave him the news about the third message from Sweden, which von Ribbentrop had not advised him about. He then passed on the Fuehrer's order for the Abwehr to set about verifying the source. Canaris was in a serious dilemma. The news of this British group, these so-called Realists, was extremely disturbing in terms of the threat it implied to Churchill's government. Even more so, it was a real threat to him and his sympathisers. He wondered how far the tentacles of the shadowy group extended... perhaps deep into the British Intelligence Services? He just hoped that the people that he was in contact with had taken care to hide their sources. He needed to do some fast thinking.

Late in the afternoon Canaris was called into the Fuehrer conference. Though not as senior as the other generals there, the white-haired, gaunt figure was always surrounded with an aura of mystery. He spoke quietly, informing Hitler that the Abwehr had no information available about any disloyal groups in the British navy. There was very little opportunity to check out the reports directly; none of his agents in Britain were close enough to senior military officers to investigate the possibility. However there was an indirect personal link to the Duke of Hamilton via a contact in Switzerland. He would see if any information could be obtained through that channel. It wouldn't be easy and would take some time. They would have to be very circumspect in their communications. There was every likelihood that British censors would read the correspondence, no matter how deviously it was routed, and the content would have to be heavily disguised.

He took a deep breath and then continued, "There is of course another possibility, Fuehrer, that this is all a British deception, and we should be conscious of that risk."

It was a clever move. As one of the guardians of Germany's intelligence organisation, it was within his area of responsibility to warn about possible British covert operations. If he could sow some doubt it might slow down the German response to the Realists' feelers, and give him more time to warn the British, even if they had turned down the meeting he'd requested. It would also give Churchill more time to deal with them.

Hitler showed some acceptance of Canaris' advice. It mirrored his own suspicions.

"Admiral, I agree with you; we must bear that possibility in mind. They didn't build an Empire based on honesty and straight-dealing. However, whether this group is genuine or not the battle is clearly swinging decisively in our favour. The RAF is offering less resistance day by day, and the British navy is, perhaps, weakening in its resolve. We shall proceed as follows." He turned to Goering.

"Reichsmarschall, tomorrow I want the Luftwaffe to launch a full-strength raid on London, to make sure that yesterday's success wasn't an anomaly. Following that we will respond to the Realists' message, in a positive manner, and agree to suspend bombing for four days. If the group is genuine it may get some of their warships out of our path. Even if it's not genuine, the Luftwaffe can use the pause to prepare for the final assault. I also want an updated report from the OKW to confirm our final readiness for Sea Lion, and giving me the range of suitable dates. I will give my decision based on those reports."

"Certainly, Fuehrer," answered Goering. "That can be done, but if I can make a suggestion, I would like to schedule the attack for two or three days' time instead of tomorrow. That will give time for our aircraft, particularly the bombers, to have minor damage repaired, so that we can have a maximum weight of effort in the attack. Then the RAF will have no choice but to oppose it with all their remaining aircraft."

Hitler accepted his point. "That's a reasonable request. I accept that change. We must make this blow as powerful as possible, even at the cost of a few days' delay – but no more. One more heavy attack before we respond to the Realists' message. That will give them all the more incentive to take decisive political action in London. Inform me as soon as the date is confirmed for the raid."

On September 8th the Luftwaffe came in force. It was the bloodiest day by far. With opposition from the RAF now much reduced, the Luftwaffe was able to commit its Stukas for the first time since July, targeting the radar stations in a series of fierce attacks. Five of the vital stations were put out of action, tearing great holes in the British defence chain. The rest of the Luftwaffe's bomber fleet streamed though the gaps, towards London, and the small number of RAF fighters was eventually overwhelmed by the sheer weight of attackers.

In London the effects were drastic. The bombers paraded over the city in textbook formations, their contrails stretching in broad swathes straight from the coast to the capital. For the first time in the Battle there were almost no signs of RAF counterattacks. They dropped their loads in dense patterns, doing devastating damage to the city and the port. Worst of all, early reports indicated that there were likely to be over 5000 dead and tens of thousand injured, almost all civilians.

Churchill was deeply depressed by the toll. It was all the more painful knowing that it had been his decision to accept this risk, an almost inevitable consequence of the Ethelred strategy.

Ismay tried to console him. "If Hitler wins this war there will be that many dead every day, Prime Minister, for months, perhaps for years to come."

The Prime Minister retreated to his room. He said he had a speech to work on, but his staff recognised that he wanted to be left alone for a time. Even Bracken, seeing him later, could offer little by way of comfort. This wasn't a hypothetical possibility they were dealing with. It wasn't some minor political crisis where a few well-chosen words or a quip could lift the mood. All around the city fires were burning; the intense black smoke choking civilians and firefighters. Dreadfully wounded survivors were being brought to temporary casualty stations. Corpses and pieces of bodies were being pulled from devastated buildings and taken to public burial grounds. This was the ugly reality of modern warfare.

The Prime Minister returned to the Situation Room an hour later to review the rescue efforts. Bracken stayed close-by, to help where he could, but also to keep an eye on his hero. Finally, as the light began to fail, the two went up to a roof-top above the Cabinet War Rooms, and gazed sadly at the blitzed city. Fires and smoke could be seen on all sides. In the air there hung an acrid smell... burning wood and paper... oil and rubber... flesh...

Churchill was appalled at what he had helped visit on his beloved London. Tears rolling down his cheeks, he spoke despairingly to his old friend.

"Does a parent left without a child, or a child without its parents, give a toss about our war strategy? What does a young man or woman, facing their future without limbs, care about our battle for democracy? How must our pilots feel, hidden away like hermits in the woodlands while our capital gets devastated; their friends, their relatives perhaps, blasted or incinerated? God save me, Brendan, what have I done?"

Bracken knew how poorly equipped he was for the role of comforting his leader or providing emotional support, no matter how much he loved him. His strength was logic; his tools analysis, scheming, intrigue. Any attempt to use those to rationalise the situation would have sounded crass. Any resort to explaining away the casualties as a dreadful consequence of war would probably have driven Churchill further into depression. But he thought that logic could, perhaps, be used to generate hope.

"They won't be able to continue this assault on London much

longer, Winston. Time is running out for them. If they're going to invade this year they've no choice but to switch ther attack back to military targets. This is, perhaps, the nadir."

Churchill did not reply. Tears still streaming from his eyes, he walked back to the bunker, entered through the thick blast door and descended the bare concrete steps. He walked slowly along the corridor, speaking to no-one, looking at no-one. He went silently to his room and closed the door.

CHAPTER SEVENTEEN

'*Germany calling, Germany calling. Why must the British people go on suffering as a consequence of Churchill's unwarranted intervention in what is purely a continental war? Why must the Luftwaffe be forced to continue its bombing campaign against London? Why should the Royal Navy suffer destruction in a war brought about by international Jewry? It is time for the realists in Britain to assert themselves. Rise up and remove Churchill and his clique. The Fuehrer wants this war to end. As a gesture of his desire for peace he has decided to suspend bombing attacks on London for a four-day period. He awaits the response of the British people.*'

The broadcast on Hamburg Radio by Lord Haw-Haw, the German propagandist, had been picked up in late morning. Its content was different enough for a supervisor in the BBC monitoring service to bring it to the attention of the Director General and, shortly afterwards, the transcript was rushed by motorcycle courier from his desk to the Cabinet Office. A recording was immediately requested and, by early afternoon, Bracken was sitting in a side room listening to it.

There was no doubt about it. It was the response, in a most unexpected manner, to the third message.

"Thank you, Lord Haw-Haw. That's just what we were waiting

for," he muttered to himself, and lifted the phone to Admiral Pound. There was a short debate about the change in the number of days that the Germans were offering to stop bombing. At Bracken's strong urging, Pound came round to accept it as a negotiation gesture by the Nazis and agreed to release a fourth warship in response.

Eighteen hours later the battleship HMS *Queen Elizabeth* raised steam in Portsmouth and, accompanied by three cruisers, put to sea. Protected by a small escort group, they headed west towards Land's End.

Chapter Eighteen

At midday, Hitler met with his command group in the Fuehrer Bunker. The movement of the ships had been monitored by reconnaissance aircraft and confirmed as not three, but four major ships, a battleship and three cruisers. Even more significantly, the Dornier reconnaissance aircraft sent out to check had been intercepted by a pair of RAF Spitfires – but had not been attacked. Instead it had been escorted at a safe distance as it went about its mission. It was most encouraging. It implied that the Realists had the serious authority, cross-service authority, they were hoping for. A favourable momentum seemed to be building. Hitler ordered an immediate four-day bombing pause on all targets within 50 km of London.

It was then time for a full briefing on the previous week's air battles. It was clear that the Luftwaffe was close to achieving air supremacy over Britain. Goering was enjoying the limelight and summarised in an ebullient manner. "Fuehrer, our fighters roam the skies over southern England. Our bombers are able to raid London and their airfields and ports almost with impunity. We have achieved the air superiority demanded by the Kriegsmarine and the Heer. The RAF is beaten. The Luftwaffe stands ready to switch its squadrons to protect the landing from British intervention, and to support the Heer in its advance."

Hitler had long learned to be cautious when Goering was waxing lyrical about his cherished Luftwaffe. He decided to moderate the mood.

"That is encouraging news, Reichsmarschall. How many of our own aircraft have we lost in the battle to date?"

Goering was slow to pick up the inference of the question.

"Our forces have suffered losses in achieving this victory, but have persevered with great determination and courage. We have been able to maintain our frontline strength by deploying reserves from Germany. Furthermore the Stuka and Messerschmitt 110 squadrons, which we withdrew in the early stage of the battle due to losses, have been restored to full strength and have been able to re-engage as the RAF opposition declines."

"I am conscious of the great courage being shown by our airmen, Reichsmarschall. How many aircraft losses precisely?"

This time Goering could not bluster. "Approximately 1200, Fuehrer, though the loss rate has declined sharply over the last two weeks," he replied, slightly crestfallen that his great achievement was being diminished somewhat by reference to the price paid.

"Mostly with their crews, I assume?" Hitler was keenly aware of the risks in bringing the fight to the enemy's soil.

"Yes, Fuehrer, approximately two thirds, unfortunately."

"Have you been able to replace those men?"

"Yes, Fuehrer. There is an excellent flow of new men from the training establishments. They have less experience than the flyers they are replacing, but in compensation, they have great commitment to the cause. And of course the RAF is much weaker too."

Hitler said nothing, and allowed Goering to try to re-establish his momentum.

"Fuehrer, despite the losses sustained, the Luftwaffe has achieved the position demanded of us. We have achieved air supremacy over southern Britain."

He sat down, and Keitel, spoke again, feeling it appropriate to associate himself with the enthusiasm of his Luftwaffe colleague. "Fuehrer, may I offer my congratulations to the Reichsmarschall on this excellent news! I know that it will give great reassurance to the Kriegsmarine and the Heer."

Von Ribbentrop was then called upon to discuss the final item on the agenda; an intriguing message from the German Embassy in Dublin.

"The embassy has received reports from several sources that serious rioting has broken out in many cities in Britain, and sabotage has also been reported. The latest information comes from Glasgow and Liverpool, from eyewitnesses to the events, and appears to be reliable. It seems that thousands of people have been taking part in peace rallies in the two cities; that things escalated and troops have been called in to defend the port facilities."

Hitler called for Canaris to join them and asked his opinion of the reports.

"Fuehrer, we had no forewarning of any unrest. However the reports from the Dublin embassy are quite specific and have been vouched for by dozens of passengers arriving from the two British ports. It seems there have been explosions and fires, in both the docks and the shipyards. There appears to have been some shooting, though we don't know by whom. I have despatched agents from London to travel to the two cities to authenticate the reports, and I have also requested Luftwaffe reconnaissance flights over both cities."

He looked at Goering, who provided confirmation.

"Those flights are in the air now, Fuehrer. We should have photographs back by 2100."

"Let me have those and the reports from our agents as soon as they arrive."

Von Ribbentrop also proceeded with an update on the news just received from Foreign Minister Ciano in Rome. Until now all that had been received from their Italian ally had been background material, confirming the general theme that there was a split of opinion within the British government and military. This morning had come more specific information; several cruisers had been recalled at short notice from the Mediterranean to the British Isles.

"To replace those transferred from Portsmouth to Scotland?"

"Perhaps, Fuehrer. It might be linked to that move."

"Does that not invalidate the theory that the Realists have real power? Are they simply shuffling the British navy's warships?"

"It is possible that the Realists are controlling it all in a masterly way. While they had to carry through on the offer made to us, to withdraw the ships to Scotland, they may have wanted to provide some cover for their actions in Britain. One possibility is that they may have portrayed the move of the four ships as part of an overall redeployment, with the units sent to Scotland being replaced by others from the Mediterranean. That way they were able to meet their commitment to us, while not causing embarrassing questions to be asked in London."

Hitler looked dubious. "If they have to cover up their actions like that, the inference is that they're not very confident about their position."

Von Ribbentrop was not in a position to argue. "That could be a logical conclusion, Fuehrer. On the other hand, it may be that there is a split developing within the British Navy. If the movement of the ships to Scotland was not fully authorised along the chain of command there may be a degree of alarm in London. So it's quite possible that the Mediterranean units are seen as loyal to the current government and are being rushed in as replacements, or perhaps to confront the dissenters."

Hitler stroked his chin, looking pensive. "Whatever is behind this, the information is becoming quite consistent. Clearly there is something afoot in England. Either it's the beginning of the split that we have been hoping for, or else we are the target of an elaborate hoax... so elaborate, in fact, that it can only have been authorised by Churchill himself. We will maintain an open mind until we obtain further information."

The two Abwehr agents did not make the train journey north. Instead their confinement continued in separate cells in the Tower of London, just ten paces away from the gallows. However two MI5 officers did make the journeys, discreetly taking notes behind their newspapers as they headed north on the different mainlines. Their record would ensure that the background details of journey times, weather and any relevant incidents could be accurately factored into the wireless reports to be sent to Germany on their return.

The wartime journeys were slow, and it was 48 hours later before the carefully prepared reports were transmitted by wireless to Berlin. Within hours of their receipt Hitler's command group had re-assembled. The photographs taken over Glasgow and Liverpool had already been scrutinised by the Luftwaffe's skilled analysts, and were now collated with the reports received from two agents. The intelligence reports were summarised by Admiral Canaris.

"I arranged for the two agents to travel north on different main lines to get as broad a picture as possible. One went to Liverpool on the west coast line, and the other took the east coast line to Edinburgh before travelling on by local train to Glasgow. They both have cover as commercial travellers for legitimate companies, which gives them the opportunity to move around the country relatively freely.

"Their two reports are quite consistent. At all mainline stations there is much intensified security in place compared with their last visits about three weeks ago. In both ports there are considerable signs of strife, with smoke seen rising in many directions. There is a strong police and army presence and the agents were not allowed into the commercial or dockside areas of either city, although they have been before on several occasions and have valid reasons to go there. They both report that, in addition to military personnel, there were many ambulances and civilian fire appliances around the two cities."

Hitler nodded. He didn't have much time for Canaris as an individual, but he accepted that he ran an effective intelligence service.

"Did they get any first hand reports from the local population?"

"Yes. Each of them spoke to about a dozen civilians, and a few police and military. They had to be very circumspect to avoid drawing attention to themselves. It seems that in both cities, trouble broke out after anti-war marches organised by trade unions. Police and troops then broke up the marches, quite violently, and several people were shot. After the shooting broke out, many of the workers headed back to their workplaces in the docks and began acts of sabotage. It wasn't organised to begin with, but militant shipyard workers and dockers have now taken over, and there is increasing confrontation with the troops."

Hitler grinned. "Remind me to show my appreciation to our friends in the international trade union movement."

There was a small amount of chuckling from the assembled group. The Fuehrer didn't often have time for jokes. If any of the attendees thought that, with 5000 trade unionists already in the concentration camps, the gibe was in poor taste, they chose not to comment.

"Have any disturbances been reported in their naval bases?" he continued.

Canaris didn't enjoy bringing good news to the Fuehrer, but had little option but to stay close to the reports received – too many other people had access for him to misrepresent the information obtained.

"There have been no reports of any. At the same time there is no indication of Royal Navy sailors being used to quell the disturbances or protect the facilities, even though there is a strong naval presence in both ports. One agent has reported rumours, although these have not been verified, that in Liverpool some sailors refused to leave their ships, when ordered to provide assistance to the troops on shore. Similarly in Glasgow our agent heard an unconfirmed report of a heavily-armed group of troops boarding a minesweeper on the Clyde, with the crew apparently being removed by force and presumably arrested."

Hitler was showing increasing interest. "Are the reconnaissance photographs consistent with that, Reichsmarschall?"

Goering responded. "They support the information provided by the agents, Fuehrer, and they also provide detailed information on the locations of the fires. They were all in the port sections of the cities, in the commercial docks and the naval dockyards. The materials ablaze appear to be mainly oil and petroleum, rubber and timber. There's not much sign of damage outside the dock area, in the business or residential areas."

"What about our wireless interceptions, Admiral?"

"There has been a substantial increase in traffic in the two ports, both army and navy signals. Unfortunately the British changed their codes a few weeks ago, so we are not able to decipher the content." Canaris had answered truthfully. He knew exactly why the British had changed their codes, but for the rest of the group it was just an unfortunate wartime co-incidence.

Canaris did add some words of caution. "Fuehrer, one should be conscious of the fact that reports have been received from those two ports only. There have been no reports from any other locations. The east coast railway route passes through Newcastle and Edinburgh, and although there was increased security, there were no signs of disturbances in either city."

Hitler curled his lip, looked down at the map of Britain on the chart table and muttered. "All revolutions have to start somewhere. Glasgow and Liverpool seem as good places as any."

He then raised his voice. "Despite the Admiral's reservations, the evidence is beginning to be quite persuasive. The disturbances seem to be significant. Something is happening. Reichminister, is there any further information coming from our sources in the Bahamas?"

Von Ribbentrop responded. "The last report was about a week ago, Fuehrer. It suggests that there is a growing mood of unhappiness in Britain. Within the British establishment there is a growing consensus that the army is in total disarray; the RAF just about finished, and the navy is next unless it takes some action. It seems that there are plans in train for a substantial increase in the number of warships based in the Americas, and work is underway to provide the necessary facilities in Canada and the West Indies."

"Nothing more up-to-date than last week, Reichminister?"

"Unfortunately not, Fuehrer. Our intermediaries have to physically journey back to the United States before reporting via our Washington embassy, and even though the people concerned are affluent individuals, they can't repeat their visits to Nassau too frequently."

Hitler was silent for a few moments, then summarised.

"We must continue to be wary, but this is beginning to look most encouraging. These reports of disturbances from our embassy in Dublin and from our agents in Britain seem credible, and have been verified by our reconnaissance aircraft. As well as which, our royal contacts have always been frank and honest in their communications with us. So if there is such a group of Realists, the question we must now consider is how to encourage them to make their move, and how we will take advantage of the situation when they do."

The conference ended in a mood of quiet excitement.

CHAPTER NINETEEN

In Nassau, the Windsors had spent the day planning the refurbishment of Government House, before hosting a small dinner party for some old friends of the Duchess from Arizona. Fifty yards away, Commander Jack Williams, ex-Royal Navy and now responsible for their security, was watching carefully from the bungalow. For several weeks his main task had been to prime the couple with defeatist messages, allegedly coming from the naval officers of almost every warship using the port. The most recent piece of misinformation fed through the Royal household had been one of Bracken's final touches, to the effect that bases were being established in the West Indies for a large number of refugee Royal Navy warships.

Now he would be more actively involved. Close to midnight he saw the American guests leave by car, obviously in fine fettle. He checked his watch. Ten minutes later his small party moved out of his kitchen, walked quietly across to the villa and rang the bell. The young maid came to the door, surprised to see the Commander at such a late hour, and admitted him. She was even more alarmed when several other figures appeared out of the darkness and bundled her, gently but firmly, into the kitchen.

"Your Royal Highness!"

Williams called loudly for the Duke, who appeared a minute later in his dressing gown, with the Duchess close behind. They both looked somewhat confused. His confusion was even greater when he saw a King's Messenger among the party in the hallway. This looked ominous.

"We need to speak to you alone, sir, urgently. We have an important message for you."

"Is the King....?"

"It's about your security, sir"

From that point, the operation proceeded smoothly. The uniforms, coupled with the obvious determination of the party, carried the process forward. With the Duchess safely escorted to her bedroom, the letter from the King was presented to the Duke. Less than two hours later, still in darkness, the Royals and their maid were escorted up the gangplank onto HMS *Cumberland*. Ten minutes later the cruiser slipped her lines and made to sea.

CHAPTER TWENTY

Three days later the Fuehrer conference took place in the Berghof, high in the Bavarian Alps. The mood was positive, with a growing number of indications that British resistance was collapsing. The RAF's fighters were offering less of a challenge every day, and there were reports of unusual naval movements at several bases. There was also a vague message from Florida that there had been some sort of incident in the Bahamas. Hitler was increasingly optimistic that things were moving in the right direction and stated that he expected to make a decision within two days.

Shortly after dinner he was informed that Keitel and Raeder wanted to speak to him about a significant development, and a few minutes later they joined him, both looking very pleased.

Keitel began to relate the news. "Fuehrer, we need to inform you of some important intelligence information coming from Scapa Flow. There seems to be a major incident in progress. It started about twenty four hours ago, when our signals people detected unusual wireless traffic in the area. A reconnaissance aircraft was sent over the base this morning. The photographs have been studied by intelligence analysts and they have concluded that there are dramatic events underway."

Admiral Raeder took over. "The units in Scapa Flow, representing about half of the entire British Home Fleet, have changed their anchorage locations in a very significant way. Normally they are positioned to allow a rapid exit to sea, to intercept any sorties by our ships, as one would expect. However they appear to have been redeployed into a formation that is more appropriate for a defensive battle, and even more significantly, against an attack from land or sea!"

Hitler was silent for a moment, and then walked over to the map of the British Isles on the wall. He looked at the Orkney Islands, just north of the Scottish mainland. "Might those movements not just be sensible precautions against an attack by our forces?" He didn't need to remind them how U-47 had penetrated the base and sunk the battleship HMS *Royal Oak* as she lay at anchor in the supposedly safe haven.

Raeder responded. "Fuehrer, by themselves they could – in theory, although it would be strange for it to happen now, so far into the war. Apart from which, our own assessment is that another direct attack on Scapa Flow is almost impossible, and we would expect the British to see it likewise. The coastal and air defences are just too strong. The attack by Kapitan Prien last year was an unequalled feat of seamanship, and the British have blocked all the access channels to make sure there is no repetition."

Keitel joined in. "It also appears that the major airfield on Orkney, at Kirkwall, has been taken over by some new group, and the runways have been blocked!"

"Do you have any other intelligence reports to support this interpretation... that these fleet movements are somehow irregular?"

Keitel answered "Fuehrer, there is strong corroboration coming from our signals intelligence staff. They have analysed the wireless traffic in the general area and discovered some very revealing facts. Almost all the traffic appears to be coming from British Navy transmitters in mainland Scotland. It seems that messages ordering new ship dispositions are being broadcast over and over again, but there are no replies, not even acknowledgements, being returned from the Scapa anchorage."

"Can we determine the content of the messages?"

"No Fuehrer. Unfortunately we haven't being able to decipher their transmissions since the British changed their ciphers – but we are able to identify the sources of transmissions, and our people can recognise the types of message. Another interesting point is that it's not just the ships at anchor in Orkney that have stopped broadcasting. So far as we can tell, all transmissions from the RAF and British army bases on the island have also ceased."

Raeder went over to the wall chart and pointed out the sites. "The only communications we can detect are broadcasts from wireless posts typically used for short range communications – ship-to-ship and ship-to-shore. These appear to be coming from Scapa Flow and the small islands around the anchorage."

"Is there any unusual activity at other bases?" snapped Hitler

"Yes, in fact the exact opposite appears to be happening in Rosyth, near Edinburgh." Raeder pointed to the Firth of Forth on the east coast of Scotland. "There is a large volume of wireless traffic between the naval headquarters and the ships there, and there are signs of several large warships getting ready for sea."

"How far is that from Scapa Flow?"

"About 300 km, Fuehrer, say ten hours' steaming."

"So, what conclusion do you draw from all this?"

Raeder answered. "Fuehrer, it is too early to be definite, but the sequence of events would most easily be explained by some sort of split within the British Navy, with the units in Scapa Flow no longer under the control of the naval chain of command."

"A mutiny?" asked Hitler.

"Not a mutiny as such. The officers and crew on the ships might still be obeying orders – it's just not clear who the orders are coming from. That's why I say a 'split'," replied Raeder.

"Is it possible to confirm that?"

"Not immediately. We have checked with Canaris, but we have no agents in the area, and obviously the British have not gone public with any information. If the ships from Rosyth sail north we will immediately be able to see whether they take up offensive positions relative to the ships in Scapa."

Hitler was dubious. "Even taking the most optimistic view, I find it hard to believe that the British ships would do us the huge service of blowing each other to pieces!"

"Perhaps not, Fuehrer, but a stand-off between the two most powerful task groups in the British Navy certainly reduces their ability to interfere with our invasion fleet, or indeed with a break-out by our naval units into the North Atlantic."

"Have there been any more messages from the Realists?"

"Not today, Fuehrer. As you know we don't have direct communication with them, so messages are taking several days to get through."

"What about Glasgow and Liverpool? Is there any further news?"

"There is no significant change, Fuehrer. There are still troop concentrations in the dock areas, though a few naval ships are entering and leaving the port. However, there's been one interesting occurrence that came after the transfer of the four ships from Portsmouth a week ago. Despite the civil unrest in the Clyde, the ships sent north were able to dock at the naval base there. That would seem to indicate some level of co-operation between the authorities who ordered the transfer, and those in control at the Clyde bases."

"What about the Mediterranean? Any update?"

"Fuehrer, three cruisers passed Gibraltar two days ago, heading into the Atlantic. Intelligence reports received by the Italians indicate that they are heading for Britain."

"Portsmouth or the Clyde?"

"That's not yet clear, Fuehrer."

"What's the latest news from the Bahamas?"

"We have been piecing together information obtained from travellers arriving in Florida. It appears that the Windsors left the island three days ago. A cruiser – our intelligence people believe it was HMS *Cumberland* – arrived unexpectedly in Nassau, allegedly to refuel. It left equally unexpectedly a few hours later, just after midnight. There were reports of unusual activity at the Windsor's villa in the late evening beforehand, and it is believed that the Royal couple embarked on the cruiser, although we don't yet have confirmation of this."

"What are the British saying?"

"They have said nothing officially, perhaps understandably. However it seems that there is a lot of confusion on the island, and there are also rumours that some of the patrol aircraft at Nassau airport were sabotaged. In any event there was a twelve hour delay before an air search got underway, by which time the cruiser was perhaps 500 kilometres out into the Atlantic, in some unknown direction. The British now appear to be sending out patrols in different directions, but the cruiser won't be easy to find. They have only a few aircraft based in the Bahamas, and the Atlantic is a big ocean. Every hour that passes makes the search area wider."

"Have any radio messages from the ship been picked up?"

"Not as yet, Fuehrer. That is perhaps to be expected. They wouldn't want to risk detection by other British forces in the area, and will probably wait until they are close to Europe before they break radio silence"

Hitler turned to Raeder. "Admiral, what conclusion do you draw from all these naval movements?"

"Fuehrer, the most logical explanation is that a large part of the Royal Navy is supporting the Realists, and is beginning to flex its muscles. They have already arranged the movement of ships away from the south coast, as agreed with us. It looks as if they have taken control at Scapa Flow, and possibly at the naval base in the Clyde. They have sent a warship to transfer King Edward VIII to a location where he can become a powerful voice in favour of a peace settlement. It appears as if the Royal Navy, or at least a significant part of it, is not convinced about the wisdom of continuing the war, and will refrain from intervening in the invasion battle."

"When do you expect them to make a move?"

"The senior officers won't come out publicly in support of the

Realists too early. There's too much of a risk that they might be removed. We expect that they'll wait until they feel the time is right... probably not until we launch Sea Lion – if that is your decision, Fuehrer. As soon as we do, we'll encourage the defectors with wireless broadcasts, calling on all Royal Navy ships to accept the inevitable and head north to Scottish ports, on the Forth or the Clyde. We will offer safe passage to those that do."

The march of events was clearly increasing, and Hitler decided to call another conference late in the evening. He started by letting Raeder repeat the information from Scapa Flow and Nassau. As the Admiral finished he asked him about the lack of information about the whereabouts of the cruiser carrying King Edward, and the significance of the radio silence.

"The lack of sightings is not a great surprise, Fuehrer. We have only a small number of U-boats in the area and a single merchant raider. I think that radio silence is also to be expected. They may not even be certain of their actual destination in Europe, as it's likely to depend on the status of any political moves underway here."

Hitler turned to von Ribbentrop.

"Have there been any developments on the political side that might give an insight into the disappearance of the Royal couple?"

"There has been some low-key speculation appearing in the American press today. Apparently a scheduled dinner between the Duke of... I'm sorry, King Edward VIII, and a visiting American film star was cancelled at short notice, allegedly as a result of the King being 'indisposed'. It's possible that the British are using that explanation to cover up their disappearance."

"Is there any further indication of who is going to emerge as the leader or spokesman for the Realists, and when that will happen?"

"There is no reliable information yet, Fuehrer, though there have been several suggestions. It seems unlikely that any leading figure will speak out before it becomes obvious that the battle is lost... the same as happened in France, when Marshal Petain stepped forward late in the day."

Hitler looked balefully at von Ribbentrop. "Petain came forward *after* the French army was defeated! Have you noticed that the British army is on the other side of the Channel?"

"It may not be necessary to defeat the British army, Fuehrer. What the army means to France, the Royal Navy and the RAF mean to Britain. Once their air force is beaten and their navy neutralised they will see themselves in the same unsustainable position as the French. As soon as it becomes clear that they're losing, that's when one would expect a new leader will emerge. It could be a military man, perhaps someone at a high level in the Royal Navy. Although it must be said that the British value their democracy highly, and it is more likely that a political figure will emerge as the new leader. It may even be someone not currently associated with the Realists. One possibility is that one of the mid-ranking members of the aristocracy will step forward."

Hitler was dubious. "All the signals that we are seeing at present are coming from the military side."

He turned to Hess "You know many of these people. What's your view?"

"Fuehrer, I remain convinced that the Duke of Hamilton is one of the leading Realists, not just the courier. As well as being a senior RAF officer he was also a Member of Parliament until recently. I think he is a more likely candidate than the other Lords who have been sympathetic towards us, such as the Duke of Bedford or the Duke of Wellington. Hamilton is younger, more energetic, and of course is a war hero."

Von Ribbentrop took over again. "There are possibilities on the political side as well, such as Halifax or Butler in the Foreign Office, or perhaps Chamberlain, although it seems that his health is poor. It certainly won't be Mosley, even if he were to be released from prison; he's much too divisive a figure and doesn't command public respect. Taking everything together, perhaps the most likely candidate would be Lloyd George, for similar reasons as Marshal Petain.

He would be seen as a wise leader, a genuine patriot who now recognizes the foolishness of leading Britain to annihilation. He is also recognised as being independent of Churchill and his policies. We learned recently that he was offered a position in the new Cabinet six months ago, but turned it down. One way or another, we expect that Churchill will quickly be deposed, once it's clear to the British establishment that his warlike approach is leading the country to disaster."

It was clear to Hitler that there was no consensus among his senior ministers, and he sought further information. "Does King George VI have any role in all this? Is it possible that he could insist on a change of Prime Minister?"

Von Ribbentrop knew the British constitution well, and was able to speak confidently. "He doesn't have that authority unless the government falls in Westminster. We think it more likely that once the battle starts going against them, the current Royal Family will leave for Canada to try to rally resistance there. As you know, the war supporters in Britain have stated that they will continue the fight from their bases in the Empire, even if Britain is lost. Our agents have heard rumours of a ship on stand-by to take them across the Atlantic."

"So, if he stays he ends up in our control and we either neuter him or depose him. If he leaves we have a replacement already identified."

"Yes, Fuehrer, as we have been planning for some time."

Hitler leant against the table with both hands, and spoke, staring at the map rather than his audience.

"Are our military preparations complete?"

"We are ready and await your orders, Fuehrer," replied Keitel.

"Give me the latest schedule and the latest intelligence reports"

"The schedule remains as we described it two days ago. Preliminary actions, diversionary moves and so on, can start on September 22nd. The units are already moving to their positions. Sea Lion can begin six days later, starting with an attack on their leadership – by which of course we mean Churchill, if we get a sighting of him."

"How would that be carried out?"

"It depends where we think he is. If we spot him at Chequers or Chartwell we'll use a special glider assault team – hand-picked men, all of them. If we believe that he's still in Downing Street we'll use a fighter-bomber raid, coming in at street level. We're confident that we can hit the building hard, but our chances of getting him won't be as high, since it's assumed that he'll be well protected, probably in a bunker of some description."

Hitler was silent for a few moments, then seemed to steel himself. He turned to face the group and spoke.

"Despite my fervent attempt to reach a settlement with Britain, their current government remains pig-headed and defiant. We have reached an impasse. Send one final, urgent message to the Realists, by radio, asking if they are ready to act. Demand their response by radio as well. If they are not able to do so, we must write them off, and get ready to act ourselves. One way or another we will now move to secure our western front before we embark on our crusade in the East. I will make my final decision in three days' time."

Chapter Twenty-One

The message broadcast on Radio Berlin was blunt.

'People of Britain, it is your final opportunity to take assertive action if you want to retain control of your nation's destiny. Rise up! Depose Churchill and his war-mongering government! Act now, before the German army is forced to act for you, in its own, very effective manner.'

Bracken and Menzies met in mid-morning to discuss the message. This time there was no mention of the Realists in it, but there was a clear urgency about the call.

"We could simply ignore it, Brendan, and let nature take its course. The clear threat is that they're about to launch the invasion if the Realists don't make their move, exactly as we want."

"You're probably right, C, but I'm still a bit nervous. There's a risk that the counsel of some of his saner advisors may prevail. Admiral Raeder, undoubtedly, will still be arguing hard against it. He's no fool, and he knows that he hasn't defanged the Royal Navy."

"So how should we respond? Is it time for the *dénouement* on Ethelred, as we've planned?"

"Nearly, but let's not expose the whole charade for a few hours yet. Hitler might still back off and blame his intelligence people for the debacle – maybe even fire Canaris, which would be a huge loss for us. We should give it one more twist, make one more grand offer and build up his hopes even further before we go for the jugular. Let's get a message together, and then we'd better check with the P.M."

Bracken stood up from the desk and began to pace the floor.

"Our preparations are complete. We are ready to strike at Churchill and his clique... Now let's think of something that will appeal to Raeder in particular."

"We could offer to withdraw the rest of our destroyers from the Channel if they start withdrawing their army from France. And maybe suggest a conference with... let's see... with the leaders of a new government and Windsor... in a neutral country, say Spain or Portugal," said Menzies.

"Yes, that's good. We don't need to be specific just who the new leader is – and actually Portugal fits rather nicely as a location. It's where Windsor was staying until quite recently, so it's a logical place to meet. We'd better put a timescale on it. Obviously all of this will take some time to organise – at least a week, let's say a few days more, so we'll suggest that, which will really frustrate him. Right, let's go on."

Two hours later they went to Churchill with their draft. He was comfortable with the script, making only a few minor alterations. He was also mentally prepared for Bracken's final remark.

"We've been thinking about who to invite from the German side, Winston."

Churchill wrinkled his nose and lips, as if dealing with a bad taste in his mouth.

"There can be no question about it," he answered quietly.

"Send an invitation to Hitler"

CHAPTER TWENTY-TWO

At the Fuehrer conference in mid-morning, the main item was the message received from the Realists late the previous evening. Von Ribbentrop opened the discussion.

"Fuehrer, they say they are ready to strike. They have offered to move two squadrons of destroyers from the south coast to Scotland, in return for us standing down two divisions in France. As soon as we start withdrawing our troops – which doesn't have to be a real withdrawal of course – they will act against Churchill. They suggest a high level meeting in Lisbon, in ten days' time, to negotiate a peace treaty."

Even Raeder was quite positive about the naval moves.

"If that were to happen it would be very positive for us, Fuehrer. It would leave the naval forces in the Channel area roughly balanced – a big improvement. Even if they changed their minds when we launch Sea Lion, it would take them a day or two to get the ships back. That's the critical window for us to get the first wave across."

Hitler looked again at the translated message, but seemed unimpressed.

"Ten days' time? Why can't they fly there tomorrow or the next day? The Reichsmarschall tells me that the British still have some aircraft left."

Goering shuffled uncomfortably at the Fuehrer's barb. Despite his frequent claims that the RAF had been destroyed, it was clear from the continuing air battles that they still had some reserves.

Von Ribbentrop continued to lead the conversation.

"The British delegation will, they say, include a Prime Minister and a senior Royal, and they have sent a specific invitation for you to attend in person, Fuehrer. The message seems to imply that there is an operational reason for the delay. Possibly one of the parties mentioned will be travelling by sea during that period. That could imply the attendance of King Edward. Or they need more time to carry out the takeover in the government. By the way, the expression they used is very significant, *A Prime Minister*, not *The Prime Minister*. Obviously the representative will not be Churchill; which would leave Chamberlain, Baldwin or Lloyd George who have held that position previously. Or it might be that they will have arrested Churchill and installed a successor, perhaps Halifax."

Hitler started to breathe heavily, clearly getting agitated. "A successor? What clown suggested that? Has there been any sign of weakening in Churchill's position?"

"None that we can positively confirm, Fuehrer. Not since the unrest in Liverpool and Glasgow, and at Scapa Flow recently."

"Unrest! That so-called unrest has led absolutely nowhere! What is happening in the ports now, Canaris?"

"Fuehrer, our last reconnaissance photographs indicate that the troops appear to have left the streets in Liverpool and Glasgow. The ports appear to be quiet. Merchant ships and naval escorts are leaving as normal." Canaris was still desperately trying to stop the invasion.

"What about Scapa Flow?" he barked.

"All appears to be quiet there. The airfield has re-opened. Several of the major warships that had taken up defensive positions there left the anchorage overnight."

"Which direction are they heading?"

"South, Fuehrer."

"South?" His face was beginning to redden.

"Yes Fuehrer, apparently towards Rosyth." It wasn't at all clear yet where they were heading, but Canaris had kept putting the question to different intelligence officers until he got the answer he wanted. It suited his case, and as long as he could refer back to a source he couldn't be accused of invention.

"I was told that the ships in Rosyth would be sailing north, to take over Scapa Flow!" screamed Hitler.

There was no response from Canaris or anyone else in the cowed audience.

"And their Mediterranean Fleet, Raeder? You're going to tell me that they've been having a regatta?"

"No, Fuehrer. The cruisers that left four days ago were detected by U-92 yesterday."

"Good. At least there is someone in the Kriegsmarine doing their job properly. Where are they?"

"About 200 kilometres west of Gibraltar."

"About 200 kilometres! Five hours' steaming time away! Why wasn't I told? Who was the fool that didn't see the importance of this? He should be shot!"

Suddenly another message was brought in. The BBC had announced, quite curtly, that Mr Chamberlain had resigned from the Cabinet on health grounds, and that Lord Halifax would be leaving to take up a new post. Unusually there were no words of praise for their long service or devotion to duty.

In the Berghof an urgent debate got underway. What did it mean? Those two were the British Cabinet members who were expected to oppose Churchill. Had the Realists made their move? Had they been discovered and defeated? Was a struggle underway even as they spoke? As they continued to debate, a further message came in and von Ribbentrop brought it straight to their attention.

"Churchill will be speaking on the BBC at six o'clock, English time."

Hitler ordered a translation to be brought to him as soon as Churchill finished.

The Oxford-educated translators began work under great pressure. They knew the importance of the message, and carefully compared their notes as they worked. Thirty minutes later the Fuehrer sat reading Churchill's speech, much of his powerful English carried skilfully across into German by the interpreters.

'The hour is approaching when we, the men, women and children of Britain, will confront the most grievous threat to our nation in our lifetime, perhaps in all our proud history. Having conquered much of Europe, Hitler's divisions now stand ready to cross the English Channel, in the futile hope of conquering this land, this scepter'd isle. They are determined to enslave us as they have enslaved others. Well let them try. The fish need feeding.

The battle will be hard, but we are strong and ready. The great nation that is Britain will not touch the forelock to that man, that monster.

There will be no surrender; that day will never come.

There will be no appeasement; those days have gone forever.

There will be no response to siren calls for realism. The only realism that the Hun will meet will be the cold steel of our bayonets and the even colder steel in our eyes.

Let us prepare ourselves for battle. Let us bear ourselves proudly.

Let us steel ourselves to see this great test through, in full confidence that victory will be ours.

God Save the King.'

Hitler stood reading the message, only slightly bowdlerised by the embarrassed interpreters. He glowered at the group around him, and raised his voice angrily.

"This is turning into a large stinkpot. For all the bravado in the messages from these Realists, there is not a sign, not a single sign, of upheaval in London. Churchill goes on radio with his warlike broadcasts, and no-one interferes. Not one person in the British parliament has raised their voice to say. *'We want peace'*. I have tried to be generous. God in heaven I have tried!! I have offered to spare their Navy; allow them keep their monarchy; even let them keep their Empire! I stopped bombing London for four days as a gesture of my good faith. What have I got in return? Absolutely nothing! A few old warships moved a few hundred kilometres away, to Scotland, from where they can return overnight. That fool Windsor has disappeared somewhere in the middle of the ocean. If he is coming to Europe, why has he not sent any messages? Do their ships not have radio? Now they ask for a meeting in ten days' time! And what will happen then? Some lackey will appear to explain that their leaders have unfortunately been delayed! 'Difficulties in travel', he'll pretend! 'Bad weather in the Atlantic', perhaps?"

He slammed his fist on the table, and shouted.

"There is always bad weather in the Atlantic!!"

"I see it all now. The British are playing for time! Churchill says that he is ready to fight. But it's all posturing. Secretly he hopes that I will fall into their trap; that I will be frightened by his defiant bluster; that I will base my hopes on this pantomime meeting in Lisbon. He knows a delay of ten days would cause us to miss the tides at the end of September. And after that the next possible date is in late October, with the winter gales approaching! There is a stench to this. This is all Churchill's doing. This is all a sham! Even their French allies call them *Perfidious Albion*. Well, two parties can play at that game. I have finally lost my patience. They will now find what kind of man I am! Send a reply to that insulting message from the Realists, whoever they pretend to be. Tell them I agree to the damned meeting in Lisbon. Let them sit there on their fat arses in London, thinking they are fooling me. As they sit there playing with themselves, I will launch the apocalypse upon them."

He took several breaths, almost hyperventilating, and turned to his generals.

"Proceed with Sea Lion – on the date planned!"

He turned and strode from the room.

CHAPTER TWENTY-THREE

The morning of September 29th broke gently over the English Channel; the sea was calm; the wind no more than a zephyr. A light fog lay on the water, painting the world a grey, pastel hue. The few souls who remained in the near-deserted villages knew that, with almost no breeze to disperse the haze, it would take an hour or two before the sun could burn through. By itself the autumnal mist was familiar, even comforting. But there was something about the scene that was disconcerting. Despite the poor visibility, not a single fog horn could be heard. In this busy part of the coastline that was more than unusual, it was eerie. As the morning wore on and the mist gradually lifted, the reason for the silence became clear: there was not a ship to be seen. It could have been a deserted seascape off the west of Scotland rather than the busy coast of Kent. Just twelve months ago this narrow patch of sea would have been alive with dozens of vessels: coasters and passenger ferries; naval ships and fishing boats, all making their way through the busiest shipping lanes in the world. Today, however, the only sound to be heard was the screeching of gulls, punctuated from time to time by the languid slap of a wave on wet sand.

The beaches were empty. Where, a year ago, children would have been playing in the sand or splashing about at the water's edge, now there was no-one; not an early morning walker or a fisherman to be seen. The nearest people were a hundred yards away, invisible, sequestered away in pillboxes and lookout posts. The bored troops looked out on beaches festooned with vicious-looking coils of barbed wire and ugly signs, warning of mines. At Folkestone beach, if anyone had entertained thoughts about risking an incursion, or thought the *Danger* signs were bluffs, the repulsive sight of a dog's corpse, lying in bloody fragments in a crater just above the high water mark would have quickly changed their mind.

The skies, too, were empty. There was only the occasional sound of an aircraft in the far distance. Even as the morning wore on and patches of blue sky began to open up, there was hardly a contrail to be seen; there was not a sign of the vast air fleets that had been pounding Britain for the last three months.

None of the grim defenders on the shore believed that the calm was more than temporary. It was just a matter of time. All along the coastline men were at their posts, watching and waiting for the expected onslaught. Further inland, at sector stations and command centres, the suspense was just as heavy. Radar controllers looked at blank screens, and plotters waited by tables that were empty of markers. On the battered airfields, tired pilots sat around their messes playing cards or lolled about in the weak sunshine, glad of the chance for some rest before the storm. The interlude had come as a welcome relief for these tired warriors, too drained by the exertions of recent weeks to worry what might happen tomorrow or the next day. They just needed sleep, now.

In the Cabinet War Rooms, there was growing apprehension that the hour was almost come. Staff were looking increasingly fatigued, not due to any physical exertions, but to tension; the tension of not knowing when it would start; of listening for any hint of a change; of jumping at every telephone call. It even affected the normally imperturbable Churchill, who went across to the Map Room in late morning to check on things, as if he wouldn't have heard within a minute of any significant occurrence.

"Still nothing?"

"No, Prime Minister. The last update was an hour ago, and there was no sign of activity on the other side. They won't be coming tonight."

It was clear, however, that they wouldn't have long to wait. The lack of aerial activity could mean only one thing; the Germans were preparing their forces for a full-out assault – if not this evening, then within a day, maybe two. It was time for the Cabinet and the Chiefs to move to the Paddock, the secret underground citadel which had been constructed at Dollis Hill in north-west London. Around the offices and corridors in the War Rooms a gentle buzz of activity was building, as people began sorting out the essentials for the transfer. For the first time since the crisis began, the full scale of the army of people drafted in to support the Cabinet became apparent; staff officers, secretaries, clerks, communications specialists, cipher clerks, facilities engineers, kitchen staff, and others whose role was not immediately obvious, perhaps security men.

It all seemed to be going smoothly enough, but, shortly before noon, Bracken came down to speak to Churchill and saw Colville standing outside the Prime Minister's office, not looking at all happy.

"What's up, Jock? You're looking a bit frayed, and the invasion hasn't even started!"

Colville nodded towards the door. "He's just thrown a complete wobbler about the move to the Paddock. The office is nearly packed, half the staff have already moved over, and now he says it's dank and depressing, he doesn't like it and he won't go until the invasion actually starts. He's like a petulant child at times. Christ, I'd rather be in the front line. I wonder if Hitler is any easier to work with. I might change sides."

"Well, as a civil servant you may get the chance soon enough," said Bracken, not encouragingly. "I'll have a word."

He knocked and went in.

"I hear you've refused to go to the Paddock, Winston. Proper order, too. A man's entitled to a bit of comfort in his work, even in wartime. The Germans probably don't have any maps showing where Whitehall is, and even if they do, and bomb us, sure what does it matter? The staff can be replaced easily enough. As for yourself, I'm sure Halifax or Attlee would do just as good a job fighting the Huns as you."

Churchill scowled at him. "In Russia I'd have you shot for that insolence."

Bracken continued, undaunted, "No you wouldn't, Winston. You'd have had me shot months ago. Probably as soon as you became Prime Minister – I know where the bodies lie buried."

Churchill looked at him grumpily and continued in similar vein, but the steel had left his voice.

"In any event, the first part of your statement, that I do not care about my staff, is a vicious calumny, vile and untrue. The second part – that Attlee or Halifax would do as good a job – is merely, I believe, untrue. If I thought otherwise I'd gladly hand over power. Alright, dammit, you've made your point. I will go. But I warn you, Bracken, if I catch pneumonia I'll hold you and Hitler jointly responsible. And if I die, I'll come down and haunt you both."

"Or up as the case may be, sir. Thank you, Prime Minister."

Bracken bowed obsequiously.

Outside the door, Colville waited, still rigid with frustration. Bracken acknowledged him, but spoke only a few words. There were things to do.

"You can continue with the move, Jock," he said, and strode past.

Colville turned and looked at the gangling figure in wonderment as he disappeared down the corridor.

By late afternoon the transfer was complete. The Cabinet, the Chiefs and their support staff settled down to their subterranean life, forty feet below a quiet suburban street; for how long, none of them knew. People began to find their way round the long, harshly-lit corridors, and gradually got used to the background noise, the hum of ventilation machines, and the chatter of telephone switches and teleprinters. Gradually an air of functionality emerged. The facilities were adequate, if basic, and the communications links to the operational commands seemed to be working well. Just off the main corridor one of the secretaries had smuggled a bunch of flowers and a picture of some pretty English countryside into her workspace. It made at least one corner of the place a bit less dungeon-like. The staff had been forced to be selective in the material they had brought over, especially in regard to personal possessions. They would be sleeping in bunk beds, in dormitories, with only a small locker each for storage. *Not as bad as a submarine*, thought Admiral Pound, as he looked around. *At least we don't have to hot bunk.*

At 1700, Churchill convened a short Cabinet meeting in the Paddock War Room. There wasn't much to discuss, but at least everyone made their way there and found their seat. Then they all moved over to the Map Room and checked it out as well. As the afternoon wore on, there was still no news. The tension was becoming unbearable. How long could they stay in this state of suspended animation, waiting for the enemy to make the first move?

Ismay was thoughtful. He could feel the sense of frustration rising; a desire to be doing something, but he had to ensure that the unexpected pause wasn't allowed to interfere with their carefully-prepared plans. They needed to be self-disciplined, and conscious not to make any imprudent moves just because of the absence of German activity. At the same time this delay was itself a change in circumstance, and they might need to tailor their plans accordingly. He spoke to Churchill. "It has to be the calm before the storm, Prime Minister. I wonder should we talk to Dowding about moving up some of the fighter reserves."

"I've been thinking about that too, Pug. It does seem the natural thing to do. On the other hand... if the Germans were to spot the movements... is there a risk that it might derail the entire Ethelred strategy? God knows we've already paid such a large price in lives... to put it at risk now... But you're right. We didn't factor such an interminable delay into our thinking. We should at least consider whether it changes anything. Let's speak to him."

A few minutes later Dowding arrived, and the discussion began about whether the complete absence of enemy activity warranted any adjustments to the plan.

"General Ismay and I have been discussing whether we should re-lease some of the fighter reserves. It would seem clear that the Luft-waffe is preparing itself for a great onslaught, perhaps tomorrow, perhaps the day after, as the curtain-raiser to the crossing. Should we do anything different to be ready for them?"

Dowding responded immediately. "Prime Minister, my men have been under huge pressure, for many weeks now. It would help greatly if we could release some extra fighters and fresh pilots from the reserve straightaway."

"I can understand your empathy with the men, Air Chief Mar-shall, but please give me something more by way of justification – especially with regard to the timing." Churchill wanted more than just a simple request before agreeing.

"Yes sir. Let me give you my analysis. The enemy is obviously do-ing its final preparation at present... last minute maintenance... pi-lot briefings and so on. After going through all that, they're pretty much committed to launching the attack soon afterwards. If they were simply to switch back to their old pattern they'd lose much of the advantage gained. Their planes and pilots would again be some-what wearied when they were most needed – for the actual crossing. As well as which, the longer they sit around waiting the more time it gives us to patch up damage and replace our losses. I think it's certain that this current limbo will be followed by the invasion."

"So, should we not just continue to wait for them, as per the plan?"

"Well, we didn't plan for such a gap, sir. We assumed that their assault would build steadily to a peak. But they now seem, instead, to be taking the time to maximise their strength before the attack. So we should probably do the same – or at least appear to. In fact, it's probably no more than they'd expect."

Churchill seemed to accept the comments. "What about the question of timing? Can we afford to wait until we see them coming?"

"I wish I could be certain, Prime Minister. It's still my personal belief that they'll hold back the main air assault until the day of the crossing. On the morning of the landings, I expect them to launch a fierce dawn attack on the radar stations and coastal guns, and then switch to close escort of the armada as it nears our coast. That, of course, means that we would spot the start of the embarkation activity the day before, and have time to move up our reserves and get ready. So we could indeed wait until they begin to embark... if I'm right."

As ever, Dowding was professional and level-headed in his approach. With unusual candour for a senior officer, he continued.

"However, to be frank, sir, there's always the chance that I'm wrong; that they might see things differently. They might decide to attack earlier, perhaps a surprise assault before embarkation starts – especially if they don't expect the RAF to put up much of a fight. That could even mean it happening tomorrow, without any forewarning. Having more fighters ready for that eventuality would be prudent."

Churchill listened intently, before commenting. "The other side of the coin is that we might compromise the whole Ethelred plan if they were to spot our reinforcements on the move."

"I accept that, sir. However at the moment there is so little German air activity – not even reconnaissance sorties – that it seems unlikely they would recognise what was happening. We could perhaps limit ourselves to feeding back the detached flights, three or four aircraft each, to the current frontline squadrons rather than releasing whole squadrons from the reserve. Even if the Germans make a pre-emptive attack at dawn and find resistance rather stiffer that they expected, it's a bit late for them to change their plans."

The Air Chief Marshall had made his argument well and Churchill was satisfied. "Alright, Dowding, I agree. On balance it seems the right thing to do. You can release the detached flights back to their squadrons straightaway... give them a chance to settle in, just in case the Luftwaffe does launch its assault tomorrow. The hidden squadrons, though, you must continue to hold back as per the original plan. We'll wait until the invaders are actually on their way and, even then, release them only in phases – just enough to protect the Navy's destroyers to start with. It is vital that we continue to disguise our strength until they set sail, both to deceive them and to conserve our strength, so that we may despatch them.

"I am determined to wait until their second wave, at the very least, is under way, before we make a serious response. Hopefully we'll still feel confident enough to let it land before we unleash our full strength. If we can wait even longer, until their third wave is on the high seas, then so much the better."

Under the strain, even Churchill was showing some hesitation. Ethelred clearly envisaged the second wave being allowed to land, and the third to sail, not just that they would 'hopefully' feel confident enough to let them. Perhaps it was just a slip of the tongue. Certainly there were no changes suggested to the battle plan.

Dowding left the meeting and made a telephone call. The orders were issued. From their hidden shelters deep in the woods and glades of rural England, the detached RAF flights were summoned. Before nightfall a hundred fighters had returned to their hard-pressed squadrons, who were delighted to see them. The planes were quickly refuelled and dispersed to shelters around the perimeters of the airfields. The fresh pilots were assigned to fly the dawn patrols in the morning, getting aloft early in case of sneak German attacks under the radar. The additional resources would give the tired front-liners the chance for an extra hour or two of sleep.

Although there was no discussion of any grander scheme, there were enough hints around for the pilots to know that something very big was stirring. There were persistent rumours of squadrons secreted away in deep cover. At twelve of the main fighter stations, the station commanders were briefed to be ready to receive another full squadron of Spitfires or Hurricanes within a day or so. Gradually they began to realise the scale of what was happening. They realised that the cat-and-mouse game they had been playing with the enemy for the last month would soon be over. It was clear that, within a few hours of the embarkation getting underway in the French ports, the frontline strength of RAF fighters facing the Luftwaffe would be more than tripled. Even if the Germans were to spot some of the movements, it would leave very little time for their intelligence people to piece together any conclusion – and much too late to turn around the juggernaut in motion in the ports. The Luftwaffe flyers would be in for a shock... and soon after them, the rest of the invasion force.

At the British naval bases, too, tension was building. In ports from Harwich to Plymouth, crews began to ready their ships for sea, excited, if anxious, about finally seeing action. For more than three months they had been anticipating this moment, this destiny. Officers and men alike shared the patriotic emotion, but the ships' captains had an even greater reason for optimism. At a secret briefing the previous day, they had been informed that the RAF would be committing an additional 200 fighters to protect them. Suddenly the odds were looking a lot better.

Late in the evening the Cabinet sat down for its final review of the day. While they knew that the invasion fleet was still in port, clearly there wasn't long to go. There was, in fact, little to discuss... the Forces were at the ready... the additional fighters had arrived at their squadrons... President Roosevelt had sent a message of encouragement. Just before midnight the meeting ended and the Cabinet members retired to catch a few hours sleep, the last they expected to enjoy for many days. Even Churchill, a notorious night owl, knew better than to keep his staff working into the small hours, in view of what was going to confront them imminently. He made the small gesture of speaking to them individually, particularly the female secretaries, who would perhaps feel least comfortable in the austere surroundings of the bunker. Finally he closed the door on his room and, save for the duty officers and a handful of security and communications staff, the Paddock settled down for the night.

The quiet did not last long.

Shortly after 0230, a door was suddenly flung open at the end of the corridor leading to the accommodation quarters. A commotion could be heard. The sergeant on duty outside the Prime Minister's room rose to his feet and unholstered his revolver, before he was able to identify the approaching figure. It was Brigadier Menzies, who was insistent on speaking to the Prime Minister immediately. The sergeant told him that his orders were that the Prime Minister was not to be disturbed unless the invasion had started.

"Sergeant, I have vital information about the invasion that the Prime Minister must hear at once. I am going in. I am unarmed. You can shoot me in the back if you want."

His words were powerful enough to get the sergeant to acquiesce. It was most unusual for the Prime Minister's sleep to be disturbed, but if Menzies needed to talk urgently...

"Just a moment, sir." The sergeant knocked on the door and went in, closing the door behind him.

"Sorry to disturb you, Prime Minister, but Brigadier Menzies needs to speak to you. He says it's most urgent." Churchill stirred from his sleep, half-raised himself in his bed and pulled a peacock-blue dressing gown round his shoulders. The sergeant held the door closed for a few moments, to give the Prime Minister time to compose himself, then let the visitor in and withdrew.

"I assume this is important, C. Has it started?"

"No sir. Something perhaps even more important..."

"Well, what?"

"An urgent message from Admiral Canaris, sir."

"Go on," said Churchill, alert, though still rubbing the sleep from his eyes.

"It says, and I quote: *'Operation Sea Lion is about to be launched. Do not let the Realists have their way. You must hold on. Hitler has ordered the invasion of Russia in the Spring.'*"

"Operation Sea Lion?"

"Their codeword for the invasion. He passed it to us some weeks ago. There was no need to spread it around."

Churchill suddenly sat bolt upright in his bed as the rest of the message sank in.

"You said Russia? Russia??"

"Yes sir."

For a moment he was totally stunned. He stared into Menzies' eyes, waiting to hear if there was any further explanation or any caveat to come. There was none.

"Can it be true? A war on two fronts! I hadn't dared hope the man could be so stupid."

All feeling of tiredness had disappeared.

"So this is why Canaris wanted to meet you! Are you certain it's genuine? How did it get to you?"

"By the usual courier, sir, completely trustworthy, though I won't go into all the details. Let's just say that with me in my role and Admiral Canaris in his, we've been able to establish a very reliable link."

"Reliable... and dependable?"

"Completely, sir, though of course for the Admiral and his courier, very risky."

"Are you absolutely confident that it is from Canaris?"

He swung his legs over the side of the bed.

"As certain as it's possible to be. We agreed a method of authentication some time ago, and he's used that. As well as which it's possible to glean quite a bit of information from the timing, and the actual wording. I know the exact route it came by, and from that, that it must have been prepared three or four days ago. Clearly he already knew at that point that the go-ahead for the invasion had been given. His note also links back to previous messages."

"The 'Sea Lion' codeword?"

"That, and also that he's familiar with all the filaments that we have been spinning as part of Ethelred. It's the first time he's referred to 'The Realists' – he actually uses the English words, which shows how aware he is of the picture that we have been painting, that the whole government edifice here is in danger of collapsing."

"So even our sympathisers in Germany have bought into the deception? Apart from anything else, that is most encouraging. But one obvious question, C, would he expect *us* to know the actual name of a traitorous group here?"

"That's a reasonable question, sir, but it's not unlikely that he would. Lord Haw Haw used the expression recently, and you used the word yourself in your broadcast a few days ago – which all hardly looks like a coincidence. They probably surmise that we became aware of the conspiracy and then ascertained the name of the group quite easily. They probably think that we'd use the same interrogation methods that they do themselves."

"What? Pliers and fingernails? Against Edward and Neville? I hardly think so!" He paused for a moment, clearly very concerned, and then looked hard at Menzies.

"Is there another possibility? You know this murky business better than anyone... could the Hitlerites have rumbled Canaris? Could they have forced him to plant a false message?"

"It's the very first thought that came into my mind, sir, but I can't see how it fits. The message was authenticated in the agreed way – which it wouldn't have been if he'd been compelled to send it. As well as which, urging us to fight on and giving us crucial information to encourage us just doesn't fit with any deception ploy that I can think of."

"Russia, Russia, Russia...." Churchill mumbled to himself, mantra-like, before looking directly at Menzies. "You realise that this changes everything?"

"I do, sir. That's why I woke you."

"Sergeant," he bellowed, "Get the Cabinet convened in fifteen minutes, and the Chiefs as well. Call Jock first and get him to help round them up."

He put his feet into his slippers and stood up.

"C, you will please join me in the War Room to convey this information. You may proclaim your total confidence about the reliability of the information, and I will support you – but banish from your mind the name of the source."

By 0315 the War Cabinet had gathered, all of them unkempt, and several looking rather disorientated. Churchill and Menzies entered the room together and sat down, as the group looked at them expectantly.

"It is rarely, if ever, a good idea to interfere with a battle plan at the very last moment. However C has just brought some dramatic information that we must discuss. Brigadier..."

Menzies relayed the news to the dumbstruck group.

"Are you absolutely certain that the message is genuine?" asked Eden.

"Absolutely. I know the origin; I know the motivation of the sender. We've received similar information from this same source, at various times in the past, via the same route. We didn't share it with you, and indeed we didn't always act upon the earlier messages due to our own doubts about their authenticity. In retrospect they turned out to be one hundred per cent accurate. Had we acted it could have made a considerable difference in our favour in both Norway and France. More recently, the information that the Admiralty naval ciphers had been broken came from this same source. Since we changed them there has been a noticeable reduction in U-boat attacks."

Eden had recognised the import of the news as soon as he heard it. "If this really is genuine, it means that we've just got to hold out for another six months, most of which is winter, when a crossing would be impossible." There was a murmur of agreement around the table.

Churchill looked at him soberly. "That is precisely why we must consider this information at once – to see whether it has any effect whatsoever on our battle plan."

Pound butted in immediately, the wise old head on his shoulders being alarmed by the prospect of a rushed, middle-of-the-night revision. "Sir, battle is likely to be joined in a matter of hours. Whether this information is true or not, it's much too late to change our plans."

"Admiral, just a few days ago were you not asking me to do precisely that, in respect of the light cruisers?"

"No, Prime Minister, I was not. I was requesting additional resources in support of the current plan."

"In this case, might it not amount to the same thing?"

Halifax was the most agitated. "Prime Minister, if I may remind you, our fears for the longer term – that we would be unable to sustain the fight on our own indefinitely – was the *only* reason that we embarked on this dangerous course. Now, unlikely as it might have seemed just an hour ago, we have the prospect of a powerful ally in the East, and our fears of a lone struggle into the future have evaporated. We must reconsider. We would never have embarked on this rash adventure, this 'Ethelred', if we'd received this intelligence earlier."

Churchill looked over his glasses at Halifax. "Be that as it may, Foreign Secretary, at this juncture we have to look forward from where we find ourselves, not backwards at what might have been."

General Dill spoke up. "Prime Minister, they may well be on their way in twenty four hours, whatever we decide upon now. It would be foolish in the extreme to do anything other than proceed with the existing plan. All the elements are in place, and our deception measures appear to have been successful. Ethelred was conceived in order to inflict a great blow upon the enemy, and that opportunity for a decisive victory still presents itself – for the first time in this war. We must proceed with the agreed plan."

"At an estimated cost of a quarter of a million casualties, General?" said Attlee, quietly.

Such a figure for dead and wounded was at the top end of the estimates, and was before the civilian evacuations and protection measures had been put in action. But the number had certainly been mentioned.

Churchill looked at Attlee for a moment, quite sombrely, clearly recognising the validity of the interjection, but anxious to achieve consensus among the Cabinet. He looked around the table at the tense faces.

"Gentlemen, if we had received this new information earlier, we might well have been working on an entirely different strategy. As it is, however, we have a plan in place, and nothing has yet been decided in this room, never mind left this room, that changes our approach one iota. However what we must decide, within the hour, is whether there's anything we could do now, and should do now, taking into account this new intelligence which might be advantageous – and which would not risk utter chaos in our battle plans."

Attlee was the first to respond. "If I may loosely quote you from some weeks ago, Prime Minister, perhaps we should forget about being the sausage grinder and concentrate on sending the meat back to the butcher. Then let the Russians take over the grinding next year."

There was silence for a moment, before Ismay spoke, reminding the group of the reality of their position. "If I might make a comment, Prime Minister, we need to be crystal clear in our thinking. The Ethelred strategy is to bring the enemy onto us, mount a stubborn defence against the early waves, and withdraw slowly as we continue to inflict heavy casualties on them. Our hammer blow is only to be unleashed only after the bulk of their invasion army is ashore. That underlying strategy affects every aspect of our deployment, our overall plan of battle, and our tactics. The only conceivable change within our ambit would be to pull the great blow forward, to try to stop the first or second waves gaining a foothold. I really believe that a clear decision on the feasibility or otherwise of that is the only issue at stake."

Churchill readily accepted Ismay's statement. "That is a profound summary, General, and should help focus our thinking." He looked at the wall clock. "The time now is almost 0345. The landings may well take place at dawn tomorrow in, let's see, about twenty-seven hours' time. If they leave it for even a few more days beyond that my understanding is that the tides start to become unfavourable. Admiral, your perspective, please. What might we change in our naval plan overnight, if we were of a mind to do so?"

Pound knew that there was a difficult conversation to come, but started bravely.

"Very little, Prime Minister. I would simply renew my request for the six light cruisers already in the southern ports to be released to me straight away. If the Germans start their crossing tomorrow, there are no other resources that I can bring to bear before the first wave lands."

"What about the Home Fleet?"

"No, Prime Minister, that is not practicable."

Churchill glared at him for a moment, then decided to move on. "I will come back to that most disturbing statement shortly. Air Chief Marshall, what might we change on the air side? Is it time to resurrect our 'Lazarus' squadrons from the woods?"

"Prime Minister, yesterday evening we moved up a hundred more fighters to provide extra cover for the airfields. We still have about two hundred ready to commit, to protect the Royal Navy's destroyers as they begin to harry the invasion fleet, and then a further two hundred or so in reserve, to cover the decisive sortie by the Home Fleet."

"Are they all ready for action?"

"Absolutely, sir, armed and fuelled – and the frontline bases designated for them are ready as well. I could move the next group of fighters up at first light, though we would need to be careful that they don't arrive at their new bases, short on fuel, just as the Luftwaffe begins its attack.

"I assume you can manage that?" Churchill commented irascibly. He didn't need to know the operational details.

"Yes sir."

"What about our bombers?"

"During the crossing we'll use our torpedo-carrying aircraft, the new Beauforts and the Fleet Air Arm's Swordfish. The crews have been specially trained for night attacks. That's about a hundred aircraft in all, and with the short distances involved, they should be able to get in a couple of sorties each before daylight. That won't stop the invasion of course, but with so many targets we can hope to inflict quite a bit of damage. As for the rest of our bombers, the plan has been to hold them back from the battle. In darkness, high-level bombers just can't see their targets, and if they try to attack at low-level, the likelihood is they'll just fly into the sea. Until now we've ruled out day attacks because of the high losses associated with them... but if we had three or four hundred Spitfires protecting them..."

"Are they ready to go, if needed?"

"Within twelve hours, sir. The bomber crews have had some training for an attack on the invasion fleet, even though it hasn't been our intention to use them this way. They had to be, or the Germans might have spotted the anomaly when interrogating POWs, and perhaps become suspicious."

"As long as twelve hours?"

"Yes, I'm afraid so, sir. The aircraft are fuelled up, but the bomb loads will have to be changed. We've been using incendiaries against the ports, and those will need switched for high explosive or armour-piercing bombs to use against ships. We'll also need to make a detailed plan of operation, plot the exact enemy locations, decide on our approach routes, co-ordinate the fighter cover and so on. It all takes time. The big difference now is that with hundreds of fighters protecting them, it wouldn't seem like a suicide mission anymore."

Although Churchill himself had raised the question about use of the bomber squadrons, he didn't want an answer based on bravado, and now played devil's advocate. "We might indeed be able to provide that fighter cover, but is it not the case that, over London, the German fighters failed to prevent heavy losses to their bomber fleets?"

"That is so, Prime Minister, but even when using our full fighter strength we rarely inflicted more than ten or fifteen per cent losses on them in any single raid. We might well regard such a level of losses as an acceptable price to pay for stopping an invasion."

Churchill was listening attentively. "Indeed we might. On the other hand do I not recall us suffering casualties in excess of fifty per cent in some daylight raids in France? Our squadrons would not last long at such a rate of attrition."

The question may have been rhetorical. In any event there was no answer. It was clear that not much had changed since the early days, when they had decided not to use the RAF's bombers against the invasion fleet.

Churchill returned to the naval options.

"Admiral Pound, I would like to come back to your earlier comments. Please explain why it isn't practicable to deploy the Home Fleet against the first wave."

Pound was certain of his facts, but now felt under great emotional pressure. He had to explain the situation clearly and persuasively to avoid a catastrophic decision being taken. "Prime Minister, the fleet is on three hours' readiness to sail, but as far as an intervention in the Channel is concerned, it can only leave Rosyth within a narrow time window on any given day. The exact schedule has been worked out after weeks of painstaking effort... sailing times, the complicated transit routes to avoid minefields, the actual engagement battle, and the subsequent withdrawal. We have missed the window for today."

He felt himself tensing up.

"And before going any further I must express my extreme concern about the way that this discussion is drifting... looking for an instant alternative to that complex plan. The decisive blow against the invasion is to be delivered by my battle fleet; four battleships, ten cruisers and their escorts – three quarters of the Home Fleet – heading south to engage and destroy the invaders. I think it important to describe that mission in some detail. The first segment is a passage down the east coast, when they will be within range of German long range bombers, to say nothing of the other threats they face from submarines and E-boats. Our battle plan is that we will have continuous protection by our fighters during the daylight hours as they sail south. And now I hear suggestions that we may have deployed our fighters elsewhere! The RAF may hope that, by throwing its reserves into the fray to protect our bombers, it might achieve a great aerial victory – but there is a real risk that our fighters might suffer heavy losses, which would then leave the cover for my ships threadbare when it's most needed."

"That is a valid objection, Admiral, which we certainly need to consider. Now if we were to decide to throw all our strength at the enemy at the earliest possible time, when could you release the fleet?" Churchill didn't seem to have been listening.

"Sir, as I have just explained, it's on three hours' notice to sail. With more than a thousand men on a battleship it takes that long to muster the crew and raise steam. So if given the order now, the earliest they could leave is about 0700. From Rosyth, in the Firth of Forth, to the Channel will take about twenty hours. Unfortunately, as you know, there's no suitable base any closer. Now here's the rub. From the time they sail, it's likely that the movements will be spotted by the Germans within an hour or two. If we despatch the Home Fleet too early – before their invasion fleet has put to sea – it's quite conceivable that they would simply put the entire operation on hold, and concentrate all their resources on destroying the Home Fleet. I don't need to spell out the implication of that. If they were to succeed, they could then simply invade us at their leisure."

Now Churchill was certainly listening, and pursed his lips. "That is a cataclysmic prospect, Admiral, which must be avoided at all costs. But is it not precisely the same risk that the fleet faces under the existing plan?"

Again Pound bristled with frustration. "No sir, it is not. Under the current plan, the timing of the fleet's departure is determined by us. It will leave the Firth of Forth at 0300 on the chosen day and, as light comes, continue its journey south under the RAF's air umbrella. I'm confident that our fighters can handle any threat from the Luftwaffe's high-level bombers, which would be operating at a considerable distance from their bases, well beyond the range of their usual Me109 escorts. My battleships will only proceed into southern waters, close to France, and within range of dive bombers and the 109s, as night falls, when the darkness will shield them from aerial attack. They will continue south in the darkness, reaching the Channel shortly after midnight, and then unleash hell for a few hours. They will attack the enemy's supply ships and destroy all and sundry. They will bombard the ports that they are sailing from. They'll wreak havoc on any beaches that the Germans have landed on. After this fierce and furious engagement, the fleet will withdraw north – back out of range of the Stukas – before dawn. That, Prime Minister, is the plan that the Naval Staff decided upon a month ago, and which has been formally approved by this Cabinet."

Pound stared at Churchill, who chose to respond calmly, deliberately ignoring the emotion in Admiral Pound's words. Or perhaps he still didn't appreciate the preciseness of the schedule.

"And would it be so different if they were ordered to sail now, just a few hours later?"

"Prime Minister, if I were to despatch the fleet now, as you suggest, we would indeed do the same great damage to the first wave of invaders. However as we withdraw north after the assault my ships would be within the danger zone for a full three hours or so of daylight. There would be more than adequate time for hundreds of Stukas, protected by hundreds of Messerschmitts, to make devastating attacks on them."

"Admiral, that is a grave warning, which I hear most clearly. However, in view of the threat to the nation the Cabinet may, with deep foreboding, decide to take that risk. Can I assume that you have already ordered the fleet to prepare for sea?"

Now Pound was having great difficulty in staying calm. "No, Prime Minister, I have not. A vital part of the Ethelred strategy, as yet unaltered, is to leave the enemy unsure about the Navy's loyalty. While I hope that we'll have a few hours' grace after we sail before the Germans realise what's happened, I cannot depend upon that. It's not impossible that they have covert surveillance in place close to the base – perhaps a miniature submarine lying doggo in the Forth, or even an agent onshore – and would recognise the signs immediately. That would destroy one of the main planks of Ethelred, the pretence that the Navy will not intervene. Unless and until I am ordered otherwise, I will make no change to our carefully prepared plans, to avoid the risk of undermining the entire strategy."

It was coming close to a direct challenge to Churchill, but the Prime Minister still chose not to react. He decided, instead, to take some heat out of the debate. "Admiral, I think your dilemma is clear. We will not make any rash decisions. Whatever else we decide upon over the next hour or so, it does seem clear that this new situation tilts the balance in regard to the six light cruisers. I approve your earlier request. You may assign them to supplement the destroyers. When you come back we will talk further about the Home Fleet."

Pound stood up. At least he had achieved something from the tense debate. "Prime Minister, may I...?" He needed to get things moving. Taking a short break from the heated discussion would be no bad thing either.

"Yes, Admiral. Just the six cruisers for now. We will take no other decisions prior to your return."

Pound left the room for a few minutes, wasting no time in case things moved on in his absence. He came back to find the debate on hold and a tense atmosphere in the room. Exchanging a glance with Churchill, he sat down and listened as the discussion moved on to the air situation.

"Air Chief Marshall Dowding, you have heard Admiral Pound's concerns. Do you have enough fighters to provide cover for both the bombers and the battle fleet?"

"It would be very tight, sir. If we were to schedule a bombing attack at dawn, our fighters might be able to provide an escort for them, then re-fuel and take off on a second mission to cover the Fleet on its way south. But it would take a lot of choreography and, as you know, things can go wrong... heavier losses than expected... sneak air attacks on our bases, possibly even with gas... parachute landings... fog. The list goes on."

Churchill persisted. "But is the Luftwaffe not likely to have its hands already full over the Channel, even if they do spot the Home Fleet's movements?"

Dowding's answer was succinct, and telling. "Sir, I don't think we should prejudge how the Germans would prioritise their targets."

Churchill accepted the comment. "A valid point, Air Chief Marshall. Hitler is well capable of sacrificing 50000 men in his invasion armada to achieve the destruction of our Home Fleet."

There was, if not an impasse, certainly serious cause for reflection as the two real issues emerged – how to employ the RAF's fighters, and when to deploy the Home Fleet.

Antony Eden had listened to the debate on the military options, and shared much of Attlee's concern about the dreadful casualties that might be suffered under the original plan. At a pause in the discussion he raised a different angle.

"There is one other factor which would come into play if we were to despatch the Home Fleet ahead of the invasion fleet sailing. It would show the Nazis that the lack of commitment they've been hoping for in the Royal Navy is a mirage. It might cause them to re-think, even at such a late stage."

"Ah yes, we forget the subtlety of our own planning," agreed

Churchill.

Eden continued, "Is it possible that we could stymie their entire invasion plan? Might it cool their ardour to see the Home Fleet heading towards the Channel, shielded by hundreds of RAF fighters that they weren't expecting? Might it be enough for them to cancel the whole thing, and focus all their effort on the East?"

Halifax and Attlee indicated their support. It was a reasonable suggestion, certainly from a political point of view. A show of strength in the face of the enemy might cause him to slink away like a defeated stag. For a few minutes the idea began to gain momentum.

It was General Dill who stepped in to quash it. "Prime Minister, I do not think that such an approach is at all wise. At no stage have we said that our forces are stronger than the enemy, certainly not as far as the Army or RAF is concerned. They have more fighters, more bombers, many more tanks. We have based the entire Ethelred strategy on surprise. Our plan is to deceive them, lull them into a sense of complacency, then use our entire strength to catch them at their most vulnerable, their army stranded like a whale on our shores or thrashing about in mid-Channel. If we now proceed to exhibit our real strength, they're likely simply to retrench, target our reserves – now exposed to view – and once again focus on wearing us down, day-by-day, week-by-week."

There was a murmur of agreement from the other military staff. Attlee also seemed to accept Dill's argument, and modified his suggestion. "That is a fair point, General. However, even if we accept that we can't just frighten him off and must respond, as planned, in a carefully phased way, could we at least limit the scope of the landings by accelerating our response? If we are robust and use all our available strength as soon as they are committed to the crossing, would it be possible to beat the first wave back from our beaches, rather than concede ground to them as planned?"

Churchill needed the military facts. "General Brooke, can you give me your opinion on the possibility of flinging back the first wave –

back to the butcher, as has been said."

Brooke spoke up, "It would be exceptionally difficult. In fact it would be dangerous in the extreme to change our battle plan at this stage, sir. Admiral Pound has confirmed that we can't bring any more naval assets to bear in time. From our discussions here, it seems that the only change that we might be able to make in the short term would be launch bombing attacks on their fleet. I should remind everyone that even as we orchestrated the secret build-up of fighter reserves, at no point did we suggest using our air power for direct attack on the enemy invasion force. Even if we did attempt that, and managed to weaken their first wave before it landed, the Germans are still likely to be able to land strong forces – paratroopers, assault troops and panzers. I am in no mind to send my men forward out of their carefully prepared defensive positions and throw them in a wild charge against the enemy."

Churchill stared at him, disapprovingly; perhaps not so much at the conclusion as the uncompromising language Brooke had used.

"So it would appear that that the Royal Navy is not able to wield its hammer, and the Army is not willing to use its sickle. Perhaps it's just as well that the Russians will be joining in."

Brooke was visibly stung by the remarks.

"Sir, with all due respect, I am not refusing to attack the landings. If such an order is given, my men will attack, with bayonets and bare hands if necessary. And I'll seek your permission to lead them myself. But my advice, as head of the Home Army, is that central to our plan is a controlled withdrawal, using carefully prepared defensive positions to inflict heavy casualties on the enemy's troops and tanks – not to attempt a *'Boy's Own'* charge across open fields."

Now it was Churchill's turn to be rebuked, if indirectly, by the reference to the children's comic. It was clear that, with the heads of the three Services lined up against him, there was no possibility of the battle plan being changed. For all the concerns that the politicians might have about casualties and damage, there was nothing more to be done. Ethelred would proceed – at the very least until the first assault wave had landed. There might then be a short period when other options might be evaluated, in a less stressed environment.

Churchill accepted that he had no choice but to concede with grace.

"Disappointing as it may be, there appears to be consensus among my commanders that nothing more can be done to avert a German landing. For the time being, unfortunately, control of the timetable remains the prerogative of the Nazis. Then let it be so. Our battle plan emerges unchanged from this discussion. Our objective remains no less than the destruction of the Huns; the survival of our nation. However let us also be aware, and grateful, that the battle may not need to be as protracted or the immediate victory necessarily as crushing as we sought just a few hours ago. I charge each of you with being ready to identify and bring to this table any opportunity, consistent with military prudence, which might allow us to achieve victory at the earliest possible time."

There was a murmur of assent, at least from a majority of the Cabinet. Churchill then raised his voice and began to speak with great purpose.

"In this new information about Russia there is something else that we have not, as yet, discussed. Something of the utmost significance. After twelve months of desperate struggle, relentless struggle, we can now see, for the first time, a vision of how this war will end – in the total defeat of Nazism, crushed between the Russian army and the British navy; between the bear and the lion. It is, perhaps, unfortunate that you cannot share this great truth with your officers and men. However you, my commanders, know the reality. You will now lead your men forward in the imminent encounter with that vision in mind; that sparkling vision of ultimate victory."

He clenched his jaw.

"Let us steel ourselves for battle."

CHAPTER TWENTY-FOUR

Even as the Cabinet meeting drew to a close, Flight Lieutenant Fowley was preparing for his mission at Heston airfield on the outskirts of London, less than ten miles from the Paddock. In the grey pre-light of dawn he walked awkwardly out to his Spitfire, swaddled in several levels of clothes. He climbed onto the wing and eased himself into the tight-fitting cockpit, carefully doing up his harness with the help of his rigger. Since the fall of France, a handful of these modified Spitfires had carried out hundreds of photo reconnaissance sorties, monitoring the build up of the enemy's invasion forces in the embarkation ports. On clear days they flew at over 30000ft where they were much too high for flak, and almost untroubled by the Luftwaffe's fighters. On days when the targets were obscured by poor weather they flew low-level, much more dangerous, missions. Then they did suffer losses.

Ahead lay an early morning sweep of the southern sector, taking in five of the invasion ports. Straight across the Channel to Boulogne, then down the coast to Dieppe, Le Havre, Caen and Cherbourg, before heading back to Blighty. It meant a flight of over 400 miles, well beyond the range of a standard Spitfire, and only possible with the long-range tank under his wing. He had done the trip dozens of times and knew the target areas intimately.

The forecast for the day was mixed, and had complicated his mission. Over Northern France there was a thick cloud layer between 9000 and 12000ft. He would have to come underneath it for the photo run. As soon as he emerged from its cover he would be exposed to the flak; dozens, perhaps hundreds of guns of all calibres as he made his pass. But at least the clouds offered somewhere to hide as soon as he had finished. He was more worried about the next leg. To the south the skies were expected to clear, with just a few patches of broken cloud remaining. Once the cover was gone he would be exposed to both fighters and flak, and he would have to make a long, hard climb up to the safety of his ceiling, six miles above the earth. Normally this would be done in the relative sanctuary of English skies, before heading out across the Channel. Today it would have to be done over occupied France. With full boost engaged, he knew that his Spitfire could climb faster than a 109. *But if they were already up there waiting for him...*

As the sky began to lighten in the east he started his engine, and waited several minutes for the powerful Merlin to warm up, before starting to taxi. He moved slowly towards the end of the grass runway, weaving from side to side to see past the Spitfire's long nose. His aircraft had been stripped of all armament and radio equipment to improve its performance at high altitude, but the extra fuel tank still made her heavy for take off, and he manoeuvred precisely to have every possible foot of space available. Carefully he ran through the final checklist, paying special attention to the engine temperature and oil pressure, and to his oxygen supply. Everything looked good. He waited.

A green Very light was fired from the control tower.

Off we go! He pushed the throttle forward and the aircraft bumped its way along the grass runway, building speed until, with a final lurch, the wheels left the ground and he began his lonely journey. He turned to port and climbed out to the south east, already rhythmically scanning over his shoulders, left and right, in case an intruder might be prowling around the airfield, looking for an easy kill. His route took him round in a loop south of London, where he could see fires still burning from the previous day's raids and could just smell the acrid smoke. Then he was over Croydon and turning towards the coast.

Fifteen minutes after take off he reached his first waypoint, a fine redbrick house in Kent, now gently illuminated by the pink morning light. It was a useful landmark on this route, though now more difficult to pick out since the nearby lake had been filled in. Many weeks ago he had discovered that it was Chartwell, Churchill's country home. Knowing that gave a special meaning, almost a frisson, to his dangerous sortie. He watched the house appear beneath his wing, and used the precise fix to check his drift. *Almost exactly on course. The Met boys had got it right; hardly any wind.* Then a less comforting thought... *good invasion weather...* He made a slight adjustment to his course, coming onto a heading of 120 degrees. As he reached the house he waggled his wings. It was both an oft-repeated good luck token and a salute to his leader. He knew that the Prime Minister was most likely hidden deep in a bunker somewhere in London, but the old habit stayed with him, a comfort. He wondered did anyone ever notice.

He set his stopwatch. It would be dead-reckoning from here to the target... 64 miles to go... just 16 minutes at his cruising speed. He pulled back gently on the stick and began to climb, easing up into the clouds. Down below he left behind, unseen, the English coast. He knew that he would soon be spotted by the German radar, but in the thick cloud he would be impossible to intercept. For now he just had to focus on his instruments, his course, his stopwatch. Twelve short minutes later, still safely blanketed by cloud, he knew he was across the Channel and coming to the initial point for his photo run. He noted the exact time on his knee pad, then pushed the throttle fully forward and watched his speed build up. He wouldn't use the boost override for now. His engine could only handle the extra surge of power for five minutes – and he might need it later. He watched intently as his speed gradually increased... 280... 300... 320mph. Checking again on the stopwatch, he counted down the seconds.

NOW!! He pushed the nose down, his speed rapidly building up to over 350mph as he descended through the cloud base and saw below him the grey-green sea.

Good... almost exactly on track... Boulogne in the distance... ease slightly left... coming up fast now... cameras ready...

Then, in a split second...

Christ almighty, look at that! What in God's name...

Straight ahead, and on both sides, were vessels – hundreds of vessels – milling about. Smoke and steam was rising from them, the plumes drifting in the light winds. In the outer harbour he could see dozens of naval craft... destroyers... flak ships... torpedo boats... all twisting about at speed, leaving long wakes behind them in the calm waters. *Shoot!* He pushed the shutter button and counted out the seconds as he roared over the armada.

On across the inner harbour... Now he could see cargo ships, dozens of them, all gavotting around in a vast maritime ballet... and barges, in their hundreds, being chaperoned by tugs into tight groups. *Come left slightly... flak far behind... keep shooting!* He was across the shoreline now. As he flashed overhead he could see the intense activity on the quay side and, in the marshalling areas, trains... vehicles... tanks... *Jesus, look at the tanks...* He was only able to imagine the long lines of grey-uniformed soldiers accompanying them, but his long-focus lens would have captured all the detail for the photo-interpreters to analyse.

The flak was getting closer. Dark grey bursts from the 37mm guns, tracer and whitish puffs from the 20mm weapons were reaching up towards him, before arching away behind. The gunners were finding it almost impossible to track a Spitfire travelling flat out.

Fighters!! Out of the corner of his eye he could see a pair of 109s. He watched nervously as they turned towards him. It was OK... they were too far away. They wouldn't catch him at this speed.

Countryside below! Finished!! He released the shutter button, pulled back on the stick and climbed hard towards the safety of the cloud base, 8000... 8500... 9000ft... Greyness. He eased forward on the stick and gently levelled out. *Should be right in the centre of the layer – safe for now!* He looked at his watch and scribbled the time on his pad, along with a few cryptic notes on what he'd seen. His report at de-briefing would supplement the hard photographic evidence from his camera. That was Boulogne... now for Dieppe. He pulled round in a wide arc to starboard, carefully watching his instruments... altitude... speed... turn and bank... Carefully he eased out of the turn and settled onto his new heading south. He throttled back to cruising speed, his heart still thumping with the stress of the high speed pass.

He still had four more ports to photograph, but already Fowley knew what he had been looking at below; knew beyond a shadow of doubt what was happening.

It had started.

Afterword

'There were indeed some who on purely technical grounds, and for the sake of the effect the total defeat and destruction of his expedition would have on the general war, were quite content to see him try.'

The Second World War Volume II - Their Finest Hour:

Winston S. Churchill

Author's Note

When the historical record is masked in secrecy, where does inter-pretation end and fiction begin? In that fateful summer of 1940 is it possible that Churchill might indeed have toyed with luring the Nazis into a premature invasion? His enigmatic words, quoted in the Afterword, offer a glimpse of that possibility and provided the inspiration for this novel. They are rarely commented upon.

In exploring that time of crisis, two figures stand out who epito-mise the hidden intrigues of the period.

Brendan Bracken was Churchill's confidante, perhaps also his Rasputin; the model for Big Brother in Orwell's '1984'. In Colville's history of his time as the Prime Minister's private secretary, Bracken is referenced more than any other individual, yet he hardly appears in Churchill's own memoirs. Bracken insisted that Churchill write him out. At his express instruction all his own papers were burned after his death. What he and the Prime Minister discussed in their midnight meetings is cloaked in mystery.

Admiral Canaris is an equally intriguing, but tragic figure. As head of German Military Intelligence, he did his utmost to thwart Hitler's ambition. It may never be known how much information he passed to the Allies, or how much disinformation to his Nazi mas-ters before he was eventually exposed. He died, naked, on a gallows in Flossenburg concentration camp shortly before the war ended.

Acknowledgements

A first novel travels a long distance from concept to reality. This road would not have been travelled but for the love and support of Dee, who encouraged me, accompanied me to many of the locations that feature and acted as my editor. She also advised me when to stop writing!

Special thanks are due to my children, who helped in different ways on the journey, and to my friends Denis Hearn, Martin McKenna and Conor McWade who reviewed the work-in-progress at various stages and contributed both enjoyable debate about the theme and valuable advice about the execution.

I would also like to thank Andrew Brown of designforwriters.com for his dramatic cover design.

For all of that assistance, the final product with any flaws, inconsistencies or errors remain my sole responsibility.

17422582R00143

Printed in Poland
by Amazon Fulfillment
Poland Sp. z o.o., Wrocław